A SYMPTOM OF MAGIC

MAGIC AND MISCHIEF BOOK 2

N. R. HAIRSTON

Cover Design by Lou Harper

Formatting by Adam Poe

Published by

FIVE STORIES OF SUPERNATURAL CURSES

Skin Cursed

Eight hours after being infected, they can control your mind. After eighteen, your life is over... Scope Agent Rye is in the fight of her life. Infected with the deadly Morillo virus, she has eight hours to get it out of her system or she'll become submissive to another forever—and the only person she can turn to has already betrayed her once.

Blood Cursed

Pacifist Delia owes much to her friends in the alternate world of Kelm. When someone poisons the Tacium that keeps them alive, she must find the culprit and stop the vicious disease in three days...or it will wipe out the entire population. With millions of lives on the line, and the disease spreading like a rising tide, can she get her pacifist family to help save her immortal friends?

Cursed in Sunlight

Leah and her partner Xavier have won big at cards, but their chance for an even bigger prize goes down the drain when their winnings are stolen. To retrieve the cash, they must embark on a dangerous journey to Cave Town where they risk being cursed forever if they're not out in 24 hours.

Cursed Breath

Every year thousands of people go missing. Coalition Agent Kerry and her team have tracked them to an alternate universe but an unexplainable sickness attacks them, draining everyone's energy. To save her team, as well as the captives, and to prevent future abductions, Kerry must face an enemy she thought long dead.

Cursed Succubus

Kia's life depends on her finding the fifth soulbar, a powerful object coveted by the First Families. They must never know she touched it, draining some of its immense power before losing it or the punishment will be extreme. But the First Families aren't the only ones desperate for the soulbar's power...an old enemy of Kia's wants it for himself and she's the only thing standing in his way.

SKIN CURSED

D rena, one of my senior agents, gave the signal for us to move in. We burst through the doors, Drena in first, then me, then the agents behind me.

The place was dark, and bedsheets hung on the windows to keep light out. A pink and blue, flower-patterned couch that had been popular about thirty years ago sat in the middle of the living room.

A blue recliner sat in front of a small TV that seemed to be on the fritz. Piled up plates and empty food cartons covered just about every surface, and the place smelled like rotten food and piss.

Garrett walked into the room, his hand over his mouth. Of dragon descent, Garrett was tall, with black spiked hair and red eyes. He was of medium build and walked with the kind of swagger that said he was past confident in his ability to do, well, anything.

We weren't exactly best friends as our opinions often differed, but there was a mutual respect there. He was a good Scope agent and as dedicated to bringing down criminals as I was. "Good grief, if they're dealing in morillo then I can't tell it. Morillo makes millionaires." He waved a hand at the disarray of the room. "This ain't millionaire living."

I kicked a half-empty milk carton out of my path and tried not to vomit at the stench. "Depending on the client, morillo can go for only a few thousand," I reminded him.

Morillo was detachable crystalline hair that came from the anus of those with capybara DNA. The government agency Albright usually handled these cases, as morillo was a national threat, and above The Scope Agency's pay grade.

Scope, the law enforcement agency I worked for, only dealt with special and major crimes, but morillo was on a level above our heads and best left to the heavy hitters.

Still we'd gotten word that an illegal operation was going on here, so Drena had made the call. We'd let Albright know, but morillo operations needed to be shut down immediately.

Morillo had many uses, but the main one was bending people to your will. If injected into a city official, or world leader, the damage could be astronomical.

"That's not pocket change, Rye. Come on, you know better than that."

I turned from him and kept checking the room. He was right of course, anyone making that type of money wouldn't live like this unless they were eccentric or they had to. "Maybe we got it wrong," I said.

"I don't think so," Drena called from the other room.

Garrett and I followed her voice to one of the bedrooms. It was a morillo lab all set up and ready to go.

A large silver work table sat in the middle of the floor. On it were three containers each holding six vials of blood. Over the top, was a mini clothesline, no doubt used to hold the morillo.

No chairs were in the room, and though every other part of the house was dirty, in here it was pristine.

My hands already in gloves, I picked up one of the vials.

No name on it, only a set of numbers. Putting that one down, I picked up another and found the same thing. "Guys, we need to look for a ledger of some type. Something they would keep the names in. He has to keep track of them somehow."

Drena picked up one of the vials and stared at it. "You," she said, pointing to me. "Check the dry surfaces in the bathroom. You," she pointed to Garrett. "Check the kitchen, all cabinets everything. I'll start on the bedrooms."

I moved quickly toward my destination, my stomach twisting in knots. This was bad, and I knew we needed to call for back-up and let our senior agents, as well as Albright, know what was going on.

The amount of blood was troubling. That meant at least eighteen people could be affected. If it was a city or government official, the person could be made to do anything, and no one would ever know that they weren't acting of their own volition.

A noise to the right, coming from the pantry area, stopped me before I could get to the bathroom. Cautiously I moved in that direction, thinking about all the havoc a morillo affected person could wreak.

If I owned a company and wanted to destroy the competition, I would simply give my blood to a morillo runner.

They would then go out to find a capybara, kidnap them, and pull the scent coated detachable hairs from their anus, which is thus called morillo. Then they would drop my blood onto the morillo.

From there it would be simply a matter of using a keeter gun, to shoot the morillo into the victim's body, where it would burrow under the skin. After eight hours, when the morillo had had time to activate, little fine crystallized hair coated in the scent secretion of the capybara, mixed with my blood, would pop up somewhere on the person's body, usually unnoticeable.

Much like thiols, which is what me and others of skunk DNA used to protect ourselves from would be attackers, the scent that covers the morillo is what puts a person under the spell. They could be made to do anything, for example, destroy their own company from the inside out, and no one would ever know the difference.

My thiols worked a little different. That awful smell that we skunks released had many uses. It could choke an adversary in a matter of seconds, but we could also turn it sweet, and put you under our spell. That one we didn't do so often as it took too much out of us.

The thing with morillo, though, was that it could only be removed by the capybara who put it there, no other way. After eighteen hours, it can't be removed, and it fuses with your central nervous system. The only way to stop it then is to kill the person who'd used their blood to have it done. The blood link would be shattered in death.

I heard what I thought was a floorboard creak, and put my back flat against the wall while I slowly stepped toward the pantry door. Another creak, this time toward the bathroom and I swung my outstretched hand that way, ready with my thiols, but was blinded by a bright light shining in my face. The only thing I could see next was the keeter gun aimed right at me.

Shit. My heart started to thump, and I ducked to the ground, hoping to find the person's feet, and knock them to my level so that I could get the upper hand.

I didn't move fast enough, and I felt it when the morillo went through my arm and burrowed under my skin. It was quick and painless. Had I not been aware it was happening, I never would have even noticed.

My mouth went dry, and everything in me stopped working. I was... Terrified. Still on the floor, I cradled my arm protectively to me as the implications of what this meant started to sink in.

In as little as eight hours, I could be under the complete control of someone else, unable to make my own decisions, and essentially a puppet to whoever held my strings.

That thought left a dry taste in my mouth. I'd been independent since I'd turned eighteen. My mother and I were close, but we'd both watched my grandmother cower before those she thought to be stronger or better than her.

She was still that way, my grandmother, and I swore I would never dance to the tune of another. From an early age, I'd witnessed her give complete obedience to whatever man she had in her life at the time, living and breathing on their whim alone.

It made the thiols in me boil, and I'd always vowed that the only person who ruled me, would be myself. That's why this hurt so much now. I refused to give my will over to another. I refused to be an empty shell, used only to carry out the orders of others.

Now capable of movement, I slowly came to my feet. I could feel the sweat dripping down my face, but I didn't care to wipe it away. I looked around, but whoever had shot me was long gone by now.

My hands went numb, and I tried to tell myself to calm down, that panicking wouldn't help, but that was like telling a dragon not to play with fire. It wasn't happening.

After eighteen hours, it would all be over. Even if the person I shared the blood link with were killed, I would still never be the same.

Killing the person would release their control, but after that much time had passed, it often left the person who'd been infected, in this case me, weak, feeble minded, and confused. I'd never known anyone to recover after a blood link was broken and they'd had the morillo in their system for eighteen hours, and I was sure I wouldn't be the first.

As long as the person whose blood affected them was alive, they were okay, but as soon as that bond was broken, and they were able to think for themselves again, it's like something became muddled in their brain. Maybe it was the trauma of having their mind twisted and shaped by another for so long. Once that person let go, the freed brain simply didn't know how to react or to whom it truly belonged.

A small tear fell down my face, and I angrily swiped at it. The only way to save me now was to find the capybara the morillo had come from and get them to remove it. I laughed, and it was a dry, humorless sound because I realized that we had absolutely no idea where to look.

2

"We are going to find who did this to you." Drena stood in front of me, her face hard, and her eyes worried. She stood about five feet six, and had brown curly hair, that she usually wore loose. At thirty-five, she was eight years my senior and one of my top mentors.

I'd learned a lot from her in the last couple of years and she'd backed me up numerous times, when I'd made some harebrained decision that no one else agreed with. They often led to an arrest, though, so if even my methods weren't standard, they worked. Drena knew that, yet she wasn't above calling me on my shit when I was wrong.

Her eyes were thoughtful. "I'm going to make a few phone calls, and we'll proceed from there. Don't worry. We are going to fix this."

I watched her go with a shake of my head. How? How were we going to fix this, because, at the moment, I saw no way out.

I tried to reach for the glass of water in front of me, but my hand shook so bad, I ended up just saying forget it. This was so surreal, that it actually seemed like a dream happening to someone else.

"Here." Garrett tried to hand it to me. We were in one of the conference rooms back at Scope. I was too much of a wreck to be seen by other agents, so we'd settled in here until I brought myself under control.

"No," I told him. If I couldn't hold the water still enough to drink it myself, then I wouldn't have it. I didn't need him or Drena spoon-feeding me and making me feel weaker than I already did.

Garrett leaned up against the table, his arms folded in front of him. Garrett's emotions ranged from very serious, to very irritated, to playful, which sometimes made me wary, as I never knew which Garrett I was going to get. Right now, he seemed a cross between serious and irritated. "We'll fix this. You're a Scope Agent, we're going to put our best on it."

I turned tired eyes his way. His words were nice, but they couldn't stop the triple knots forming in my stomach. If we didn't find the capybara the morillo had come from, this could be the end of my life as I knew it. "Damnit!" I slammed my fist down on the solid wood table, then jumped to my feet, not knowing quite what to do with myself.

My skin itched all over, and I knew if I didn't do something quickly, I would go out of my mind.

Garrett raised a brow, but didn't say anything.

"Okay," Drena said, walking back into the room. "We're needed at the Albright Agency."

The Albright Agency was a large, sleek, silver building with fourteen floors. Inside everything was black, silver, and immaculate. The whole place smelled of lemon disinfectant that I strongly believed was reapplied every thirty minutes.

We were led to a third-floor conference room by one of the guards at the front desk. The walls were painted silver with black diamonds. It looked nice and professional, to my eyes anyway. The floor tiles were black with silver diamonds, and I thought the contrast was nice, but it almost made me feel like I was inside of a puzzle.

The fresh lemony scent carried to this room, and gave the impression that a germ wouldn't last two seconds up here.

A table big enough to fit about thirty sat in the middle of the floor, with a large whiteboard and projection screen in front of the room, making me wonder if we would be given some type of lesson while we were here.

I sat down, with Garrett and Drena on either side of me. I put my hands on the table, but couldn't stop wringing them, so I put them in my lap where no one could see.

My heart was beating so fast you would have thought it was competing in a marathon. I'd made a life for myself in the last couple of years, carved out exactly who I was and wanted to be. All of that was at risk now and I just didn't know how to handle it.

The door opened, and two men and two women walked into the room. Their movements were stiff, and their faces looked severe. I guessed Albright agents didn't know the meaning of the word relax.

Both women and one of the men took a seat across from us.

The ringleader, or the one in charge rather, went to the front of the room and I cringed when I saw who it was. He was a tall muscular twenty-eight and had shaggy black hair that kept falling in his face. He also had a smile so beautiful and sexy that one look at it could melt away any problem I was having.

Jax, my love. Well, sometimes anyway. I swallowed hard as I stared at him, all strict and professional. My gut twisted even more as cold fear gripped me.

I never wanted him to see me like this. Not that he wouldn't do everything in his power to help me. It's just that we'd been down that road before when he'd helped me shut down an illegal skunk oil operation, and I had no desire to revisit it.

I'd been at my most vulnerable then, and Jax had been great. Still, there was no way I wanted to make a habit out of this. I didn't like feeling weak. Jax and I worked best when we were on equal footing.

"To start off," he pulled down the projection screen, never turning our way, "the three agents who came into the room with me," he said, no doubt addressing myself, Drena, and Garrett, "are a part of your team now, and will be taking point on this. I will not be involved, so you will defer to them."

Drena, who knew exactly who Jax was, looked at me and raised an eyebrow. I ignored her, but knew that I would be deferring to no one. I started to say as much but realized it was in my best interest to keep my mouth shut. I didn't want to unnecessarily upset the agents who potentially held my life in their hands.

Jax kept his eyes straight ahead. "There are three top morillo runners on this side of the Hemisphere. If morillo operations are going down, you can bet these three know about it." He clicked a small silver device in his hand, and three pictures popped up.

One, a tall, forty-something, lanky man, with glasses, that looked like he'd be just as at home on a street corner as a jail cell. The caption underneath read Darren Womack.

Another, a short woman whom I put to be in her thirties. With high cheekbones and short black hair, she looked intelligent, cunning even. Like she'd been around the block a few times and now stood at the top of her game. Maze, no last name given.

The last man looked to be in his thirties as well. He was of average height and a little on the slim side with a mustache and receding hairline. I could easily picture him sitting on the couch all day drinking beers and flipping channels. Lucky. He didn't seem to have a last name either.

Jax clicked through three large mansion-style houses. "This is where they live. We believe them to have a few judges and higher ups in law enforcement in their pockets or under the spell of morillo." He sighed his irritation. "Right now, we have no way of knowing, but we are working on it."

He turned around and his eyes locked with mine. He never changed demeanor, but I could see the surprise and questioning look flutter across his face. "You," he said, pointing to me. "May I speak to you outside please?"

The agents that had come in with him all looked a little shocked, and I figured that this must have been highly unorthodox behavior on his part.

One of the women he'd come into the room with was slim, with short brown hair and had the look of one of those people who were all work, all the time, no fun in between. Right now, she eyed us both, a curious expression on her face and I got the impression that she wanted to say something but didn't believe that now was the time. Perhaps she'd talk to Jax later.

The other woman was average height and weight. She seemed the type that would stay up all night holding the hand of a victim until they felt safe enough to be alone. She had black hair and her green eyes bore into Jax back as if she was trying to will him to look her way.

The man he'd come in with had red hair and green eyes. He was of medium build, and seemed nervous, as if he was just waiting for something to go wrong. He cleared his throat and straightened his tie, a clear sign that he was uncomfortable.

"Now hold on a minute." Garrett started to rise, eyes set on Jax. Drena put a hand on his arm and quickly whispered something in his ear. Garrett blinked at her, then sat back down without another word.

I got up. My head may have been held high, but my skin was still crawling from what I knew to be beneath the surface.

"Be right back," Jax said as he closed the door behind us. He pulled me into the empty room next door.

I leaned my back against the wall and he came to stand in front of me, his face only inches from my own. His voice came out almost accusatory. "It's you. You got hit with the keeter gun." It was more a statement than a question.

I looked at him, unable to speak. His eyes read concern, but his jaw stayed tight. I took a deep breath and shuddered as I lay my head on his chest, tears flowing freely now.

He quickly wrapped his arms around me, making me feel safe and secure. So much so, that I scooted closer, just to be more in his warm embrace.

He kissed the top of my head. "We're going to fix this," he said softly, pushing thick course hair away from my face. "Hey, we've handled worse, right?"

We hadn't, not really, but just hearing his soothing voice and words of comfort were enough to lull me into a false sense of security.

Jax was here, so nothing could go wrong. I wrapped my arms around his waist and pulled him tighter to me. We shared a quick kiss, then I put my head back on his chest, never wanting to let go.

"I don't know what to do," I finally croaked out.

His grip on me tightened, and I knew he was just as nervous as I was. Strangely though, having him here beside me, made me feel for the first time since I'd been shot, that maybe everything was going to be okay.

When we walked back into the room, all eyes were on us. I didn't give anything away, taking my seat, and pulling my chair up as if I hadn't just been in the next room crying my eyes out.

Jax went back to the front of the room. "So, I think I'll take point on this after all."

Though no one objected, I could see the eyes of his agents stray my way.

Jax cued up a picture. It was one of the mansions he'd showed us before. This one was a shiny white, and the yard looked to be about the size of two football fields. He clicked on the picture of the tall man with glasses again. "Darren Womack. This is his home, as near as we can tell."

He pointed to the red headed man he'd come into the room with. "Fred, go ahead and put the team together. We need to be ready to move out in fifteen minutes."

Fred's eyes bulged, and he cleared his throat. "I'm... I'm sorry, sir, but move out where? We don't have warrants for these places. You'll never... I don't think... It'll never stick."

Jax licked his lips, one of his tells that he didn't give a fuck what you thought. If they'd worked together for a while, then Fred probably already knew this. "Doesn't matter if it sticks. I just want to bust up as much of his operation as we can." That and find the capybara whose morillo had infected me. If he were one of Darren's, he'd be somewhere close. Once you had a capybara, you never let them go.

The woman with the black hair raised her hand.

Jax looked weary as if he knew she was ready to call him on his shit. "Tonya?" His eyes slanted in a way that said he knew exactly what she wanted.

"Ummm, what the fuck are you doing? Or have you finally lost it?" she asked.

Jax grinned brightly, and I furrowed my brows, wondering what she meant. "Do you have any suggestions, Tonya?"

She gave me, Drena, and Garrett an inquisitive stare, then

turned back to Jax. "Nah, boss. This is your thing. Just make sure you know what you're doing and that it's for the right reasons."

Jax thought about what she said. Her eyes watched his every move, and I suddenly realized that I liked this woman a lot. She wasn't afraid to stand up for herself. She knew this was fucked up and didn't mind pointing it out to Jax, who was obviously her superior.

"I hear you," Jax said, then took a careful glance around the room. "Anybody else have something to say? Cynthia?" He looked at the woman with the short brown hair and she shook her head. "Good, then let's get on with it?"

Drena leaned over and whispered in my ear. "You know who could help out with this don't you?"

I blinked, sure she wasn't suggesting who I thought she was. "Are you crazy? I'm not going to see *him*," I whispered back, my skin already beginning to crawl from the mere suggestion that I visit Cam.

She fiddled with her pen, her eyes saying a lot more than her mouth. I gave her an incredulous look because she was serious. She really wanted me to go see the best friend who'd betrayed me and who'd used the pain and derogation of other skunks to salve his own wounds and further his illegal agenda. "No thank you." My voice brooked no argument.

Drena didn't give a damn about any of that. She kept right on talking as if I hadn't said a word. "I think seeing shaggy here," her thumb cocked to Jax, who happened to be in the process of pushing unruly locks out of his face, "has made you forget how important this is. He can't protect you any more than we can if we don't know what we're dealing with."

"Cam was a drug dealer," Garrett said, leaning over to join in the conversation, uninvited.

Something weighed heavily on my chest when he said that. I didn't like it. I could say it. I knew it to be true, but when other people said it, pointed it out to me, it just really made my thiols boil. "I know who he is, which is why I don't want to see him," I said through gritted teeth.

Neither Garrett nor Drena looked convinced. "He's been your best friend since you were kids. Look, I get it. But until you accept it…" She let the rest trail off.

Garrett wasn't so soft with his words. "I don't care if you accept it or not. Cam ran one of the biggest skunk oil operations we've ever seen. Those three," he pointed to the faces on the screen, "run the biggest morillo ones. They have to know each other. You know that they do."

I put a hand under my collar, as I was beginning to feel hot there. "You think they have secret clubhouse meetings? Or maybe they give out drug dealer of the year awards? You think so?" Deflection, thy name is Rye.

Never one to pussyfoot around, Garrett gave it to me straight. "And how is this helping you? This pie in the sky willful foolishness? How is not using every resource at our disposal helping you? Stop being a coward, and get off your ass and go talk to your boy before we walk into that first house and run into a situation we can't get ourselves out of."

I stood abruptly, my hands shaking at my sides, and my skin feeling like it was on fire. They were right, yet I'd never wanted to tell two people to fuck off more in my life.

I wiped sweat from my brow and tried to contain my trembling. I looked down at the two forcible expressions staring up at me. It must have been easy for them to sit there and judge.

It wasn't their hearts that had been broken. It wasn't their best friend who'd torn down years of trust and love. It wasn't them who'd started to doubt themselves because if I could be so wrong about Cam, there was a lot else I could be wrong about too.

I took a deep cleansing breath and straightened my spine,

putting some of the steel I'd lost back into it. "I'll meet you there." I said it loud enough for everyone in the room to hear and began my walk across the floor.

Jax watched me go, a thoughtful look on his face, that said he knew exactly what I was ready to do, yet he made no move to stop me.

3

Cam was being held in Moraid prison in Wayfaix county. It was a twenty-minute drive to get there, and I called ahead and used my Scope credentials to hurriedly pass through the front gates. The prison was set in the country, miles away from any residents or businesses.

Moraid was a large building, no different from any other prison, except here is where those in law enforcement who'd committed a crime were kept, for their own protection, far away from the general population.

I rolled up to the guard house and handed over my Scope badge. They'd already been informed that I was coming, so after taking a look at it and giving it back, I was waved right through.

The guard in charge of me while I was there was named Gern, and he led me to a narrow room, with multiple chairs lined up on either side of a large plexiglass window. Cam was already sat there waiting for me, and I wondered if they'd brought him out the moment I'd called.

Apparently, they hadn't told him who'd be visiting because his eyes widened with shock and excitement when he saw me. I took a deep breath and promised myself not to let past attachments cloud my judgment.

Cam had on a bright orange jumpsuit, and his black hair was pushed back from his face. Like all skunks, Cam had that wide white stripe running down the middle of his otherwise all black hair.

My hair was the same. We could try and dye it, but no matter what outrageous colors we used, it still remained bushy, and jet black, with that stripe of white.

That fact that we could never change our hair color made us easy targets for those in the skunk oil business, like Cam. Skunk oil was the fat taken from the lateral glands in our backs.

Consumers often paid thousands for just a few ounces. It did everything from healing broken bones to getting you so high you didn't come down for days. It was also known that rubbing it on your penis or vagina before sex would have you coming for hours. Some even used it as a contraceptive.

This was something we were hunted for. Not openly, as the Scope Agency showed no mercy on those who dealt in the skunk oil trade.

Still, skunks like myself and Cam were a target, only he'd become the hunter instead of the hunted. He'd done to our kind what we all feared the most.

He'd captured other skunks and drained them of their oil, which was a painful process and often left us unable to walk for days, sometimes weeks. He'd turned their worst night-mares into reality and I'd never forgive him for it.

I tried to look hard and unaffected as I picked up the phone. "I need your help." I didn't want to linger on pleas-antries, because asking him how he was, or any such ques-tions, would imply that we were still friends, which we most certainly were not.

His eyes took me in, watching my every movement, as if

amazed at my mere presence. I grounded myself by remembering the faces of some of the skunks we'd freed from the cages he'd kept them bound in.

I remembered how they'd been half starved, their spirits broken. I remembered the smell of urine, feces, and vomit. I remembered how I'd felt when I'd first discovered them, and that strengthened my resolve and made it easier to do what I had to do. Which was act indifferently to the man seated before me, whom I'd once loved as much as my own life.

He was still smiling and seemed amazed that I was actually there. "I'm so happy to see you, Rye. Anything you need. Anything I can help you with." He seemed so eager to please, and that had never really been a part of Cam's personality. I wondered what had happened to him since he'd been in here.

I cleared my throat and told myself to focus. I hadn't come here for that. Cam had known exactly what he was doing, and my time was running short. "What do you know about the morillo trade?"

His smile faded and concern lit his eyes. "I know that it's something better left for Albright, and not something Scope can easily handle. Rye, I hope you aren't getting mixed up in any morillo cases."

He looked around, to make sure no one was close enough to hear, then gripped the phone tightly, his face serious and fierce. "They are always looking for more people in law enforcement to infect." I thought about the fact that had I not actually seen him shoot me with the gun, I wouldn't have even known I'd been infected, and I wondered how many others they'd gotten that way.

Cam was still talking. "If you get a tip, on a house, or a dealer or anything, just hand it over, because it's probably a trap to infect as many of you as they can." He took a breath. "Don't follow the lead. Give it over to Albright, they are better able to handle this type of threat."

My eyes shifted to the floor, only slightly, but we'd known each other too long, been a part of each other's lives for too many years, for it to go unnoticed.

"Rye," he said, and everything in me exploded. To say my name like that was just disrespectful. That tone the was one he'd used when I felt scared or alone and trusted only him to comfort me. It was the tone he'd used when we'd graduated from high school and college. The same tone was used when we'd first gotten our Scope badges.

It was a tone used for intimacy and friendship, and we had none of that anymore. I took a deep breath as something inside me shattered. I didn't want him to know how he affected me. To talk, would be to betray that to him. So, I just sat there and didn't say a word.

He didn't push it, but I know he must have known. His voice was serious, and his eyes held sorrow. "I'll find out what I can, but the top three, they have safeguards in place. If you're after one of them, then one of their contacts in law enforcement have probably already let them know. Keep that in mind, before you plan your raid."

I nodded and started to get up, but his voice stopped me cold. "It was good to see you, Rye. I hope this won't be the last time."

I looked at him, at what he'd become, and thought of all the carefree days of our childhood we'd spend playing hide and seek, kickball, and name the thiols.

Those times we could never go back to, my eyes watered as I hurriedly walked away, vowing I would never come to this soul-sucking place again.

Jax was waiting for me as I exited the prison and I rushed into his arms, just happy that he was there.

He wrapped me up in a hug and kissed the side of my head, brushing hair out of my eyes. "Figured you could use a friendly face." His grip on me became furious and protective, and I loved that he knew I wasn't as unaffected by Cam as I sometimes pretended to be.

I basked in the glow of his comfort for one moment longer before pulling away. "I'm fine. Learned one or two interesting things."

I repeated all that Cam had said to me, and he nodded. "I wish you'd let me know before you went barging in there. I could have told you all of this."

I hit him with a glare, and he relented, throwing his hands up. "Come on, you only have a few hours left."

4

W e rolled up to the front of Darren's mansion. Between Albright and Scope there were twenty of us all together, and one thing we all had to keep in mind, was that he may have been warned that we were coming.

I used my thiols as a protective shield, and it wrapped itself around my whole body, something I wished I'd thought to do when I'd first heard the creak of the floorboards and got hit with the gun.

I wouldn't be able to keep it up for long, but knew I needed it until we were sure no one with a keeter gun was in the house. A shield was dangerous because it took too much energy to keep activated, which is why I never really used it.

Except in the case of someone like Drena, with turtle DNA. Her skin hardened, but it was natural to her and didn't cause a problem. When she put up her protective shield, nothing could penetrate that barrier.

Garrett covered himself in fire, but like me, he would start to wane if he kept it up too long.

Jax had no such protection, but he was quick and fast, and I prayed that would save him.

A loud bang sounded from behind the house. "Around back," Drena said, looking at the length of the mansion. "Best to go straight through. No way can we make it around this thing in time to see anything."

Garrett dropped his fire shield, and his green speckled wings unfolded from his back. He grabbed me by the arm. "We'll look from up top."

We flew up, the wind ripping through my hair, and Garrett's grip around my waist tight. We hovered just out of sight, on top of the roof. What we saw were three men and three women in the back of the house. All were moving at a fast pace, as they loaded up two white vans with crates and boxes.

One of the women, a tall redhead, put a box in the van then turned to the short brown-haired dude behind her. "Where's the stock?"

He pointed toward the mansion. "Lined up and waiting."

She looked in the direction of the house and shook her head. "Then let's get 'em outta here." She spat on the ground. "Should never have been here in the first place. I told Darren, you never keep nothing that can incriminate you at home." She shook her head again. "You just don't do it."

The man chuckled as he loaded more boxes in. "Boss is going to do things his way. He don't care what nobody else thinks. Thought you already knew that."

Garrett loosened his hold on my waist. "Use your thiols," he said before completely pulling away and firing back up his protection shield.

I shot thiols out of my hand to keep myself floating in the air, but it was wobbly and unstable. This wasn't something I did often, as the fear of falling was too great. Still today was a day of firsts, so I'd at least try to stay upright. "Let's do this."

We flew straight for them. My thiols couldn't hold me and I fell to the ground hard, tumbling on to my side.

Pushing down the pain, I jumped back up immediately, not wanting to give them the upper hand.

I hit the brown-haired man with thiols and wrapped it around his neck, choking him until he passed out. At the same time, I squeezed the woman's waist, making her arms flap, until I weakened her enough to deliver a punch straight to her face. She fell to the ground and didn't get back up.

That took care of two of them, but we still had four to go. Garrett pointed a straight line of fire into one of the men's eyes. The guy screamed, grabbed his face, and slammed into one of the vans, before falling.

Drena came from one side of the house, agents behind her, while Jax came from the other, part of his crew behind him. Knowing they could more than handle the three that were left I carefully entered the house.

The door was opened, and they still had boxes waiting to be loaded into the vans. I popped the top on one box and saw stacks of morillo. In another were blood vials. Closing that one, I signaled for Tonya to come over. "This is what they were trying to hide, but they spoke of a product too. I don't think they were talking about this." I pointed to the multiple crates and boxes littering the hallway floor. "I'm going to look a little further."

She looked back to where Albright and Scope agents were busy taking the last of Darren's people down. "I'll come with you for back up."

We crept through the house, backs against the wall. We'd only gone a few feet when my nose detected a slight earthy smell, and my ears picked up the muttering of scared voices. I gestured toward a door up ahead. We stepped slowly that way, taking extra care to be quiet.

Tonya held up three fingers, and I nodded. On count, we burst into the room, to find a group of ten capybaras. They were all lined up against a gray brick wall, a long, thick, silver chain linking them together. Each had a bag at their feet, as if they'd been instructed to gather their belongings.

The room smelled musty, as a small place with too many people often did. Five bunk beds took up the majority of the floor, all fitted with thick covers and blankets which made me think this was where they'd been held.

Unlike the skunks that we'd found in the basement of the warehouse that Cam had been keeping, these people were clean and looked like they were fed regularly. Also, they showed no signs of abuse or neglect.

The fear though. That was the same. That identical look of despair that had dulled the eyes of my fellow skunks now took up residence in the eyes of these capybaras.

A fire roared in my gut because both groups had been at the mercy of a heartless coward, who would do anything to line his own pockets, with no care for the damage he caused others.

I softened my face and talked as calmly as I could. "We're here to help." I didn't drop my shield, but I held up my hands in a non-threatening manner. "We're going to get you out of here and back home to your families."

A woman at the back of the line, with short brown hair, wearing cut off blue pants, and a gray sweater, looked at us, relief filling her eyes at first before confusion and trepidation took over. I looked around and saw that most looked unsure and frightened, as if they didn't believe we were really there to help. I couldn't say I blamed them for being doubtful.

Tonya showed them the Albright badge around her neck. "We're only here to help." She sniffed the air, her wolf senses kicking in. "I can smell your fear, and it's okay. It's okay to be scared, but we're not going to hurt you."

She had this under control, so I quietly traced my steps backward, not wanting a stampede of agents to come in and shake them up again. I needed to warn them off.

Outside, the remainder of Darren's henchman had been handcuffed, but the man himself was nowhere in sight.

"We've got a team clearing the house," Jax said to me when I walked up.

I nodded. "Let them know to stay out of the kitchen on the bottom floor. There's a group of ten capybaras there. Tonya's trying to calm them down."

Jax gave the command through his com. "We won't know much until we go through it all, but it looks like he kept most of his records here. Intel tells us that he's paranoid, makes his whole crew strip down completely naked, cavity searches and all before they're allowed to exit or enter his home."

I looked at his men and women now being loaded into Albright vans. "Not a pretty picture."

Jax's eyes followed mine. "No. It's not. Look, we'll have someone interrogate them and go through this stuff. If they find anything of use they'll let us know."

"Good." Now on to the more immediate problem. A quick look at my watch told me we only had about five hours before I would no longer be myself.

I closed my eyes for a second and tried to calm my nerves, that by now were doing a good impression of jumping beans. "Where to next," I asked, anxious to get on with it.

Jax gave a glance around to make sure all was secure then put his hand on my arm. "Hey, we're going to fix this, okay? Next house is Maze. I don't think it'll be gift wrapped like this one. Of the three she's the smartest, but we won't know anything until we get there."

Drena and Garrett joined us, but it was Drena who spoke. "More Albright and Scope agents are on the way, ETA is three minutes."

Jax nodded. "We'll leave most of them here. I have another team already staked out and ready to move on Maze."

Garrett and I looked to Drena. As our senior officer, it was her job to tell us what to do. "I've got a crew headed that way too. Garrett, Rye, and myself will follow. The other Scope agents can stay here."

Tonya emerged from the house, taking slow, careful steps, the capybaras right there with her. Most of them looked nervous and scared, but her soft voice and gentle coaxing seemed to be getting the job done.

Jax watched for a second and seemed to come to a decision. "I'll take Fred and Cynthia with me. Tonya, I think can help with the care of the capybaras. They seem to trust her. Her best attribute is relaxing victims so that we can actually help them."

I checked my watch again, and Drena gave me a sad smile. I closed my eyes, not wanting to see the same loss of hope in her eyes that was starting to fog up my own.

Growing up as a skunk, you learned to live with a certain amount of fear, because the threat of being captured for your oil was always real.

This was something else, though. This was a complete loss of self. This was worse than seeing my grandmother lose herself in the next faceless man.

My very existence was at stake and once those eight hours were up, life as I knew it would be over.

5

It took us about ten minutes to get from Darren's house to Maze's. As soon as all teams arrived, Jax gave the command. Just like before, we put up our shields.

Maze's house was just as big as Darren's, but instead of white, it was blue and red brick. Garrett and Sam, who was an Albright agent with fly DNA, checked the perimeter. "Clear," Garrett said when they landed back beside us.

Jax nodded. "Alright people, keep your shields up and let's go. You have your positions, so let's move in."

We went in the front door two by two and spread out. My heart sat in my throat as I went from room to room hoping to find something on the capybaras whose morillo now invaded my body.

We had the house cleared in a matter of minutes and found nothing. Not one person, not one strand of morillo or vial of blood. Unlike her colleague, Maze preferred to keep her house completely free of any signs that she was one of the biggest drug dealers in the world.

Jax ran a frustrated hand down his face then pointed to a tall skinny man, with reddish brown hair. His yellow-orange eyes told me that he had bear DNA. "Lim, you're the best tracker I've got. Sniff around and tell me what you find."

The man's nose flared as he sniffed through the air for a bit then shot up the steps.

Jax watched him go. "Whatever scent he picks up we'll follow."

Trackers could often sniff out anything, but what differentiated the good ones from the bad ones was deciding which scents to follow and which weren't worth the effort. Everybody made mistakes, but a good tracker was right more often than they were wrong.

Lim came back down the steps and shot out of the house. We ran behind him, Jax pointing to agents as we went, telling who to stay and who to go.

Lim jumped into his car, and we hurriedly followed. We drove behind him for about ten minutes before he stopped the car on a bridge, got out, and began to sniff the air again.

Then he stopped, his confused eyes straying toward the water, and my breath stopped as I thought he'd lost the scent.

But no, he gave a wave of the hand, then dived into the river. Only those with bear DNA could keep the scent after it hit the water, which is another thing that made them excellent trackers.

Garrett rose a few feet off the ground. "I'll follow and see where he's going."

Drena watched him swim then turned to Jax. "You think he's on to something?"

Jax watched Lim's long strokes as he sped through the water. "He usually is."

Garrett dipped lower, and Lim pointed and said something to him that made him take off back toward us. "The house is just around this bend here. "Follow me."

We hopped back into our cars, and drove for another five

minutes, but stopped when we got too close to our destination, wanting the element of surprise to still be on our side.

"It's the blue clapboard up ahead, the one with all the people on the porch," Garrett let us know.

We waded through the bushes, getting a good look at our surroundings. "How do you want to play this?" I looked from Drena to Jax.

Drena's eyes drifted to the house. Five men and three women sat on the porch, listening to music, eating, and drinking. "I say we storm the place. Take 'em down quick and hard."

Jax talked into his com for a moment, then his eyes set on mine. "You good with that plan? Just run up in there like we own the place?" He had a twinkle in his eye, and I knew he was trying to assuage some of my fear.

I gave him a small smile to let him know that I appreciated the effort. "Whatever it takes." I was completely serious, and from the look on his face, he knew it.

I would never allow myself to be at the mercy of another, to have no control of my own actions. I'd rather be a dead skunk than a subservient one.

Jax stared at me a moment as if trying to read through me. I looked back, eyes as open and honest as I could make them.

"Okay," he said after a couple of seconds, eyes never leaving mine. "So, we storm the place. On my count."

We went in hard and fast. The people on the porch acted about how we'd expected. At first surprised and confused, looking around trying to figure out what was going on, then fists went up, and the real fighting began.

I left them to it and slipped into the house, my thiols up as a shield. If they had capybara here, then I meant to find the one who'd infected me. I walked slow, clearing the living room then the bedrooms.

Nothing. My heart sank and hope became a foreign concept. This house too had been a dead-end.

The sound of screams and the smell of fire had me running back up the hallway. I looked out the window and saw lights and powers sizzling through the air.

That was fine, Scope and Albright had it under control, what I needed was a clue on who'd done this to me.

I went back down the hall and checked the house again. Keeping my shield up was draining me, so I leaned against the wall and tried to catch my breath. I wouldn't drop my shield though, no matter how bad it got.

Not that I could be infected again. Once taken over by one morillo, you were immune to all others. My problem was that this morillo hadn't taken me yet. So if we found the capybara it belonged to, and got them to remove it, it still left me open for another attack. Which was a real threat, because the last thing I needed was to have to hunt down yet another capybara, to remove yet another strain of morillo from my body.

The creak of a floorboard forced my attention back up the hallway. My footsteps were soft and my movement light. I crept toward the sound and stopped when I saw who it was that stood before me.

Maze. Her body was turned toward the kitchen, but her head was tilted as if she was keeping track of what was going on outside.

"Walk one more step, and it'd be your last." Her voice came out mocking, yet serious, causing me to freeze where I stood.

Slowly she turned my way. "Still creeping through houses unguarded and alone." She watched me closely, looking for what, I didn't know. "I would have thought you'd had enough of that by now."

No need to conceal myself any longer, I walked

cautiously into the room, keeping my senses open for any oncoming attacks. "So, it was you who did this to me," I accused.

She looked amused as if we were playing a game and she'd just thrown out the winning hand. "Was it? Now why would I do that?"

"Why would you need a Scope agent under your control? Oh, I don't know." I waved my hand through the air. "I can think of a million reasons."

Her amusement was gone, and now she just looked bored. "Really? I can't think of one."

Something about the way she said it, that and her whole demeanor put me on edge. Something wasn't right here. I wasn't seeing as...

She kicked me hard in the chest, moving faster than my eyes could follow.

I stumbled back into the wall, my chest on fire from the pain. She'd stunned me enough to make me drop my shield, and before I could get it back up, she was on me again.

Her long nails clawed at my face, making me scream out in agony as she ripped at me over and over again. I put my hands up and tried to defend myself, but she flipped me over so that I was face down on the floor. She then sat on my back, and I tried not to panic as the thought of being suffocated floated through my mind.

She pulled my head up by my hair. My neck muscles strained, and my throat felt as if it was ready to detach from my body. Her voice was hot and rushed as it whispered in my ear. "I'm not going to kill you, pretty girl. We've still got plans for you. Once the morillo sets in, well, then I won't have to do this."

Before I could respond, she got a tighter grip on my hair and slammed my head into the floor. I think I honestly saw stars as my head began to swim. I tried to use my thiols to propel me up, but I'd already been weakened by the use of my shield, so the only thing that came out was a small puff.

I swallowed down my fear and pushed back, trying again to throw her off me, but by now my head was spinning, and blackness was beginning to creep under my eyelids.

A thumping sound from beyond the kitchen caught both of our attention, and she was off me in a flash, running in that direction.

Thankfully my com was still in my ear. I knew if I called for them, my fellow agents would be here in a second. That's just how we rolled, we always had each other's back. It was one of the things that made me proud to be a Scope agent.

I gave off a weak, pitiful "help," then tried to get to my knees, and from there, to my feet.

I at least wanted to be on equal footing with her when she got back. My head was still spinning, and I pushed down the small amount of vomit that had made its way into my mouth. I needed the element of surprise. That was the only way to get the upper hand on Maze, I figured.

I brushed myself off and wiped hair from my face. Blood clung to my hands, and I knew I'd have a bunch of bruises later. I started a slow limp in the direction she'd gone, determined to get her before she had a chance to get me again.

I'd probably only made it about two feet when Drena, Jax, Garrett, and a handful of agents came bursting through the door.

I'd started to lean to the side, my vision going in and out. Drena quickly wrapped an arm around me and hauled me up. "Maze. She went that way." I pointed to where the noise had come from.

Jax and Cynthia shot off in that direction. "Is the house clear?" Drena asked me, and I nodded.

"As far as I checked, but there was a noise by the kitchen.

Don't know what it was, but Maze seemed in a hurry to get there. Hey, at least it stopped her from bashing my head in."

My legs went weak as a steady pool of blood dripped from my face. Drena tightened her grip, unwilling to let me fall.

Another crash sounded, then Jax and Cynthia came back with their hands up. Maze and about twenty of her crew walked behind them. "Get over there." A big guy pushed Jax and Cynthia our way.

Jax came up beside me and slipped a hand around my waist, causing Drena to let go. I didn't want her to. To be honest, I needed the support of both of them to stay upright. "What happened?" I asked Jax.

He turned deadly eyes toward Maze and the people with her. "Got a room as big as a football field, just a little past the kitchen. Full of capybara. I didn't get a chance to count how many."

Maze said something to her crew and then turned toward us. "Well, what do we have here? Is this the best that Albright has to offer these days?"

Jax looked a little startled as his eyes traveled the length of her body. "You're not Maze," he finally said, causing mine, and every other agent's head to snap his way. "Where's the real Maze?"

I wondered if Jax had hit his head as well. He'd shown us pictures of Maze before we'd come, and this was most definitely her.

She smirked at him, and I felt something in my stomach drop. The look on her face was pretty much an admission, but her words contradicted that, though only barely. "Of course, I'm Maze. Whoever else would I be?" Her sly smile gave it away, and I realized we'd been played big time.

She turned back to her crew. "Kill them all except for the one infected with the morillo."

They charged us, and Garrett made a ring of fire, engulfing us in it and keeping them out. I grabbed tighter to Jax. "My back," I said, hoping he'd understand.

A short heavyset dude rushed the fire barrier and Jax held up his hand and use his power the pull the man's spine out. The guy's jaw went slack before he fell face first to the floor.

Another man came, this one tall and muscular. Garrett breathed fire into the man's eyes, causing him to scream and back away.

Drena and Cynthia also helped with the fending off while Jax turned his attention to me.

"I don't have anything to put the liquid in," he said, looking around as if something would reveal itself in our circle of fire.

"Right pocket," I said, turning a bit so he could get to it. "Never leave home without it now."

Jax took the small vial from me, squeezing my hand as he did so. "Tell me when, ok?"

Drena, whose skin was still a hard protective shell, was blocking every attack they launched at us, but one must have slipped through, because blue light landed by my head, burning the ground beside me. "Now!" I said.

I turned to my side and put my hands between my legs, hoping that any thiols that leaked out would hit me and miss everyone else. Some thiols always came out when someone removed the fat from the lateral glands in a skunk's back. It was the only way to get to the skunk oil though, and right now I needed it if I had any chance of making it out of here alive.

The pain was excruciating, and I bit my bottom lip until he finished. "Mostly my head, that's where the pain is."

He began to massage the oil into my head, but I knew the quickest way for me to heal was to drink the stuff. "Give it here." I reached out my hand for the vial, and he fitted my fingers around it. I took a deep breath and then swallowed the skunk oil whole.

It tasted bitter, like cooked leaves and it tingled as it worked its way through my system. The effect was almost immediate. Within seconds my vision cleared, and my energy came roaring back. Had I not drunk it and just let him rub it in, I would have still healed, but at a much slower rate.

Maze and her squad had us crowded in, and some were close to breaking through the ring of fire.

I surged up, using my thiols to balance me in the air. I jumped high enough to go over the fire ring. Fist raised, I brought it down hard, right on the fake Maze's face. After that, all hell broke loose.

She stumbled back but didn't fall, so I started a relentless rain of blows onto her face. One of her minions came at me. Of frog DNA, he jumped, mouth opened wide, intending to incapacitate me with his spit.

I rolled out of the way, waited until he landed, and then kicked his legs out from under him. After that I quickly shot a line of foul smelling thiols into his mouth.

He gagged, grabbed his throat and fell off to the side. A big man with hammer hands, of beaver descent, landed a smack across Drena's face. With her hard shell protecting her, she didn't even flinch.

Instead, she put both hands together, to make a mega fist, and hit him square in the stomach, sending the man flying across the room.

My thiols back to its top level, I aimed toward the mouth and ears of anyone who came toward me. I made sure to make it sour enough to leave them writhing in pain and out of the fight.

More Scope and Albright agents came, and soon the fake Maze and all her people were in custody.

Now we only had to free the capybara and hopefully find the one who'd infected me.

The kitchen was a mess of pots, pans, and silverware. From the smell of crab legs and shrimp, someone had just finished cooking. My stomach growled, and I realized it'd been hours since I'd last eaten. That didn't really matter though because the thought of food turned my stomach inside out.

I checked my watch and saw that we only had three hours left to save me.

Jax and Cynthia led us to the room with the capybara. It was as huge as a football stadium. The walls were off-white while the floors were solid wood. Dozens of bunk beds lined the walls, with small ottomans in front of them.

It was a little cluttered with clothes thrown over beds and on the back of chairs. Two or three hampers sat at the foot of every bed. Some were empty while others seemed to be over-flowing.

It smelled of fruit soap and strawberry shampoo in here and one look around told me why. There was a door toward the back of the room labeled bathroom, and as I walked closer, I saw that it held a shower, tub, and sink.

I'd counted over twenty capybaras when I'd come in, and for the most part, they seemed apprehensive, not knowing if we were friend or foe.

"We're not here to hurt you." Garrett held his hands up. "We just want to get you home to your families."

"Rain!" a woman in the back shrieked. I put her age at around forty but knew I could be off by a few years either way. She was tall with brown hair, hazel eyes, and a nervous face. She looked clean, as if she'd just recently used the shower and I looked around and noticed that most of the men and women here looked the same.

Their clothes were worn, but still looked decent. Also, I

noted that not one of them appeared to be starving or malnourished. Just like with the capybaras we'd found at Darren's, these too seemed to be in good shape.

I wondered if it was easier to get more morillo out of them this way. Or maybe a capybara's morillo was most powerful when the body was well taken care of. It was something I'd definitely be checking into later. That is if I had a later, I remembered, rubbing a hand down my face in an effort to cool my nerves.

"Rain," the woman said again, pointing at me. "You smell like Rain."

The guy standing beside her sniffed the air and let his nose lead him until he was standing right in front of me. Judging from the bit of gray at his temples I put him to be a few years older than her, but they were of the same height and had the same nervous glint in their eyes. "She's right. You smell like our brother, Rain." He looked at me as if waiting for me to explain myself.

The woman came over as well and stood next to her brother. Jax, Drena, and Garrett stopped what they were doing and came over to listen.

The woman patted her hair down, seeming a bit self-conscious now that all eyes were on her. "My brother was at home last I saw him." She wiped tears from her eyes and the man beside her squeezed her hand while wiping his own. "It's the only thing that's gotten me through this, knowing that he was okay."

Her face crumbled and she buried her head in her brother's chest.

Even though I now had a name for the person whose morillo I carried, I took no pleasure from it. Watching Rain's brother and sister break down in front of me was hard, because I didn't know if I could help them or myself. "We're going to find him," I said, with no idea how to do so. "We're going to find him and bring him back to you. What can you tell us about your brother that would help?"

Drena gave me a sharp look for making promises that I might not be able to keep, but I ignored her and took down what information I could.

They told us of a night club, not far from here. I'd heard of it, drove past it a couple of times, but never stopped to go in. "No time like the present," I mumbled as I followed the last of the capybara out of the room.

More Scope and Albright Agents had arrived and began loading the capybaras up in the vans they'd arrived in. They'd debrief them, get them medical help if they needed it, and then help them get home.

I watched Jax, Drena, and Garrett talking to the other agents around us and wondered how much longer I'd be a part of this. I looked down at my ticking watch and knew that my time was running short.

6

From the outside, club "Explosion" looked like any other nighttime spot. Neon lights lit up the small square building, techno music blasted from inside, and the parking lot was full of cars. Two bouncers stood at the door, both of capybara descent.

Both were big, and broad chested with more muscles than they probably knew what to do with. One had short red hair and the other black. They stood in front of the door, blocking us when we tried to enter. "What's your business here?" the one with the black hair asked.

Jax pulled out his Albright badge and showed it to them. The two men gave each other an unreadable look and then stepped aside to allow us entrance. As we walked through, I saw one of them speaking into a com, letting someone named Jem know we were there.

"So, I guess we talk to Jem," I said to no one in particular.

Inside the place looked nothing like it did outside. The music sounded far off and in another room. The lights were bright, and it was easy to see brown walls and a paneled floor. It smelled of sweat and pine which wasn't that unpleasant a scent.

The place had about fifty people inside, all capybara. They turned to stare at us when we entered, and a few stood.

I took in how all the tables had been pushed together as if they were having some sort of meeting. The tables held maps, and notepads, and papers.

Though this was a bar, few here seemed to be drinking alcohol. Most had juice, water, or soda in front of them. I got the spooky impression that what we'd just stumbled upon was something they definitely didn't want local law enforcement to know about.

One guy, tall, with a bald head and deep-set brown eyes, stood and walked our way. "I'm Jem." His eyes traveled over each of us. "What can we help you with today?" He looked at me and nodded. "Sister."

I figured I still smelled like capybara and that's why he was confused. "Oh, I'm not, I'm..." I trailed off not knowing what else to say.

He looked at my thick, course, black hair. "Think I know a skunk when I see one, but you are a sister all the same. To the capybara anyway. Who else knows what it's like to be hunted and sold for simply being yourself, to be used to make others money. Who else knows the fear of a loved one not showing up on time, of being out of contact with them for too long, fearing they've been captured. We are partners in this."

I nodded because he couldn't have been more right. No one else knew what it felt like unless your species was a target as well. It was easy to sit on the sidelines and judge, but until you yourself were faced with what we went through, you couldn't possibly understand.

He must have read as much on my face because his shoulders relaxed just a little as he stared at me. "Figured Rain was missing. Haven't seen him around here in a while. Had some of the guys check out his house, and the only thing they found of interest was this."

He walked over to the table and ruffled through some papers before coming back with a faded flyer in his hand. I took it from him and read it over. It was for a new textile company set to come to town, and this was a call for job openings.

Jem took the paper back from me. "Saw this all over town. Don't have a count on just how many capybaras they've trapped this way, but I believe it to be more than a few."

"Have you been to the address given?" I asked, noticing that it was only a few blocks away.

He nodded. "More than once. Nothing. Whole place has been shut down, and wiped clean."

"Dammit," I cursed under my breath. So close, yet... Oh, of course, they wouldn't still be in the same place.

Jax's phone rang, and he took it out of his pocket and put it to his ear. He listened for a couple of seconds and then seemed to perk up. "Good job. That's good work right there. Okay, talk to you later."

He hung the phone up and then turned to us. "At least three of the capybara from the house we just left remember being in a house on East Thompson before being moved.

"They said they were being held by Lucky, the third dealer on our list before they were transferred to the fake Maze's house."

East Thompson was a street about three miles long. It would take forever to search each house, and a quick look at my watch told me we only had two hours left.

I took a few steps back as my breath started to close in on me. Reality hit me square in the chest, and I realized that we might not be in time to stop this thing. Then, my life, my life would be over.

Jax gave my arm a quick squeeze. "Nobody's giving up today. We've still got time. Lim can track the scent. If you smell like Rain, and he's in the vicinity, then Lim can track him." I nodded, choosing to put my trust in that instead of dissolving on the floor into a fit of tears.

The one thing I couldn't figure out though was if some of the capybaras had been with Lucky, how had they ended up with the fake Maze?

Had there been a turf-war, an overtaking? The answer to those questions would probably answer many more.

Jem watched us closely, but I noticed he didn't say a word. He was probably hoping to suck up as much information as he could before one of us noticed.

When Jax spoke again, it was Jem he addressed. "We'll be sure to stop back through, try to bring you any news that we can. I know it can't be easy, not knowing if your loved ones are all right or not."

Jem ignored Jax and turned to me. "We'll be thankful for any information you can give."

Once on East Thompson, Lim took a good whiff of me and began to sniff around. We were at the top of the street, and so far, we'd found nothing. "Let's go toward the middle," Drena suggested.

We took slow steps that way, Lim sniffing the air the whole time. We were probably partway through the middle when his ears perked up, and he looked at Jax. "That one, boss." He pointed to a brick house with blue shutters. Blue and white patio furniture sat on the left side of the porch, and a blue swing hung from the rafters. It looked nice.

"Is he in there now, or he's been in there recently?" Jax asked.

Lim shrugged. "Don't know about now, but in the last twenty-four hours, yeah."

Jax talked into his com, telling all the other agents where to join us, then turned to Drena. "How do you want to play this?"

She shrugged. "Like we have every other time, straight through the front door. We don't have much time."

Jax turned serious eyes my way. I could see the worry etched into them and I knew that he feared for me. My stomach rolled, and my mouth went dry because this truly was the end of the line.

"What do you want to do, Rye?" he asked me because it was my life that hung in the balance.

I didn't have to think about it. "Straight through the front door."

I heard a jingling sound and then Garrett was beside us. "Don't forget these." He held up a set of metal linked chains in the shape of diamonds. "You did so well with these last time. I just thought…"

Yeah, last time when I'd nearly beat my best friend to death with them. "Nice present," I said with no humor at all. I yanked the chains from his hand. "Asshole."

He didn't seem fazed by my temper. "You'll probably thank me later."

Jax gave me a "what will it hurt" look, and I jerkily wrapped them around my knuckles and took off running for the front door. I didn't bother to knock. Instead, I kicked it open and burst inside.

The house was quiet and smelled of oranges and smoke. The only thing I saw while running past was the black and white checkered furniture in the living room. The walls were a pristine white, and the floor had a deep rich black carpet on them. I walked through the kitchen and into a back room of sorts.

A young man, who gave the look of someone who'd never ran into a problem that he couldn't solve, stood in front of a table with vials of blood on it. Up above was a clothesline of morillo. He had short black hair and was of medium height and slim build.

He had headphones on and danced around happily as he held up a strand of morillo. I watched for a moment as he checked something in his notepad, then checked one of the vials of blood.

He stopped for a second, then dropped the vial and the morillo, and sprung through the air, right toward me.

I ducked, but didn't move fast enough. He hit me and knocked me to the ground. Stunned, I held up my arms and tried to ward him off. We struggled for a few seconds until I saw an opening and used my thiols to knock him back.

Jax and the others came running into the room, Lim leading the pack. I came to my feet unharmed and raised a hand to let them know I was okay.

The man lay on the ground, and one of the Albright agents grabbed him up and stuck magic binding cuffs on him, ignoring his struggles as he led him outside.

"Rain's in the ceiling," Lim said. "We need to try and find a trap door."

We all spread out to look. After about two minutes, one of the Albright agents shouted that she'd found it in one of the bedrooms.

She already had the door to the attic down when I walked into the room. I thought there'd be steps or something, but there wasn't anything to grab ahold of. I knew it would be a bumpy ride, but I had no other choice but to use my thiols to get to the top.

The smell hit me as I floated up, and I covered my nose to keep from choking. The scent of too many unwashed bodies in a confined space had me gagging.

Once through the small opening, I landed wobbly on a solid wood floor. The first thing I noticed was that this was much bigger than any attic I'd ever seen. It ran the length of the house, and there were probably a hundred dirty and dingy twin sized beds covering the floor.

The walls were wooden too, as were the horizontal studs connecting the floor to ceiling. It didn't look sturdy and I got the feeling if a strong wind came it would topple it all over.

Covers hung over the windows, blocking any sunlight from getting in and giving the place a dark and desolate feel. Three buckets, all overflowing with shit and piss sat a few feet in front of the windows and it was obvious that they weren't emptied on a regular basis.

Whoever had done this was disgusting, and I wanted nothing more than to rip them apart. The capybaras were mostly in their beds. Some lay huddled under the covers, while others gave me cautious looks as if I was there to exploit them even more.

All looked to be dirty, unwashed, and underfed. One man looked to be nothing but a bag of bones. His skin was stretched so tight that I wondered how he was even still alive.

Something in me broke in that moment, and thiols shot from my hand. I aimed it for the window, which blew open as a result, the sound loud and sending out an echo.

By now Jax and the others had made it up. The look of horror on their faces matched my own.

Footsteps from the dark half of the attic had sounded when the window had shattered, and now those figures came into focus. A gang of them, at least thirty, with Lucky and Maze leading the pack.

"Look, Maze," Lucky said, gesturing toward us. "We have guests."

I looked at Jax to get his reaction and saw that he looked

as shocked as I felt. "So, you two are working together?" I asked.

Lucky looked at me as if I'd been a naughty child. "You may have abandoned your best friend for getting in the drug trade, doesn't mean I had to, not when I could simply join."

Anger and hurt clouded my good sense, and I opened my mouth and shot thiols straight into his eyes. He let out a scream, and before he could recover, I shot thiols at Maze too.

She jumped out of the way, then raised a fist and dropped it, causing her whole crew to charge our way.

The capybara whose morillo I carried was somewhere in this room, so I planned on fighting like hell until I found him. No way was I getting this close only to fail.

I shot a stream of thiols out, wrapping it around three of them like a lasso. I then quickly turned it sour and sent a line of it straight into their nostrils.

Their eyes bugged, the inhuman smell suffocating them from the inside out. They dropped to the floor, and I hurriedly pulled it back, wanting only to knock them out, not kill them.

Two men approached from Jax's left, he held his hands up, and they screamed in agony, as he stripped every piece of hair from their bodies. Eyebrows and all. They looked naked, hairless, and the way their faces contorted in pain when they fell over, I knew it would be awhile before either of them made a peep.

One man tried to hit Drena, and she blocked it with her shelled arm, then jabbed an elbow to his face, followed up by an uppercut that dropped him immediately.

Garrett tripped one guy up with a small ring of fire while blasting another through the chest.

A tall man with a crew cut dipped behind me before I could stop him, and put a hand around my neck, choking me so hard I couldn't move. A woman came in front of me and kicked my face hard.

My head snapped back, and I tasted blood in my mouth. My throat tightened, and I started to lose air. I had to find some type of way to get away from them. I'd come too far to have it all end now.

The chains on my hands jingled as I clawed at his hands, trying to remove them. The sound calmed me and reminded me that I did have another weapon at my disposal.

The woman raised her leg to kick me again, and I loosened the chain from my fist and swung it, hitting her in the face, and knocking her off her feet. She wouldn't be down for long, so I swung the chain behind me and hit the guy holding me as well.

The metal made a tinkling sound when it landed, but it wasn't enough to make him let go.

The woman rose to her feet, and I was starting to lose strength as his hold on me tightened. She came at me again, and I let myself go slack in his arms, eyes closed as if I'd passed out.

He gave off a satisfied "done" and tried to push me to the floor. As soon as he removed his hand, I sprung up and used my thiols to lift me in the air until I was behind him. I then brought the chain to his neck and wrapped it around, while shooting thiols out of my eyes and into the woman's face.

He gurgled and gagged, hands pulling at the chain, while her eyes bulged and they both dropped to the floor, passed out.

More agents entered the room, and pretty soon we had it all under control. I took a deep breath, happy it was finally over, but knowing it was bittersweet for the capybara that had been captured and their families who hadn't known if they were dead or alive.

Jax came up beside me. His shirt was torn and his hair a

shaggy mess. His face was bruised on the right, and he had blood on his neck and hands. I raised my eyebrows at him.

"You should see the other guy," he said as his eyes raked me over, no doubt checking for bruises.

"I'm fine," I said, trying to catch my breath.

Drena had dropped her shield but looked as out of breath as I felt. "Thirty minutes," she said, looking at me.

Something went hollow in my chest, and I looked at my watch. She was right. In thirty minutes, I would officially belong to someone else. We needed to find this Rain now.

The agents were busy loading up Lucky and Maze along with their crew. Someone had found a ladder and they were using that to get them all down.

Garrett no longer wore a shirt, and his pants were all but ripped off him, but other than that, and a few cuts and bruises, he seemed okay.

Cynthia's hair was a mess, and her clothes just a little askew. Really the only sign that she'd been in a fight was the bump forming nicely on the side of her head.

The room was all but cleared now except for the capybaras and a few agents. Lim's nostrils widened, and he started to sniff the air. He went for a tall guy, with black hair and dirt clinging to his head. The man sat watching us with wide-eyed terror on his face.

I guess after witnessing the fight we'd just had, and after being held captive so long, they had no idea who they could trust. I walked a little closer until I was just a few feet in front of him. "Look, we're not here to hurt you."

I held my hands up, and then quickly put them down when I remembered they were covered with a metal chain, and that was my usual way to launch a thiols attack. "I think I have your morillo in me, and I really need you to remove it."

Drena and Jax came to stand on either side of me. The

man's eyes shifted to his right, and the look of terror on his face increased.

"What's he scared of?" Jax wondered out loud.

It wasn't just him. The other capybara in the room seemed to be looking at that same spot. I walked a little closer and really got a good look at the man and woman sitting on the bed beside him.

Before I could completely figure it out, the man jumped to his feet and wrapped his arm around my neck.

"Twenty minutes," the man whispered in my ear, and everything in me told me that this was the real Lucky. Seemed like him and Maze both liked playing "hide and seek." "Twenty minutes and you'll be under our control."

I elbowed him in the stomach, my chains clinging as I did so. He let out a whoosh of air, and I squirmed out of his arms, then wrapped the chain around his neck, forcing him to the ground.

"Of course, now that everyone knows you've been infected, you're really of no use to us. Maybe we should just kill you now," he said from his spot on the floor.

He kept saying we, which made me look at the woman he'd been sitting beside. Her eyes met mine, and the spark of victory in them, cobbled with the angle of her nose, and the height of her cheekbones, told me exactly who she was.

"Maze," I shouted, pointing at her, at the exact moment she sprung up, dragon wings flapping. She flew toward the open window, but Garrett was on her in a second, Drena and Cynthia backing him up.

He tackled her to the ground, and Drena put a boot to her throat, while Cynthia brought out the cuffs. Maze smiled when they led her back toward the rest of us. "We'll be out in a manner of minutes. You really think your jails can hold us."

Jax's face stayed impassive. "We'll see."

Once the real Maze and Darren were handed off, the

capybara in the room seemed to let out a collective breath of air. Jax put a hand around my waist and kissed the side of my head. "We can end this now," he whispered.

I nodded, hoping he was right. Garrett, Cynthia, and Drena began to help with getting the capybara out of there, while Jax and I stood in front of Rain. He still sat on the bed, his eyes exhausted, and his shoulders slumped. "Please, help me," I said. "I know you've been through an ordeal, and what happened to you isn't fair, but please, if you could please take this out of me, you're the only one who can."

He came to his feet, an unreadable look on his face. "Sister," he said looking at me. "Sister." At first, I thought he was asking about his own sister, and then I remembered that Jem had called me that as well.

Sister, because as skunks and capybara we both suffered for something we had no control over, something we were born with that made us a target.

"Sister," I said, nodding at him to let him know I understood.

His face turned to one of acceptance, and he raised his hands and began to mumble under his breath. The air went out of me, and I fell to my knees as my body began to shake. A cough started in my throat, and soon I was hacking and vomiting, my stomach clenching as it tried to expel everything I'd ever eaten in my life.

My arm felt as if it was on fire, as skin slowly peeled back, and the morillo began to rise to the surface, guided by Rain. What probably only took a few seconds, felt like an eternity, but finally, he was done and I was morillo free. Relieved, I lay on the floor, panting and gasping for air, my whole body now on fire.

"It'll pass in a couple of minutes." Jax was beside me, his arms wrapped around my waist.

I looked to Rain, who by now was one of the only capybara left in the attic. "Thank you. Your brother and sister are waiting for you, as are Jem and the rest of the bar."

His eyes lit up, and for the first time, I saw a look of hope on his face. A tear escaped his eyes as he watched me. "You really found them? My family?"

I nodded, still trying to catch my breath, but happy with how many people would be united with loved ones today. "Yeah, we really found them."

7

W e had gone in without warrants, so a lot of what we'd found didn't stick, but the capybara's stories of how they'd been taken and held against their will did.

Albright along with Scope got credit for bringing down three of the largest Morillo operations ever. The capybara we'd captured freely gave up the names of those who'd they'd been forced to infect, while causing the morillo in those individuals to go dormant, thus ending the power, held over them.

From what we could gather, both Lucky and Maze had searched for years, and in many states, before finding people who looked enough like them to pass as body doubles.

The doubles had been trained and paid well, and from how they'd fooled us, I'd say they'd earned that money. Too bad they'd never have an opportunity to spend it.

I, myself ended up taking a week off work. Just the thought of what could have happened, what almost had happened, was a little too much for me to bear.

I'd been in sticky situations before, but nothing that had brought me so close to the edge.

I imagined all the people who'd unknowingly been infected had an even worse time of it, and counseling had been set up for them, as well as for the capybara who'd been held captive.

Jax was with me tonight, and for the first time in a long time, I allowed myself to relax just a little.

"You know you really scared me there for a minute," he said. Jax sat at the kitchen table, a bottle of beer in his hand, two large pizzas in front of him. I hadn't seen him in a week, not wanting to be bothered with anyone. But tonight, I'd called him over, and he'd picked up the beer and pizza on the way.

I took a swallow of my own beer, enjoying the burn as it went down. "Really?" We were playing connect four and I picked up a red chip and placed it into a slot that blocked his black one from winning.

"Really," he said, pulling me down onto his lap.

I bit into a slice of pizza, the cheese so gooey and filled with sauce that I closed my eyes, and just gave myself a moment to enjoy it. "How were you going to get along without me?" I teased.

He waved a hand through the air as if it was nothing. "Oh, I'm sure I could have found someone else who likes cold beer, hot pizza, and connect four."

I ran a hand through his tangle of curls, enjoying the feel of them on my fingers. "Asshole."

He smiled, but when he looked at me, his eyes were nothing but serious. This time I saw the fear that he must have felt, at thinking he would lose me forever. "Yeah, but I'm your asshole."

I put the pizza down, and placed my hands on either side of his face, kissing him softly. "That you are, babe, that you are."

BLOOD CURSED

1

―――――――

"This is the best thing I've ever tasted," Klenaya said, twirling spaghetti noodles around her fork and scooping up plenty of sauce before shoving it into her mouth.

Kyle had four different types of soda sitting in front of him and a fifth one in his hand ready to drink.

I chuckled and shook my head. He seemed fascinated with the stuff. "You said that last week when we ate hot chili for the first time. What's it going to be next?" he asked her.

Klenaya and Kyle were twenty-one-year-old twins. Their skin was a dark brown and they both had bone straight blue-green hair that hung loosely around their shoulders. They each had bright purple eyes that lit up every couple of seconds, but even more so when they were excited.

I'd met them when I'd been thrust into their world, and alternate universe, by my ex-boyfriend Greg and one of his cohorts. I was back home now, but the two often slipped into my universe to visit.

Klenaya and Kyle's world, was ninety percent water, and

the people living there had bodies made up of between seventy-five to eighty-three percent water.

See, that's the thing. I may not have had anything else going for me, no job, no friends, but I could control water, and anything that had water in it.

I'd always thought it to be a useless power and so had the kids at school who'd ridiculed me daily about it. I never fought them, though I realized now that I could have.

Still I'd been too paralyzed with fear to make a move against anyone back then. I shuddered, shaking my head, not wanting to go down the route of bad memories and torturous school days.

Kyle and Klenaya's universe was a big world made up of multiple countries. Greg's country, Langunda, bordered the twin's country Kelm. Greg and the other Langunda had thought to use me and my water powers to take over Kelm so that they could get their hands on the precious tacium.

Tacium was a blue powdered substance that gave the people of the twin's world immortal life. They could be hurt, they could even have their faces ripped off. I'd perform this action on Amber myself when she'd attacked me. Amber was a Langunda like Greg, and she'd worked with him to hurt and deceive me.

The tacium in her had made sure her face had grown back and she'd stayed breathing. The stuff was in everything from their food to their building materials to their clothing.

Tacium made everything faster, last longer, so that the only thing that could kill them was going too many days without it. They were addicted to the stuff. Their world, much like ours, was made up of multiple countries and rulers, yet every one of them would die without the tacium.

Tacium was naturally produced on Kelm, where the twins lived, so that's why Greg had wanted to take it over. The ones who controlled the tacium controlled the whole universe.

Finding out after years of being with him that it'd been the only reason he'd talked to me in the first place, thinking he could use me to overtake the tacium, had left a bitter hole in the pit of my stomach that was just now starting to heal.

Klenaya had saved me, saved me and Leon, the policeman that had been brought along for the ride.

Leon sat across from me now, sipping his coffee and watching Kyle down soda after soda. He frowned. "I can't even imagine what you're doing to your kidneys right now, Kyle."

Leon had helped in saving the tacium from Greg and his people, saying that the cop in him just couldn't stand by and do nothing. I, on the other hand, had needed a little more convincing.

Kyle gave Leon a look that said he didn't care one bit, and proceeded to down another.

I laughed and took a sip of my soda. It felt good being here like this with them and I really enjoyed their company. Before going to the hospital, a place I'd been sent after Greg had mind warped me, I hadn't had any friends. Greg had been my whole world, and in my eyes, he was all I'd needed.

Growing up, my sister had been my only friend, and now she was on the Isles with my mother, hundreds of miles away from me.

The Isles was a place full of powerful beings and my mom had been born and raised there. They didn't believe in violence on the Isles and my mom had taught me not to fight, to always take the passive approach.

This of course had put a damper on Greg's plan for me to help him take over Kelm, but he'd done small things to try and bring about anger in me and get me to fight. He'd had me beat up in an alley once, another time he'd had me robbed.

All in an effort to bring out the inner fighter in me.

When that hadn't worked, he used his mental power to warp me into shooting him, thinking a little time in jail was all I needed to resort to violence. That hadn't worked either, as the teaching of the Isles was engraved deep within my soul.

I'd believed him to be immortal, which he had been, but no one had believed me and they'd placed me in a mental hospital instead of jail.

My mom and sister hadn't helped me out of it and they could have. I think I must have needed to learn something from the experience, because I saw no other reason they would let me waste away for five years in a mental hospital knowing I was innocent.

I let out a sigh, and wiped a hand down my face. They'd never even come to see me. Something else I didn't understand.

It had been difficult then and it was difficult now, being here without their support. I hadn't talk to either of them in so long.

Kyle chugged more soda, while Klenaya finished her meal. Letting the past go, I decided to focus on the future instead.

"So, what do you guys have in mind for today?" I asked because I knew they were up to something. They always had the whole day planned when they came to my world.

It'd been three months since we'd taken down Greg and his people, and they'd been coming here fairly often since then.

Klenaya got that sneaky look on her face, and I knew whatever it was, it would be something dangerous and hair-raising. They were thrill seekers, the both of them.

Leon knew it too, if the suspicious glance he shot between the two were anything to go by. "Look, I just got off work, so take it easy on me, okay." I couldn't tell if he was joking or not, but from the expression on his face, he knew that taking it easy with these two was a lost cause.

I picked up a breadstick and broke a small piece off and began to chew. Garlic flavor exploded over my tongue, and I savored as much of it as I could before washing it down with grape soda.

The twins and Leon were chatting about the last movie he and I had taken them to, and I watched on and smiled. Their happiness and excitement at seeing new things filled me with a special kind of joy, one I'd never really had before.

It was always nice seeing their eyes light up, well more than usual, because they had even more of a glow when they saw or did something that interested them.

Like going to the movies, skateboarding, or learning to ride a motorcycle, all things they didn't have or couldn't do back on Kelm. I enjoyed spending time with them a lot more than I thought I would, and I believed Leon did as well. He never seemed bothered when they came up with new and creative things to do, and he always seemed to be relaxed and enjoying himself when we were all together.

"We want to go to Growl for the day," Klenaya finally said. She finished the last of her spaghetti and pushed her plate away, looking at both Leon and myself with a big grin on her face.

Leon sat down his coffee mug with a resigned sigh and turned to her. "And what's on Growl?"

Kyle waved his hand in a nonchalant way and Leon and I shared a look because we knew what was coming. "Look, we just found out about it a week ago. They have battle fireworks, and we'd like to see them."

I almost spit out my soda to keep from laughing, and Leon did let out a chuckle. "What?" he asked, looking from one twin to the other. "Come on, I couldn't have heard you right."

Klenaya put her elbows on the table, and clasped her hands in front of her, eyes shining brightly. "You see, they take these fireworks, and base them on real people and fighters, sort of like the games we play on that box here when it's on the TV." The Wii and Xbox is what she meant, but I saw no need to correct her.

"You're not explaining it right." Kyle scowled at her. "And not every firework is based on a fighter, some are original creations."

"Then take over." She gestured at him. "Like you always do."

He ignored her sarcasm and sat up a little more in his chair. "See they are programmed with all these fight moves and predictions. Then, when you release them, they light up the sky like fireworks, and, you have a controller. Just like you do on the box here, and you battle the other person, using kicks, jabs, fists, and whatever power your fighter has."

Leon's ears perked up, and he actually seemed interested. "So, the fireworks have the body of a fighter, is it different colors?"

Kyle nodded. "Each fighter has its own distinct pattern."

"So, what do you get if you win?" I asked, getting a little intrigued myself.

"You win a money prize and a chance to advance up in the games," Klenaya answered quickly before her brother had a chance to say anything.

Leon looked at them, a small smile on his face and I knew they'd already won him over. "Well, what else do we have to do today? Delia, what do you think?"

What did I think? Something no one had ever really asked me until I'd met these three and it still filled me with small bits of confidence every time they did. "Why not?" I said, giving in as well. "Like Leon said, what else did we have to do today?" They were going to go whether we joined them or not, so I figured we might as well go along.

2

Like others of their universe, Klenaya and Kyle both had the ability to open portals. Klenaya opened one now from my world to her and Kyle's, so they could get their recording devices, as they didn't want to miss a minute of the fight.

Leon and I waited in the living room while they scampered off to get ready, and it was probably five minutes before a distressed looking Bale came walking up the hallway. Bale was the twin's father and also next in line to rule Kelm. Right now, he walked with his bald head bowed, as he talked distressingly to himself.

Leon and I passed a look between us, but neither of us said a word. Yama, the ruler of Kelm, came in behind him. Yama had purple hair that reached to his shoulders. That, along with his piercing red eyes always put the word "debonair" in my mind whenever I saw him. He zeroed in on me the moment he entered the room. "Delia, Leon, you have no idea how happy I am to see you two."

He wasn't surprised that we were there since it seemed like lately, we were always there.

"What's up?" Leon asked. He sat on one of the many couches in the room, hands folded in front of him, shoulders hunched. His red hair was brushed to the side, with a little extra up top and then the rest combed over.

Bale stood with his back to us looking out the window, his head still down.

Yama took a seat on the edge of the couch where I sat. His usual cavalier manner was gone, and his shoulders strained tight with tension. I'd never seen him worry about anything, really, so I knew this had to be serious. "Lamink is a country six hours away by boatcar. It along with the three countries beside it are faced with something we never thought we'd see here. A sickness so potent that even the presence of tacium is not enough to stop it."

He took a deep breath, but the tension in his shoulders remained. "It's spreading like wildfire, and it is only three countries away from Kelm. Another couple of days and everyone here could be infected."

My chest tightened at the thought of him, Bale, and the twins being infected with a disease that even tacium couldn't heal. I wanted to help, wanted to do anything I could to stop it. These were my friends now, and I wasn't ready to lose them. "What can I do?" I asked.

He ran a hand over his face as the twins came back into the room. Bale called them over to him, and from the devastated look on their faces, I assumed he told them.

Yama pointed to the water flowing beneath our feet. "We believe it's water based. That's what we've been able to narrow it down to. I've been asked by the leaders of those other nations to offer you two a deal."

Leon's head snapped up as if he'd thought he'd been exempt from this conversation altogether. "What?" he asked the other man, a little warily I thought.

"Fifty thousand a piece of your nation's dollars if you will use your water skills to try and pull the disease out," Bale said, walking fully into the room and away from the window. He turned to Leon. "And you are to back her up." He shook his head in a way that said he thought this whole thing was a very bad idea.

"Just how would you get your hand on a hundred thousand dollars from our world?" Leon asked, not bothering to keep the skepticism out of his voice.

Yama gave him a look that said he really should know better. "We have banks and investments in many worlds." He gave Leon a quizzical look. "Does this really surprise you?"

"What about the people that are already sick?" I asked.

"We're talking thousands of people here," Yama said. "No way can you pull the virus out of everyone. All of our top scientists are working on a cure, but no one really knows what it is. If it is water based and you're able to pull it out and isolate it, then that would go a long way toward helping them find a remedy."

I didn't have to think about it. This was the kind of thing people of the Isles used their power for. This was the kind of thing my mom and sister would be proud of me for, the kind of thing that made me proud to have the power that I did, if it meant I could help others with it.

I gave Leon a look that let him know he didn't have to do this and I wouldn't think any less of him. "I'll do it," I said, looking into Yama's deep red eyes. "I'll do it."

3

Leon decided to join me anyway, as did the twins, who were of legal age, so there was nothing their father could do to stop them, no matter how much he tried.

I was happy to be honest. The thought of going alone terrified me and over the last couple of months I'd come to depend on these three for moral support, probably more than I should.

Rangord was the leader of Lamink. We were told to go see him first, and he'd give us further details.

"Kind of wish they would have told us we'd be sloshing through even more water than what's on Kelm," Leon said, looking down at the liquid that reached a bit above the ankle.

"It's only a few inches more," I laughed.

"You can drown in a teaspoon," he deadpanned.

Klenaya locked the doors to her boatcar. "About four countries over the water is to your waist. Three countries from there and the water is over your head, and everyone has gills and fish tails."

Leon stepped high as if trying not to get his pants too

wet. "So, what you're saying is, I should shut up and stop complaining?"

She threw her hands up. "I didn't say it. You did."

Kyle tilted his head back and looked up at the large building before us. "This place is huge."

I agreed and wondered what we'd have to deal with once we got inside. The place was a palace, as big as the one the twins lived in. It looked like something out of a Disney fairytale, and I expected a weeping princess to come running out at any minute.

The whole thing looked to be made of blue crystal, and the sidewalk leading up to the front door seemed a couple of miles long. No other buildings were around, as only trees and bushes surrounded the place.

The door was white crystal and matched nicely with the blue of the castle. We knocked and were immediately let inside.

A tall man, dressed in pink and brown led us to a large room, and once we were inside, he closed the door, never uttering a word.

Thinking that he'd been more than a little rude, I took in my surroundings. The walls were painted a beautiful ocean blue, matching the water on the floor.

It looked so stunning that I almost felt as if I was on a tropical island somewhere instead of standing in a room in a palace.

The only other thing in the room were a few chairs, and a lone man sitting upon a throne, looking down at us.

I blinked and nudged Leon who gave me a brow raise to let me know we were on the same page. To say I was surprised was an understatement. We'd been coming to this universe for a while now, and we'd yet to face anything like this.

This spoke of absolute power, and I hadn't thought that

was something they practiced here. Even Yama had a council, and from what I could tell, a lot of decisions were put to a vote. Very rarely did he decide something solo.

The man walked down the steps, his eyes never leaving us. He looked to be about thirty, and he had pale skin and brown hair. He was of medium build but stood about six feet tall. "I'm Rangord," he said, bowing to us. "Pay no attention to that." He waved at the throne. "That was just something one of my predecessors set up, and deemed whoever ruled Lamink must sit there at least three hours a day."

He led us to a set of chairs a few feet from the throne. "Anyway, my time is up, so let's talk."

Another man walked into the room. He had purple hair, dark skin, and yellow eyes. He looked to be in his late twenties.

Rangord turned to him and pointed. "Ah, here he is. This is Flynn, next in line to rule Lamink."

Flynn didn't seem all that pleased to see us, and he turned his enquiry to Rangord. "So, this is them?" Rangord nodded, and Flynn gave us a distasteful look. "Waterwhisperer that saved the tacium from the Langundas. Guess you've come to our land now to show us how it's done." He took a seat three chairs down from Rangord.

I cleared my throat and tried not to look hurt. I hadn't been expecting a warm welcome, but that had been down-right cold. I was here to help, so I wasn't sure what this Flynn's problem was.

Rangord gave him a stern look. "Calm your mouth, Flynn, they mean us no harm."

Flynn didn't look all that impressed. "Yes, strange crea-tures from another land who always seem to pop up when-ever there's trouble are nothing to be suspicious over. Judgment's still out on them." He looked from Leon to myself, making sure we knew exactly who he was talking about.

Klenaya's voice was full of acid when she spoke, a tone I'd never really heard from her. "If it wasn't for them then we'd all be begging for tacium at the feet of the Langunda. Is that what you really want? If yeah, then maybe you should join them in the take-away. If not, then maybe show a little respect for the people who risked their lives so that we could have one."

His hands stayed clasped in front of him, and he looked utterly bored with her speech. "All hail the conquering hero. Come save us from ourselves. Whatever would we do without her."

"Die," Kyle said, his jaw tight as his eyes locked on Flynn. "When the Langunda chose to starve us of tacium. We would all die. Is that not clear enough for you?"

Flynn started to say something else, but Rangord raised a hand to forestall any more talk on the subject. "Who cares about what you're talking about, Flynn? Our people are dying, and you're mad that we didn't all die months ago?" He gave the other man a curious look. "Really?"

"You," Flynn said, voice brittle. "You should care."

Rangord straightened his shirt, which made me think he just needed something to do with his hands. "Well, I don't." His attention turned. "Are you really just going to sit there and say nothing." He pointed to a guy sitting back in the corner. He had his feet propped on the chair in front of him, and so far, he seemed to be enjoying the show.

My eyes went wide when I saw him, because, until that moment, I hadn't known he was there.

When he finally stood, I noticed both twin's heads snapped his way, and they had the most unreadable expressions on their faces. Fear? Awe? I really couldn't tell.

He stood a little over six feet and had skin just a shade

lighter than my own. His hair was long, full, and wavy. It was black, mixed with silver, or was that silver mixed with black? I couldn't really tell.

He walked with power and self-awareness that dared anyone to challenge him. The twins never took their eyes off him, and I couldn't figure out if it was fascination or intimidation.

He looked down at Flynn once he reached where we all sat. "Are you done?" he asked the other man.

Flynn gave him a hard look, and I figured there was no love lost there. "I was just..."

"Shhh." The man put one finger to his lips in a hushing motion. "None of that. As our supreme ruler said, people are dying. Or is your little tirade more important than that?"

Flynn swallowed hard, and then hung his head, putting his hands in his lap, not saying another word.

Rangord pointed to the new man. "This is Lamink's chief investigator, Iiann. He'll be assisting you while you're here."

Iiann took a seat beside Rangord, but he looked at us. "I'll take you to the house where the first case appeared."

"House?" Klenaya asked, brows furrowed, looking from Rangord to Iiann.

"Shouldn't they be quarantined or something?" Kyle asked, finishing his sister's thought.

Iiann's eyes traveled over one twin then the other, holding their unblinking attention. "Did I say he wasn't? Or did I just say he was at home, with no further implications?"

Klenaya pursed her lips, and Kyle's eyes turned to slits.

"Okay," I said, hoping to ease some of the uncalled for tension in the room. "So, we go see patient zero and then what? I try to pull the virus out of him?"

Rangord answered for Iiann, who was still caught up in a staring contest with the twins. "Yes, then we'll go from there."

I sighed and came to my feet. I could do without the extra hostility, and I hoped that Iiann coming with us wouldn't be too much of a problem for Klenaya and Kyle because, at the moment, they really didn't seem to like the other man.

This was serious business and it hit me in the chest that if we couldn't stop it, everyone I'd just talked to would soon be dead, including Kyle and Klenaya.

4

Before leaving Rangord's, we were all given protective suits that fit us from head to toe. The material wasn't plastic, but it wasn't quite cloth either. Instead, it was more like a mix between the two, but a little on the squishy side. Whatever it was, it fit perfectly, and I found after a few minutes, I hardly knew it was there.

The house we went to was small, white, and had no front porch. It looked like it could use a good pressure wash, but other than that, it seemed to be in good shape.

Since there was no porch, we had to stand on the steps in order to knock on the door. An older lady with gray hair answered. Short, and a little on the heavy side, her face looked weary, and her back was slightly bent as if she was trying to keep herself from falling over. "He's back there," she growled by way of a greeting.

We followed her in, the smell of milk and butter hitting my nose immediately. On the stove, a single pot boiled and I wondered if she was making potato soup. The living room was only big enough to fit a brown couch and recliner that looked like they may have been in style here twenty years ago.

It was clean in here, and I got a homey sort of feel. The place felt lived in, and I could easily imagine these people moving here in their early twenties, raising a family, and year by year making the place more their own.

We walked past the small kitchen, and into a narrow hallway, with beige walls, and water lapping at our feet. "In there." She pointed to a closed door. "I ain't going in there. I've seen enough of him today." With that, she walked back up the hallway and left us to it.

Klenaya watched her go, her mouth opened just a little. "Not one for small talk, is she?"

"And what would you like her to say?" Iiann asked, turning around so that he and Klenaya were only inches apart.

Klenaya eyes zeroed in on his. "She could give us more facts about his condition. Warn us about what we're prepared to see."

Iiann put his hand on the knob. "Why? I've already done that. Would you like to hear it again?"

Kyle came to stand beside his sister. "Don't be a dick," he said to the other man. "She was just asking a question."

Iiann turned to face Kyle, so close I was sure their breath mingled. "Does your sister really need a knight in shining armor?" He looked at Klenaya. "I'll say she's more than capable of handling herself. I'd bet on her." His eyes gleamed when he said it and something told me he knew exactly what he was doing.

Kyle's eyes turned deadly. "My sister is not some prize to be bet on. You'd do well to remember that."

Iiann's lips quirked up into a smile. "And you, Kyle? What would one get if they bet on you?"

Kyle's hands fidgeted at his sides. "Just open the door," he said through clenched teeth.

I held Leon back as the others entered the room. "Is this going to be a problem? I feel like we're caught in a game that only those three know the rules to."

Leon put his hands in his pocket and bounced on the balls of his feet. "Who knows what any of them are thinking. I'm not getting in it, and you shouldn't either."

I nodded because he was right and there were more important things to deal with right now. The room was so small that it only fit one full bed and two small dressers. There was no room for anything else. In here the walls were the same beige of the hallway.

We stood lined up in front of the bed, with barely any room between us. I'd been the last to enter and had had to stop for a minute to catch my breath.

It smelled like open sores and unwashed bodies in here. So much so that I kept my hands tight at my sides to keep from putting them over my mouth and nose. I didn't want to be disrespectful if I didn't have to.

The man on the bed was all skin and bone. His hair was gray and thinning, some of it laying in gray chunks on his bed. He had his blanket half off him, one small leg peeping out. He was covered from head to toe with open sores and blisters, each running over with pus. Even his face and mouth were covered, and I could only imagine the pain he felt.

He looked horrible, and I swallowed hard and tried not to let it show on my face.

On the wall hung a picture of a fit muscular man, standing proudly beside the woman who'd opened the door, both smiling brightly. Iiann followed my gaze. "That's what he looked like a few weeks ago, before the disease took hold."

I put a hand over my mouth unable to stop myself. The

difference was astounding. My eyes shone, and I knew then, that I would do whatever I had to, to see these people well again.

Kyle and Klenaya stood side by side, their faces drawn and tight.

Iiann squatted in front of the bed. He dipped his hand in the water from the floor and gently massaged it onto the man's head. When he spoke, his voice was low and soothing. "Hey, Beck. Rangord sent some people to help you." He repeated his action with the water, making slow circles on the man's forehead. "They're the ones who saved the tacium, and they've come all this way to lend us a hand, pretty cool huh?"

I was a little shocked at his gentleness as I hadn't thought he had it in him.

Beck gave no indication that he heard the other man, as his eyes stayed closed and his body unmoving. Iiann rose to his feet and nodded at me, his face resigned yet hopeful.

I cleared my throat and then sat in the seat that Iiann provided me. "I'm going to touch your arm," I whispered. "I hope that's okay." I reached out and laid a hand on one of his sores. It was seeping pus and felt wet and icky under my fingers.

Not sure if I could do this, but still willing to try, I closed my eyes and searched for the water in his body. It only took me a second to find it.

I could clearly see the water flowing through him, but all of it seemed to be connected to the blue powder that was tacium. Knowing there was something else there as well, I closed my eyes and tried to focus on it.

After some careful maneuvering, I was finally able to grab hold of it. It was green and yellow and seemed to be eating the tacium and attacking the blood cells.

I flexed my hands and tried to use the water to pull it out.

Sweat broke out on my face, and my hand started to strain, but no matter what I did, I couldn't get it. Every time I tried, the blue powder of the tacium reached up and knocked me back.

I blinked hard, trying to process because that had never happened to me before. My powers always worked when I needed them to, so this was strange, to say the least.

I licked my lips and decided to try again. I got the exact same results. The virus just wasn't budging, no matter what I did.

"I... I... can't..." I stuttered, still trying to understand what was going on. "It's like the disease is attacking the tacium and keeping it from working, yet every time I try to pull it out, the tacium stops me. I don't get it."

Iiann sighed heavy, his hands on his hips. "We figured something like that was happening." He ran a hand through his hair. "Nice to have confirmation, I guess."

Leon stared at Beck, a pained expression on his face. "I thought tacium was supposed to protect you from something like this."

"Normally it would," Iiann answered.

"I think," Klenaya said before Iiann could continue. "Based on what I've seen so far, that this is poison." All eyes turned to her. Some looked shocked, others like they'd already come to the same conclusion. I had to agree with her. I thought we were most certainly dealing with a poison of some sort.

Klenaya looked thoughtful for a minute. "Delia, did it seem a part of the tacium, or separate?"

I thought back on it. "Some of it was definitely mixed together."

"So," Kyle said, taking up the narrative. "The person who did this probably made the poison using tacium."

"Which means that the tacium will do its job and protect

the poison and everything around it," Iiann said, a hard edge to his voice.

Leon's eyes stayed on the figure on the bed. "Will getting more tacium into those infected overpower the poison?"

Iiann shook his head. "Tried that on a few people. It didn't work."

"Who in their right mind would poison the tacium?" I asked. "Something you all need to live." It seemed a particularly stupid thing to do, and it made me wonder just what type of game was being played here.

Iiann thought about it. "Had to be someone who has access to it."

Kyle's eyes lit up. "Also, someone who could make sure their supply was untouched."

"So that's who we need to talk to, the companies in charge of collecting the tacium from Kelm and the companies that sort it once it's here," Klenaya finished.

Now the three seemed to be in sync. I looked to Leon and he shook his head and held his hands up in a way that said he wanted nothing to do with it. I gave him an "Oh really," look and then turned back to Iiann. "Can we talk to the Laminks that handle the tacium?"

We went to the Stalling company first. It was on a busy street, and the large brick building looked to be about three stories high. The place bustled with activity, as people seemed to go in out of it at a rapid-fire pace.

We were shown into a room where two men, one tall, the other short, both with black hair and pointed noses, sat at a large table surrounded by chairs. Both looked to be sweating bullets, as if they'd been called to the principal's office and didn't know how to handle it.

The walls were a deep navy blue and looked freshly painted. The room smelled of old cloth and dye, and I figured this was some type of fabric company. "Thank you for calling ahead," the shorter man said. The two men looked so much alike that I was sure they were brothers.

"We've assembled the workers who last dealt with the tacium, but that was weeks ago. The next run, of course, goes to Mildins Enterprises, and then the Tacons company takes over."

I took in what he said. Apparently, a different company did the run every cycle. I wondered why. Maybe so that each business could make money, or perhaps it was for security purposes.

Thinking on it, I figured it was probably both reasons that kept the tacium switching hands every trip.

Iiann walked around the table, giving both men a curious look.

"What?" the taller one asked, his voice low and nervous.

Iiann stopped walking and looked at the man. "Where are they?" His voice was quiet but scathing.

"Where is who?"

"The people you assembled to talk to us," Klenaya answered.

Kyle went to stand in front of the taller brother. "Why are you still in here if you have no more information to provide?"

The man cleared his throat. "It's our job to make sure the integrity of this company…"

"Trust me on this, Raymond, you don't want to finish that sentence." Iiann stood with his hands behind his back. "Go now, before I bring you up on obstruction charges."

The man paled and rose from his seat, running a nervous hand through his hair as he did so. The shorter man stayed rooted to his spot.

"I don't need you either," Iiann said. "I prefer to talk to your workers alone." The shorter man's lips tightened, showing his displeasure, but he still left without another word.

After only a few seconds, three men and two women shuffled into the room and took a seat.

Iiann stood off to the side, two fingers stroking his chin, watching their every movement. "Tell me what was different," he said once they'd finally gotten settled.

"Sir?" one of the men asked in a confused tone.

Iiann walked toward them, a stern look on his face. "This last run to get the tacium. Tell me what was different."

The five looked at each other, none seeming to know what to say. "It was routine like always," one of the women finally said. "We delivered the fingen and picked up the tacium."

"Fingen is what makes our carboats run. The only place it grows is here." Klenaya let myself and Leon know. I gave her a small nod, so she'd know I appreciated the information.

I thought back to a few months ago and remembered Yama saying that all countries in this universe had something of value that they traded for the tacium. I guess for the Laminks, it was this fingen.

"Were you stopped by anyone?" Leon asked, reminding everyone in the room that he too was an investigator.

A different man answered this time. "Only regular checks, nothing unusual."

Leon thought about it. "Where you present the whole time? Whenever anyone checked the tacium, were you right there to watch them?"

"As you know it is required," one of the ladies answered, looking at Iiann. "We did everything by the book." She sniffed and held her head high. "Tacium's too important to do otherwise."

Both investigaters gave the group assessing looks, but it was Leon who spoke. "How many stops did you make? Going from Lamink to Kelm?"

"None," one of the men said.

Leon looked skeptical. "No bathroom breaks? No food stops? Nowhere were the tacium could have been left unattended for a bit?"

The first woman who'd spoken shook her head. "We take the fastest boatcar there is. It doesn't take us long to get to Kelm, but even if it did, we have a bathroom on the boatcar and bring along plenty of food and drinks. No reason at all for us to have to stop."

They certainly had their bases covered, I thought as I looked the group over, not sure if they were being truthful or not.

Iiann asked them a few more questions, stopping only when he seemed satisfied that he'd learned all he could. "Don't tell anyone about this conversation, and if you think of anything else let me know. If something more pops up, I'll be back." He opened the door, and the group hurriedly shuffled away.

"Well," he said as the last one filed out. "I guess we go to the sorta now."

5

The Sorta place was a large gray structure with a slew of garage doors, all attached to the building. A keypad functioned as a doorknob, and Iiann punched in a code, causing it to open.

The place was huge, with metal walls and water flowing everywhere. It smelled like steel, metal, and sweat in here and I wrinkled my nose, not enjoying the scent.

Tacium was divided into multiple sections, each with a different name on it. "It's sorted into divisions, then neighborhoods, then families, and places of business," Iiann helpfully supplied. "Everyone needs the tacium to live and this way we can be sure it's all distributed evenly.

Men and women with small electronic devices in their hands went about the checking and sorting. Three women and two men walked the floor, and from the way they directed the others, I assumed they were the ones in charge.

One of the men saw us when we entered and alerted the other four. "Iiann," he said. He was tall, tan, and had a long green ponytail down his back. "Are you in the business of giving out tours now?" His eyes roamed over Leon and

4

myself. Kyle and Klenaya I assumed he knew as the daughter and son of Bale.

Iiann's face stayed impassive. "Didn't come here to chat, Owen. I want to know who's had access to the tacium recently."

"You and everyone else with a code," one of the women spoke up.

Iiann nodded and looked up toward the ceiling. "I need the videos of the last couple of weeks. I want to know who's been in here. Especially if they came when no one else was around."

The five shared an uneasy look, and Iiann caught it right away. "What happened?" he asked, tone bordering on dangerous.

"Had a little glitch a couple of weeks ago," a different woman said.

Iiann's expression hardened, and he took a few steps closer, managing to look both menacing and authoritarian. "What happened?"

It was one of the men who spoke this time. "Cameras went out for about ten minutes. It's gotten jerky in the past. Last time was about ten months ago. We thought maybe it was that again. But if something's wrong with the supply, then maybe that's why."

Leon rubbed a hand down his face. "You have to have a code to get in. Is there any way to check usage that corresponds with the camera outage?"

One of the women typed away on her device. "It happened at twelve nighttime and the only code used was the one you just put in."

Surprised, I quickly turned to Iiann, who only nodded. "I work directly for the Sted. That's where you first met me. Where Rangord lives as well as Flynn. Everyone who works there has the same code."

"Like Flynn?" I asked, remembering the man's bitter face when we'd first arrived in Lamink.

"He didn't do this," Iiann practically growled at me.

The venom in his voice surprised me, but if he wanted me to believe in Flynn's innocence, he'd have to try a little harder. "How could you possibly know that?" I really wanted to know.

It seemed strange that he would defend the other man, especially after witnessing his behavior toward us earlier. He didn't want us here investigating, that much he'd made clear.

Iiann's eyes lit into mine, a small storm brewing inside them. "Because I do, and Flynn has no ambition to be any more than he already is. Why would he do it?"

"Perhaps," Klenaya said, coming to stand between us. "You should back away." She put her hand to Iiann's chest and gave him a gentle push.

His eyes went from her brother to her and then back to me. "Someone in the Sted did it. Of that, I have no doubt, but it was certainly not my brother."

Shock rendered me speechless. Did he say? "So, Flynn is your brother?"

Righteous indignation covered his face. "And if I thought him guilty, I would arrest him myself. But he's too loyal to Lamink and to the Sted." He said it like that was the final word on the matter, and he didn't care to hear anything else about it.

Leon let out one of those deep breaths that said he didn't like what he was about to say but would say it anyway. "You're too close to this. We can't leave him out just because you say so. Any good investigator should know that."

Iiann gave him a look that would freeze water, then punched the code in as if the numbers themselves had done something to offend him.

His lips stayed tight and hard as we rounded the corner to

the street we'd left the boatcar on. The water sloshed under my feet, as my boots swished through it.

Once we reached the parking lot, the air suddenly turned tense. Something was off, and I could feel it in every bone of my body.

A man leaned against Iiann's car. He was dressed in all black and had his arms folded in front of him. I measured Iiann's demeanor, which was relaxed and non-hostile. That made me breathe a little easier. Apparently, he knew who this was and didn't see him as a threat.

"You know I wouldn't have believed it unless I saw it with my own eyes." The man rose from the car, feet about an inch apart and hands tight at his side. He was of average height, muscular, and had a bald head.

His face was hard and unforgiving. "The tacium is our life, Iiann. Why would you work with these interlopers to destroy it?" He sounded hurt and disappointed.

Iiann took a calculated look around. "Someone set us up," he said as we continued to walk forward. "Gillum wouldn't have come alone. We're surrounded."

6

It was smart. Making it looked like we were the ones who'd poisoned the tacium so the real culprit could get away scot-free. It took a cunning mind to come up with that and once again my thoughts turned to Flynn.

The twins and Leon hadn't said a word, and I figured they were probably coming to the same conclusion that I had.

Gillum walked toward us, hands held tight at his side, his face a story in rage.

Leon straightened his shoulders and stood a little taller. "What is it that you think we've done?" he asked the other man.

Gillum answered Leon, but he never took his eyes off Iiann. "Saw you go into the Sorta, I'd been advised what you were there to do." The disappointment was clear in his voice. "I would have never believed it, had I not seen it for myself." He said this last part very low, with clear disbelief in his voice. "Why'd you do it, Iiann? Why'd you poison the only thing that makes us who we are?"

Iiann gave the man a hard stare. "Are you listening to

yourself, Gillum? I mean really listening, because you sound ridiculous."

As soon as he said it, we were surrounded by men and women in gray and black uniforms. Their bodies popped with energy, and they glared at us as if they wanted nothing more than to rip us apart. I assumed they were the local law enforcement, either that or some posse Gillum had thrown together.

If we didn't do something, this could turn ugly fast. "Wait a minute." I held a hand up. "We just left the Sorta and harmed nothing or no one. All you have to do is send one of your people in to check."

"I don't have a code to get in," Gillum said. "And they don't exactly answer knocks at the door, but he already knows that." He pointed to Iiann.

"Well, Iiann knows the code, we'll all go around there together, and then you'll see."

He chuckled like he thought I was trying to fool him and he'd already one-upped me. "I know he did the poison weeks ago, today was just to check in with his contact on the inside, and that person is not about to admit to their part no more than you people are."

"Fuck it then," Kyle said, using words he'd recently picked up in my world. "Let's fight."

"No!" I held my hands up again, to stop anything from happening, but Gillum's group charged anyway. I didn't want to do this, hadn't come here for this.

Iiann looked at me in disgust. "Put your hands down and your fists up, there is no reasoning with brutes who have already made up their minds."

As if to prove his words as true, something hard and cold hit me in the face and sent me spinning. I landed on my back, my face stinging. I swallowed hard and told myself that everything would be okay, we just had to make them understand. When I looked up again, I was dismayed to see the fight already in progress.

A woman with her arms raised in attack mode headed straight for Klenaya. Klenaya shot light out of her eyes and cut a big gash in the woman's leg. The woman's eyes went wide, and she fell back into the water, a pained look on her face.

I had to remember that these people were immortal and the woman's leg would soon heal.

Kyle was in hand to hand combat with two Laminks, but for now, he was holding his own. Blocking punches and getting in quick jabs, he seemed to be enjoying himself more than anything else.

Leon used his power of telekinesis to flip one guy on his head and twist the arm on another.

Iiann's pupils glowed blue, and he began to speak in low rhythmic tones. He turned eyes on a man in a red shirt, and the man gasped as his face became marred with scratches and blisters, unable to stop them from growing he fell over into a small ball and began to whimper.

I came to my feet, hoping to be able to put an end to this, but something cold and wet hit across my face again. It stung like acid and caused me to stumble back. A man and woman stood in front of me glowering. The woman held an iron pipe in her hand and had it raised to hit me again. The man's eyes glowed orange as he started to chant under his breath.

Flashbacks to Greg doing the same thing echoed through my mind. As much as I wanted to stay in control, I knew that I couldn't. I would not be taken that way again. I jumped back out of the way of the pipe as she brought it down hard toward my face.

Rage hardened me as the man continued to chant. I would not go down this road again, I vowed. Never again. My hair started to blow back, and my feet rose off the ground. "Nstee yee ghu!" I said speaking in the ancient language of the Isles. I opened my mouth and hollered like the wind, blowing back the man and woman in front of me and a few others as well.

"Leste mau klm grol?" My voice now sounded hard and had a distant echo. I lifted the man and woman who'd attacked me and rose them in the air. I used the water in the man's system to squeeze his heart, and the water in the woman's to close in on her lungs. They both gasped for air, so I squeezed harder, not to kill, but until I knew they would no longer be a threat to me, and then I dropped them to the ground.

I screamed again, then created a tidal wave knocking the remainder off their feet and hurling them behind me. Then I heated the water and watched as steam and fog both rose. It was enough to blind them so that we could get away. "Let's go," I shouted to Leon and the others. "I'll hold it for as long as I can."

I ran to Iiann's car, and we jumped in. When he tried to start it all he got was a clicking sound and then nothing. "They must have disabled it while they were waiting for us to come out," Iiann said, still fiddling with the controls, trying to make it work.

"Just tell me which way," Leon said, buckling in. "I'll get us there."

"Here," Iiann said, pointing to the right.

Leon closed his eyes to better direct his telekinesis, and in a second the boatcar, with us in it, was floating through the air, in the direction that Iiann had specified.

Iiann continued to give directions until we ended up in an alley, where the water was dirtied by trash and debris.

I looked around, not sure if I was seeing right. I'd been to many parts of this universe in the last couple of months and never had I seen dirty water. In fact, most of the water we walked through looked clean enough to drink.

So, seeing it look so disgusting now left a bitter taste in my mouth and made me wonder why someone hadn't bothered to clean it up.

Klenaya looked around, a huge frown on her face. "Hmm, why are we here?"

Iiann looked at her in disbelief. "Would you rather be back there?" He pointed in the direction we'd just come from.

"Let's just…" Leon opened the car door and got out.

"No one knows about this place," Iiann said as he exited the car.

Though I didn't like it, I resigned myself that we would be staying here for a while. The smell alone was enough to make you hurl. If I didn't know any better, I'd swear we'd landed smack in the middle of a sewer. Still, I'd gladly endure this if it meant I didn't have to fight anymore.

I wasn't proud of myself for what I'd done back there, but knew I hadn't really had a choice.

Taking in my surroundings, I saw that we were in front of three buildings, all side by side. They were white brick, but like everything else around here looked dirty and in need of a good washing.

Iiann went to the first one and punched in his code, causing the whole side of the building to rise in the air. I balked and saw that Leon looked as shocked as I felt. I hadn't seen any doors, but that still didn't give me reason to think the whole building would open before us.

Iiann turned to Leon. "Could you?" He pointed to his non-working boatcar.

Leon raised his hand and guided the thing inside, landing it onto a large concrete slab that looked like it was made for just that purpose.

The space was small, but it still held a ragtag blue loveseat that was scratched and marred. The couch was purple, and I got the feeling if I sat on it I'd sink to the floor. The walls were blue and gray, but looked to be peeling and in need of a good paint job.

There were no windows or doors, but there was a small kitchen. In it sat a mini-fridge balanced on a short wooden table, a small black microwave also on the same table, a mini sized stove that looked like it'd been built for a five-year-old, and a sink that held clumps of dirt and hair. There wasn't much space in the kitchen either, and I wondered if one could turn around in there without bumping into a wall.

It was disgusting, and I wondered if anyone had ever tried to cook a meal in there. I certainly wouldn't eat anything that came out of that kitchen.

Off to the left was a bathroom, and that, thankfully did have a door.

"We need to regroup." Iiann leaned against a counter in the kitchen, watching us all with cool eyes.

Kyle sat on the car, his feet dangling off the side of the hood. "What we need is to talk to Rangord. Or do you think he's been corrupted too?"

Iiann thought about it for a second and then his eyes went large. "Flynn," he said, voice filled with fear, eyes searching frantically around the room as if his brother would suddenly pop up. "We have to get to Flynn."

"And if he's the one behind this?" I asked because I had to. He may trust his brother, but that didn't mean I had to.

Hot eyes turned my way. "Then I'll deal with it," he said through gritted teeth, his voice coming out like a growl.

Leon sat on the loveseat, shoulders hunched, mind working. "We don't know the situation. Don't know if Rangord and the others have been turned against us." He thought about it some more. "Surely Rangord and your brother don't believe we poisoned the tacium. That wouldn't make much sense unless someone they trust is whispering in their ears." He looked to Iiann as if he could provide the name of said person right away.

Iiann didn't look convinced. "My brother would know better than that, as would Rangord, but I agree we need to proceed with caution."

"So, what do we do?" Klenaya stood by one of the chairs in the room, her body rocking back and forward in a way that told me she was anxious for something to happen. I didn't want her or Kyle to worry, but I didn't know how to fix this.

Besides, I agreed with her, sitting here talking was getting us nowhere, while the disease continued to spread.

Kyle patted the hood of the car. "Well, what do we do for transportation, because this ain't going nowhere."

Iiann walked into the bathroom, making sure to leave the door open. He punched some numbers into a keypad across from the sink, and the wall opposite opened into another room, with three boatcars. They too sat on giant concrete slabs, one blue, one red, and one black.

Boatcars looked something like one would expect a small space ship to. They were sleek and modern, and could fly through the sky, as well as maneuver through the water.

"These work fine." He walked to the black one and then gestured for us to join him. "We need to talk to Rangord. See what he's been told." He opened the doors, and we all piled inside.

We drove to a spot where we could see the palace from the sky.

Guards surrounded the whole thing, from the roof to every side of the building. It hadn't been that way when we'd left, so it had to have something to do with Gillum thinking we were traitors.

7

Iiann didn't seem all that worried as he took in the extra guards blocking our way into the palace. "Rangord probably did this for show. He knows we're not involved, but it has to appear to the people of Lamink that he's doing something."

"So, we don't go in?" I asked. Seemed like our only way out of this mess was through that building, so not going in wasn't an option.

Iiann stayed looking ahead. "No. We have to go in. We just have to find a way to do it without causing more damage."

"What do you suggest?" Klenaya asked.

"There's a way to get in through the north side of the palace, put in there in case a rebellion ever took place. It's a quick escape route, but we can use it to get inside. Only myself, Rangord, and three others know about it."

"What are you trying to say?" Kyle asked.

Iiann took us higher in the sky, and I could feel my head start to spin at the change of altitude. "That Rangord knows that we are innocent and he'd have made sure that way was clear, no matter what he had to do."

"I hope that you're right," I said under my breath, but he still heard me because he turned to stare my way.

"I know what I'm doing, Delia." He landed the boatcar a good distance away from the palace and then opened the door to get out. "Come on," he said, turning around to face us. "Well, come on."

We walked for about ten minutes through woods and forest. Finally, we stopped at a large Redwood, and Iiann began to feel around on the bark. Once he found what he wanted, he tapped two times, and a small portion of the tree opened up to reveal a min-keypad. He pushed in some numbers and then stepped aside.

The tree split in half and a small yellow floor stood in the middle of it, a keypad in the wall behind it. I looked around and wondered if any of the other trees housed such contraptions, and if they did, where did they lead to?

We stepped inside, and I tried to not be wary, but I'd never ridden an elevator that was stuffed inside a tree, so it was a little stomach turning.

Iiann pushed in some numbers on the keypad, and we started a slow descent down. I held my breath the whole time, praying this thing was safe.

It only took a couple of seconds for us to come to a smooth stop. I breathed a little easier thinking that hadn't been half as bad as I'd thought it would.

When we got out, it was to a hallway with two elevators sat side by side. We got on the second one and rose all the way to the top.

This time when we got out, we were inside a small sitting room that held a mini-round table, and two chairs. "Rangord's private study is right through there. He would have left that empty as well, so that we could pass through with no disturbance," Iiann said.

When we entered the room, Rangord was on the floor holding his cheek, an angry Flynn standing over him. A broken glass lay shattered beside Rangord, and I wondered if Flynn had thrown it at him in a fit of rage.

"What happened?" Iiann went to his brother's side as if he was the one in need of assistance.

The twins helped Rangord to his feet.

Flynn cracked his head from side to side, his eyes boring into Rangord. "He tried to make me drink the foul liquid in that cup." He pointed to the shattered glass. "When I refused, he brought in three guards. Two held me down, while the other forced it down my throat. As soon as they left, I punched him in the face." He held up his right fist and shook it as if to illustrate his point.

Iiann's body went rigid, and the slow, controlled way he turned to Rangord made my body go cold. His rage was palpable which left no doubt that he believed his brother one hundred percent. "What did you do to him?" he asked, his voice low and dangerous.

Rangord straightened his clothes and went to take a seat behind his desk. "Flynn is indispensable to me." He held his hands out in front of him, and I wondered if this was where he took up for the man who'd clearly assaulted him. "I'm not sure I could run this place without him. So, he stays no matter what else happens."

Klenaya's eyes turned to slits, and she took a couple of steps toward the desk. "What are you talking about?"

Rangord didn't look at her. Instead, he focused on Iiann. "I gave him the cure to the poison, and that's one less person you have to worry about getting sick. Well, two if you count me." He sat back nonchalantly in his chair as we all stared at him in shocked silence. "Me and a few others."

My mouth went dry, as I tried to understand. I'd put all my money on Flynn being the culprit, yet here Rangord sat, freely and rather proudly admitting to it. My head started to spin, and I wondered why he would do this to his own people.

He was already in charge. What more did he want?

"You have the cure?" Klenaya asked, and from the look of horror on her face, I knew her thoughts were with Beck, who was currently wasting away to nothing, his wife there for it all.

"You have the cure, and you do nothing to help your people?" Kyle asked in disbelief.

"Because he's the one who started it," Iiann said. His voice held a shocked wonderment as if he himself wasn't sure he believed that.

"You sent Gillum after us," Leon accused. "Hoping to lure us back here, so that you could do what?"

Rangord turned to me, and the hatred in his eyes was enough to make me flinch. What had I ever done to this man? I didn't even know him. "I wanted the rainmaker to know that she cannot save us this time. I wanted you all to witness that I alone hold the key to stopping this and at the moment I am not inclined to do so."

Flynn stood rooted to the spot as he blinked at the other man. "You poisoned the tacium and put us all at risk? Why would you do that?"

"Because he wants something." Klenaya walked over to Flynn and waited until he nodded his approval before massaging small circles into his back, trying to calm him down.

"You're willing to risk the lives of everyone in this world..." Kyle started, then stopped as if he too was at a loss.

It was difficult to understand, and I didn't buy that it was simply a quest for more power. As number one ruler of

Lamink he had power, and besides, my gut told me that this was about so much more than that.

"Because what he wants is priceless," Iiann said, answering Kyle's earlier question.

The smug look on Rangord's face told the truth of those words, and I felt my anger rise at his deception. People were hurt and dying, and yet here he was reveling in it all.

"What do you want?" I asked, my voice unable to hide my fury.

"Who are you now?" he asked me. "Such a weak little girl cowering beneath Greg's feet. For years, we watched you and laughed at your stupidity. It was my idea to have you mugged." He smiled at the memory as if he'd gotten a particular amount of pleasure from that one.

I'd made peace with how Greg had treated me a long time ago, but this right here was like a slap in the face and served to open a wound that was just beginning to close. My fists clinched, and it took everything in me not to rip that smug look off his face and shove it down his throat.

Leon came up behind me and placed a hand on my arm. "Don't let him do this. Don't let him win," he whispered to me.

My voice shook when I spoke. "Why?"

Instead of answering, Rangord stared at me, eyes intense, face hard. Something told me if he could get away with killing me then and there he would. Which made me wonder once again, what I'd ever done to make him hate me so much.

His tone was brittle when he spoke, and I would have sworn he had acid lacing his throat. "You tore my mother's face off. Did you feel powerful when you did that?" He cocked his head to the side. "Do you still feel powerful now?"

His mother? It took me a minute, but once I took a closer look at him, I noticed that same sloped nose and drawn-in cheek bones. "Amber," I said my voice barely above a whisper. "You're Amber's son."

He nodded, his eyes taking on a stormy look. "Do you know that she hasn't eaten in weeks? That she refuses any tacium and that she'll probably be dead in a few days?"

"Do you realize the amount of people you've hurt by poisoning the tacium or do the lives of your people not matter at all?" Iiann asked, an incredulous look on his face.

"I care about my mother as I'm sure everyone in this room cares for theirs," Rangord answered. "Free her, and I will see that everyone affected gets the cure. Leave her to rot, and I promise you, she will not die alone."

Flynn's eyes shined as he looked at the man who'd been his boss and ruler of his country for who knew how many years. "And you thought I would condone this? Rule with you while everyone I loved died? Are you really that delusional?"

Rangord seemed unaffected by the scolding. "You want to live. What's delusional about that?"

My feelings where a jumbled-up mess, but I did have one question. "How do you expect me to get your mother out of jail?" Because that's what this whole thing had been about, right? A get out of jail card for his mom issued by the person responsible for putting her there. I gritted my teeth. There was no way I was letting Amber back loose in the world.

She'd helped Greg in hurting me. It'd been her along with Greg who'd first flung Leon and me into this world. They'd put us in a cell and the only way we'd escaped was by using my water powers.

Klenaya had scooped us up then and we'd gone on to help her and her people defeat Greg and Amber and stop them and their country from taking over the tacium.

Amber had been especially vicious when she'd attacked me, beating my face into the ground, and stomping me. I'd let it go on as long as I could, the teaching of the Isle's telling me not to fight. Finally, I couldn't take it anymore, so yeah, I'd ripped her face off and left her on the ground withering in agony.

I wasn't proud of it, but I'd done what I'd needed to protect myself and I wouldn't apologize for that.

Rangord watched me with cold eyes. "I want my mother offered a pardon so that she can leave without looking over her shoulder. In exchange, I won't poison anyone else, and I'll release the cure. Renege, and I'll release the poison in waves."

"Still not understanding how I fit into all of this," I said.

"You will convince Yama and Bale that you can't save them from this because you can't. They need to understand that. You came here, you failed, now it's my turn. As long as they think they have you to turn to, they won't do what needs to be done. Knowing you can't help, really leaves them no choice but to release my mom or watch millions die."

He ran a calculated hand over his chin. "Bring me back their answer, and we'll go from there." He turned his chair toward the window, his way of saying the conversation was over.

I stood there for a moment, wondering at the gall it took to turn his back on a room full of enemies. He was so sure his plan would work, and it only strengthened my resolve to make him pay for every single person he'd hurt.

There would be no get out of jail free card for his mother, of that I would make sure.

8

W e made it to Iiann's boatcar without incident. Which was a relief, because at the moment I didn't know how much more I could take.

Leon buckled his seatbelt, and the furrow of his brow told me how pissed he was. "He's not going to stop the disease no matter what we do. I hope no one seriously believes otherwise. He's got a plan in his mind, and nothing we do or don't do will stop it."

I'd thought the same thing, but I still didn't know what to do about it. There had to be something, though, I refused to believe that the only answer was to let the tormenter Amber go free.

Leon must have read my mind. "How about we go back to Kelm and give Bale and Yama a chance to come up with something," he suggested.

I smiled, and gave his hand a small pat because that was the best answer I'd heard all day.

Iiann started the car, and we rose in the air. "If he has a cure, Kelm or one of the other countries should be able to come up with one as well." He pushed a few buttons on his control panel, and we started to move. "But..."

"Not soon enough," Kyle finished for him.

———

It was dark when we entered back into Kelm. We'd already called ahead, so Yama knew we were coming. As ruler of Kelm, it was ultimately his decision on whether Amber went free or not. We hadn't given them any details, deciding it was best to do that in person.

Bale sat at the kitchen table playing a board game by himself, a grave expression on his face as if he feared the worst and was just waiting for confirmation.

Yama sat in the living room, his hair was combed back from his head, making him look suave and sleek. He looked that way a lot, at least when I saw him anyway. He also had a calculated glint in his eyes, as if he knew we brought bad news, but he was already thinking of ways to turn it back in our favor.

He stood when he saw us and motioned for us all to take a seat. Bale joined us from the kitchen and Yama waited until everyone was seated before he began to talk. "From the way you sounded on the phone, I take it that it's not good news."

"No," Iiann said.

Yama pointed at Iiann. "You, I understand being here. You are chief investigator, but what of your brother?"

Flynn came to his feet. "I can go into another room if it's going to be an issue, though I don't see why it would be. I am second to Rangord so what is your problem?"

Ah, there was the sass of the Flynn we'd met when we'd first arrived in Lamink. It was actually good to see him get some of his bearings back.

Yama's voice stayed calm as he spoke. "I don't have a

problem. I just worry that the situation is a lot worse than we'd originally thought if Rangord feels the need to send his best here to Kelm. That, or either Rangord himself is the problem."

"Rangord is Amber's son," I said, cutting through the talking, getting straight to the point. "Did you know that?"

"Amber probably has hundreds of children. We are only allowed to reproduce in twenty-year stretches. Once those kids reach a certain age, it becomes impossible to keep track of them all. Unless you're the parent of course."

I stared at him wondering just how many children he'd produced and he stared back with an amused look that told me it was none of my business.

"You maybe should have been on top of this one," Iiann said, his voice brittle and hard. He kept a critical look in his eyes as he told Yama and Bale all that had happened so far.

Bale let out a breath when Iiann finally finished. "There is no reasoning with the man, then. That much is obvious."

"What about his mother?" Flynn asked. "Would she be more receptive to helping stop him?" He stood as if ready to go and talk with her right now.

Yama apparently approved of this. "You and your brother are welcomed to try," he said to the other man.

Bale came to his feet. "I'll show you to the takeaway."

They stayed gone about thirty minutes, and when they came back, all three wore grim expressions.

"Well, it was worth a shot," Klenaya said, picking up on their mood as soon as they hit the door.

"What did she say?" Kyle asked.

"That she'll only talk to Delia," Iiann answered.

Leon came to his feet, objecting immediately. He'd seen how shaken I'd been earlier when Rangord had mentioned the mugging, this was probably his way of protecting me. I appreciated it, but also found it a little condescending even though I was sure he hadn't meant it that way.

He was a cop, and his natural instinct was to protect, and I could never fault him for that.

"Is okay," I said, looking up at him, and he raised a brow as if asking me if I was sure.

I nodded because it wasn't even a question. Thinking back to Beck and his wife my mind was made up before I even opened my mouth. "Lead the way," I said to Bale.

I gave Leon's arm a gentle squeeze as I walked by letting him know that I'd be okay and not to worry.

He would anyway, though. We'd become great friends since leaving here that first time, and usually hung out at least two to three times a week, and always when the twins visited.

I followed Bale out of the house and down the street. "It's quicker if we walk," he said, easily keeping pace with me. "Guards will be watching the whole time, and you can leave whenever you want." He looked at a small electronic device in his hand. "We have a log of her visitors, and Rangord's not on it, but plenty of his brothers and sisters are. Any one of them could have told him about their mother's condition."

I nodded, glad for a chance to stretch my legs and enjoy the cool air. Not many people were out, but a few passed us on the way. Water danced around our feet, and I'd been here enough times, that it didn't really bother me anymore, not too much anyway.

The building we walked into was beige and almost as big as the house Bale lived in. "Just finished building this to hold some of the Langunda," he let me know as we went through the multiple security checks that would take us to the prison cells.

I stayed close to Bale as we walked through the halls, almost fearful of getting mistaken for an inmate and being made to stay. It was foolish I knew, but I'd been through it all before and just couldn't shake the feeling.

We finally came to a locked door at the end of a long hallway. Guards stood all around, but no one said anything. Bale punched a few numbers into the keypad. Once it opened, he motioned me inside. "It's the last one on the left." He stood away from the door as if he had no plans to enter.

The cells were more like rooms. The only thing standing between them and freedom was a large plastic wall. From what Bale had told me, it was made with tacium, so it was strong, and it blocked their powers.

That gave me a little relief, but not much. The cells were a luminous white and each held a bed, dresser, toilet, sink, microwave, mini-fridge, table, and one chair.

Some inmates lay on their beds reading, while others sat in their chair looking around. More than a few stared at me with hard eyes as if I'd destroyed everything good in their lives. The stares were so intense that I had to resist the urge to turn back toward the door. I knew they couldn't get to me, but it still made me self-conscious.

"You're not coming?" I asked Bale as he still hadn't moved from his spot on the other side of the door.

"She doesn't want to see me," he answered. "The only person she wants to talk to is you."

I nodded and tried not to flinch as the cell doors closed locking me away with a bunch of angry Langundas. I took a deep breath and kept my head high, as I walked to the end of the hall.

I gasped when I saw her, because the woman in this cell was a poor reflection of the woman I'd met a couple of months ago.

Where her hair had been long and full before, she was now pretty much bald. The few strands she did have, hung in loose, lifeless lumps around her head.

Her face was sunken in, her lips wrinkled and tight. Her eyes looked huge as if her face had all but shriveled away. She reminded me of the crypt keeper, from that old TV show.

She smiled when she saw me, a grin as evil as the woman herself. "How does it feel?" she asked, her face grainy and hard. "To become what you always feared."

I gave her a stony stare, not willing to play her mind games. I was my own person now. I made my own decisions, and I wouldn't let her, or anyone else take that away from me. "Your son is set to kill thousands unless we release you, but let me be the first to tell you, you're not going anywhere. We want you to tell him to stop, and then maybe Yama could work out better accommodations for you."

She smiled that crooked grin again. "Bout time one of them did something. I was starting to think I would have to rot in here. Son, you say? Tell me, which one of my lovely boys has brought about my freedom."

My eyes squinted as I looked at her and I wondered if this had been her plan all along. Starve herself until she could guilt one of her children into reacting. Well, she tried it, I'd give her that, but it wasn't going to work. Not if I had anything to do with it. "You're not going anywhere, but you need to call your son off," I told her again. "I'm sure something can be arranged to make your stay here a little better if you do."

"So confident and sure, aren't you?" She laughed, a hollow, empty sound that left my ears ringing. "I made you who you are, you know that? Without me, you would have never found the will to fight. Show your gratitude and let me out of here and take me to my son." She was delusional.

"Give it up, Amber," another voice said. "She can be as stubborn as a stubbed toe when she sets her mind to it." I stiffened because I'd know Greg's voice anywhere. It took everything in me not to turn around, but I was determined to not show weakness in front of either one of them. "Delia babe, it's so good to see you," he purred.

He wanted a reaction, and I'd be damned if I gave him the satisfaction of getting one from me.

Amber crossed one leg over the other, a pained look on her face and I imagined how brittle and weakened her bones had to be by now. "Take me to my boy," she said again. "I'll tell him to stop this and let everyone live."

Watching her, I knew without doubt that I was looking into the face of a predator. My skin started to itch, signaling it was time to go. The thought of staying a second longer made my stomach roll. "Goodbye," I said, hoping I'd never have to come back. She wouldn't stop her son. Knowing her, she'd probably join him.

I turned to walk away and Amber and Greg both started to shout obscenities. I ignored them and just kept my eyes on the door. The faster I got out of there, the faster I could breathe again.

Once on the other side, I took a large gulp of air, glad that I'd made it without breaking down. I felt exhausted, like I'd just walked a marathon and hadn't had food or drink for days. I wiped sweat from my face and vowed no matter what, I was never going in that room again.

9

When we got back to Yama's, Amber's words still rung in my ear. She'd been so smug in trying to get under my skin, and here I was letting her.

In her mind, she'd created me, and made me become something I'd never wanted to be. I tried to fight the accuracy of her statement, but it played havoc on my mind to the point where I stood up and abruptly excused myself to the bathroom, leaving Bale to explain the gist of our visit.

I made sure the door was firmly closed and then threw cool water on my face, trying to block out her words. Why, why was I letting her get to me?

I was my own person. I made my own decisions. Her words should mean nothing. Yet, somehow, I couldn't shake them.

I felt a small headache forming, and I sat down hard on the toilet, trying to banish everything about the last thirty minutes from my mind.

"The only power she has is that which you choose to give her." My mother's voice was a surprising and soothing presence in my head. She must have sensed my distress and decided to reach out from her home on the Isles.

I closed my eyes and called out to the water in her, to the large bodies of water that surrounded the Isles, hoping to get a clear connection. "Mom. I don't know what to do. I can't get her voice out of my head."

"The only voice talking to you now is me," she answered.

I sighed, not knowing how to articulate my words, but sure that she could read my mind and figure out what I wanted to say anyway. "So many people are going to die, Mom." I sniffed, hot tears running down my face.

I hated being like this, so easily broken, yet I knew no other way to be. It was how I'd been raised, and I'd carried those same thoughts and feelings into adulthood.

My mother spoke again. "The blood of the Isles runs through you. I am connected to you. Use it." Then she was gone, and I was all alone in the bathroom, tears still flowing, wishing for the first time in a long time that I had my mother here to comfort me.

I took a few more minutes in the bathroom trying to school my features before walking back out. All eyes turned to me when I entered the room, and I guess I must have looked a sight because I got concerned looks and some careful eye avoidance.

I tried to not let it bother me. I was who I was, and I was done apologizing for that.

Yama sat at the kitchen table now, his keen eyes watching me. I didn't know why, but I got the distinct impression that he knew everything going on inside my head, but respected me enough to let me work through it on my own.

Bale stood by the door talking to Iiann and Kyle. I didn't know what they were talking about, but I assumed it was about the disease.

Flynn sat across from Yama at the table. He had a small

electronic device in his hand that he kept looking at. Meanwhile, Klenaya and Leon seemed caught up in their own conversation.

I took a deep breath and walked into the center of the room. I thought long and hard about what my mother had said and hoped I was making the right decision. "I think…" I said, then stopped to clear my throat.

The room became deathly silent as the others turned my way. I swallowed around the lump in my throat, trying to tell myself I could do this.

I hated being the center of attention. It always took me back to grade school when I'd been the butt of every joke, and every day wanted to curl up into a small ball and disappear.

My heart sped up, and I wrung my hands together and told myself to focus. Amber had shaken me more than I cared to admit, and dammit, I couldn't let her win. I wouldn't. "I think I know a way to defeat them."

"Are you sure about this?" Leon asked, concern etched across his face. We were climbing out of Iiann's boatcar and on our way to deliver Rangord his answer. Bale, Yama, Klenaya, and Flynn had ridden in Bale's, ride. While Kyle, Leon, Iiann and I had taken Iiann's.

We all stood by the tree now, deciding that Flynn would take his group first, then Iiann would take ours. "I'm not sure about anything," I answered Leon's question. "But we have to try, right?"

I could tell from the way his jaw tightened, that he didn't like it, but he readily agreed. Nothing was worth leaving these people to the mercy of Rangord's disease. Nothing.

"If this doesn't work we still need to expose Rangord. We

can't let him get away with it," Iiann said as we waited for the first group to go down.

Kyle stood leaning against the tree. "People's loyalties lay with the tacium, not one person."

Iiann agreed. "A threat to the tacium is a threat to us all, and Rangord knows that. Not one person would back him if they knew what he'd done. Not one."

Iiann looked at his watch and then back at the keypad. The light on it turned green, and he pushed in the code. Once it opened we all stepped inside.

Yama and the others waited in the small room preceding Rangord's study. Yama's eyes landed on me as I walked off the lift and something in them gave me the strength to do what I needed to do.

"Ready?" Flynn asked, his hand hovering over the keyboard.

"Yes," I said, speaking for everyone.

He took a deep breath and seemed to steel himself, before pushing the buttons that would take us inside Rangord's private study.

The man himself sat behind his desk looking over a small screen and smiling. His eyes turned our way when we entered, but he didn't seem all that surprised to see us.

He pointed to the device on his desk. "The first man I had you go see has almost expired." He smacked his lips together. "Once the first one is gone, the rest will quickly follow." He turned to Yama. "Are you ready to let my mother go?"

Yama looked at him, his face unreadable. "I came to make sure that you join her. We'll put you in a cell right across from her if you like."

Rangord tapped a finger to his lips. "And what will the other leaders say when they find out you had a chance to stop this but didn't? What will you tell your people when it spreads to Kelm? One life in exchange for so many. Is it really that bad of a deal?" He sounded like a used car salesman trying to convince an unsuspecting customer to buy a lemon.

Yama's eyes locked with mine and I felt something break deep inside me. Something in them held a power that spoke to my soul. "Do your thing." His voice was rich and full and held a confidence I wasn't sure I deserved.

I closed my eyes and let my mind flow to my mother, my sister, and every other person on the Isles. I envisioned it, the way it had been the last time I'd been there. That had been many years ago, so I envisioned it how it was now.

I sent my thoughts, my emotions, my feelings rippling through the water reaching out to every person there and letting them know I needed their help.

I was a daughter of the Isles, and they would not deny me. A whole world dangled precariously on a needle threaded by a madman, and they would not abandon it.

My body shivered as the force of their power reached out to me and entwined with my own. I smiled when I felt it, felt them, my mother, sister, grandmother, father, uncles, aunts, neighbors. I'd never experienced anything like it, and I finally understood what the phrase "drunk with power" meant, because that's exactly how I felt at that moment.

My hair flew straight up, and I could feel my eyes begin to glow, energy encased my body and lifted me in the air before bringing me down again. My heart pounded relentlessly, and I had the feeling I could take on ten men if they were to dare try me.

A small chant started in my head and grew louder by the second. "San shang loo loous glore, san shang loo loous glore," I said, over and over again.

Somewhere in the back of my mind, I heard a door slam and a scuffle break out. I opened my eyes only minimally, not wanting to lose my connection to the Isle.

Gillum stood by the door, a man and woman on either side of him. I could hear Rangord talking, though it sounded far off.

Gillum's eyes lit blue, as did his companion's and they began a rhythmic chant of their own. Their voices sounded hard and strong as they walked in unison farther into the room.

Iiann and Flynn came to stand on either side of me, their eyes glowing as well, as they too started to chant. I closed my eyes and focused on the Isles and bringing their strength forward even more. "Esste, losta, grurlo," I said, feeling the power flow through me. "Esste, losta, grurlo."

Iiann and Flynn continued their chant, and together we walked toward the other three.

"Esste, losta, grurlo." Wind blew through the room, knocking everyone and everything back, except for the six of us doing the chanting.

My feet lifted off the ground, my hair sticking straight up. I let Iiann and Flynn deal with Gillum and his crew while I focused on the poison currently working its way through the nervous systems of so many people.

I got the code of the poison and threw it back to the Isles to decipher. They threw it back a second later, having worked out the riddle to removing it.

We needed to make the virus attack the tacium, then once the tacium was weakened, we could separate the two and dissolve it.

In record time, with the mental powers of the Isles, we searched every person and every piece of tacium they'd ingested. Energy crackled around me as we focused on snatching the poison from the tacium, then from the people it'd infected.

We also searched every piece of tacium in this whole

universe, including what was still in Kelm. We took no chances on any of it being affected.

"Esste, losta, grurlo, esste, losta, grurlo," I repeated over and over again my voice getting louder every time I did so.

Sparks shot off me, and I threw my head back, and my whole body began to tremble. "Esste, losta, grurlo." We kept going, didn't stop until we had every stitch, every inch of poison in that whole universe, including Rangord's hidden supply. It appeared as a large angry mass in the shape of a ball. It floated in the air, hovering just above the country Lamink.

"Esste, losta, grurlo! Esste, losta, grurlo!" The ball of poison shot out of this universe, into empty space where one last powerful chant finished it for good, causing it to dissipate into nothing.

Exhausted, my knees buckled and Iiann and Flynn caught me before I hit the ground.

Rangord's grief filled cry brought us all back to the present. I reached out to the screen he'd been looking at earlier and turned it around so that everyone could see what had him so upset.

The first man we'd gone to see, Beck, was now sitting up on the side of his bed. He was screaming for his wife, asking for food, water, and tacium to make him feel better.

Relief flowed through me, and I'd never been so happy to hear a man scream in my life. He was alright, which meant that the rest of them were alright too. But just to be sure, we did a few more checks of those who were known to be infected. They were all healing fine. Which is all I'd wanted from the start. It made me feel good knowing that we'd saved so many people.

It only took Gillum a second to assess the situation and realize that he'd been on the wrong side. Rage filled his face, so much so that when Rangord jumped over the desk to attack, it was Gillum who took him down, with a small chant and a fist to the face.

Rangord fell with a thump, knocked out cold by one of his own men.

Leon and the others still watched the screen, where Beck now ate with gusto, while his wife looked on in shock and relief.

"You did it," Klenaya said. She made to hug me, but my knees gave out again, causing Leon to put an arm around my waist and pull me up.

"Yeah, we did it," I agreed.

10

"Oh, look at that one." Klenaya pointed in the sky, where a firework in the shape of a lion hung, looking strong and menacing. Facing it was an even bigger firework shaped like a bear.

The lion's body was made of blue and red sparkling lights. The eyes were a dark green and the paws the same color.

The bear had sea blue eyes, and its body was silver and black. They both let out an ear pounding roar, and I jumped back, surprised that they could do that. The twin's eyes lit up as they watched and I figured it was worth it if it made them this happy.

I too was happy. Happy that we'd stopped the spread of a deadly poison and happy to know that my mom and the rest of my family on the Isles hadn't turned their backs on me, no matter how violent I'd become lately.

I smiled at Leon, who looked to be having as much fun as the twins were.

We would have both helped out, fifty thousand or not, but I knew it would be foolish not to take the money. Especially on my part, since I was out of work at the moment, and could use the boost in cash.

"This is just the first one," Leon said, his eyes straying back toward the fireworks. "That means there's more to come. I'm going to take pictures."

I laughed and pulled out my phone, figuring I might as well record this as well.

My hand paused before I took my first photo, and I thought of Rangord, a man willing to do anything to set his mom free, no matter the consequences.

Well, he was with her now. In a cell right across from her, as promised.

As next in line, Flynn had taken over rule of Lamink, and when we'd left, he'd been in the process of putting his council together, though the whole thing was still a little bittersweet for him.

Gillum had seemed wrecked, knowing that he'd almost contributed to the destruction of tacium, but Iiann had assured him that not knowing all the facts, he'd only done what he'd thought to be right.

Now whether Iiann really believed that or not, I didn't know, but he had agreed to stay on as chief investigator and help his brother out, so I felt that Lamink was in good hands.

It had taken a few days for my body to recover from the strain of having the power of the Isles, as I wasn't meant to hold anything that strong. Leon had had to get back to work, but I'd stayed a few days on Kelm, trusting Yama and the others to look over me until I felt better.

That had been a week ago, and the twins had been sending Leon updates every day I was there. On the third day, they'd brought him for a visit, but he hadn't been able to stay long because duty called.

Today was his day off and since the twins had pretty much memorized his schedule, they'd picked today to come to this universe, Growl, to see the fireworks. Leon was a detective, so even his days off were not always days off, but I was glad he was here now.

I got the camera on my phone ready, as three whistles started to blow. I looked at the twins, who were almost jumping in place they were so excited and I realized that it made me feel good having all four of us here together like this. To be honest, I wouldn't have it any other way.

CURSED IN SUNLIGHT

1

I threw out the ace of diamonds and watched the faces of my competitors turn sour as if they'd just downed a gallon of vinegar. Xavier gave me a slight smile from across the card table, and I knew we were on the same page.

I hadn't seen him since the night we'd had to fight for our lives in Pear Town together. I'd pretty much gone back to life as I knew it after that whole fiasco.

Twist, the other person who'd been with us, and who'd certainly been hurt the most, hadn't come back to Jinx's (the gambling spot where he worked as a floor runner) for two weeks. Eventually, he'd come back, though, he seemed to be a shadow of his former self.

The night we'd first met, Xavier had told me he wanted me for a big game where it was twenty thousand just to sit. I didn't have that kind of cash, and I'd told him so outright. He'd agreed to front me the money on the chance that we'd actually win.

Well, we'd been victorious, but in winning, we'd advanced to the next round. Something I hadn't known, as I thought I'd be able to just take my twenty and go.

This time it was forty to sit, so I again had to borrow twenty from him. Which made me kind of ill, and I showed it by shooting him a hard stare every few seconds.

Looking at it on the flipside, though, there was eighty thousand dollars up for grabs. Twenty, of course, would go to Xavier, but that still left me sixty to play with. More money than I'd ever seen in my life. My bills were in tatters, but I was a gambler, so my bills were always on life support.

Winning here could pay off a few of my larger expenses, as well as allow me to be more selective in future games. I was at the card table every night. Being sick or even just tired didn't matter. If I didn't play, I didn't eat. Winning this money would help to alleviate a lot of that pressure.

***

The tournament hall was a large space that fit over a hundred tables easily. All around us the games went on, not only spades, as many contests took place at once.

The floors were burgundy carpet and the walls a crisp white. It wasn't the best combination I'd seen, but then things here looked more vintage than what I was used to, so I really wasn't a good judge. Every couple of feet were large floor to ceiling windows that let the sun in and provided ample light. Not that the carefully placed chandeliers, that seemed to be above every table, weren't doing a good job.

Because so many people were crowded in here, the only thing I could smell was body odor and sweat. The place wasn't too noisy, as most people here concentrated on the games.

I looked down at the table, and my spine tingled with excitement wondering if we could actually pull this off. Besides my bills, I also needed a new car, as my old one had broken down a few months ago. I figured I'd purchase a nice used one for about three grand, and still have enough to keep my rent and utilities paid for a while.

Just thinking about it put a big smile on my face, but that quickly vanished when the man beside me, a big fellow named Earl, with red hair and a beard, threw down the three of spades, effortlessly cutting my diamonds to shreds.

I looked up to Xavier in a panic. I would have never played the ace of diamonds if I'd thought Earl still had spades in his hand. Shit. I took a deep breath and tried to keep my head in the game.

This was the last hand and what happened here decided who won tonight's tournament. Xavier seemed unbothered and tilted his head to the side in a way that said, "It happens."

Yeah, it'd certainly happened to me before, but not with eighty thousand, ready to slip through my fingers.

Xavier only had one card left as did Earl's partner, Tenana. She was a tall woman, her skin the same color light brown as my own. She had on a white shirt, and her hair was in a kinky twist that was natural and flowing. It looked good, and I made a note to ask her about her hair game later.

Xavier looked from Earl to Tenana and then smiled and threw his last card out. I held my breath, as this was the difference in me walking away with everything or nothing.

A seven of spades hit the table, and I almost jumped from my seat. Xavier raised a brow that said I was stupid to be worried in the first place. Well fuck that, he still had money if we lost, I didn't. I turned from him, back to Tenana. Her face was stone cold, giving away nothing.

She looked at the cards already on the table and then at her own. The smile on her face, and the way she slammed the card down, like one only did if they were victorious, made my stomach sink to the floor.

Why had we had to advance to the second round anyway? Why couldn't we have just walked away with the first win? I heard noises around the table, but I was so caught up in my downward spiral that I paid them no attention.

I couldn't believe we'd come this far only to lose. Not only that, but I was used to playing with food and lots of alcohol. Here, none of that was allowed on the game floor, not even a glass of water.

"Leah!" Xavier said my name as if he'd been calling me for a while.

"What?" I said, not able to keep the bitterness out of my voice. It wasn't his fault, we'd played as a team, a very good team mind you, and we'd lost as one as well.

"Look at the table, darlin'."

I sighed loudly, letting my inconvenience show. Then nearly lunged from my seat when I saw that the only thing she'd thrown down was a five of clubs.

"I was just fucking with you," Tenana said, a disappointed smile on her face. "Had to get back at you somehow, right?"

The only thing I could do was nod, as at the moment I seemed incapable of speech. There were three floor runners to each table, making sure the transitions went smoothly, and there were no problems.

One was a short guy with black hair, dressed in the blue slacks and yellow pocket shirt uniform of the tournament hall. "Don't forget the house takes three percent. Come on. I'll verify your win so that you can advance to the last round tomorrow."

Last round? You mean we had to do this shit again? I looked to Xavier, but he held his hands up, feigning innocence. I ignored him and turned back to the floor runner. "How much to sit at the game tomorrow?"

His brows drew together as if he wondered why I was

here if I didn't know the rules. Good question, to be honest. "Games start tomorrow night at seven, sixty to sit."

My shoulders slumped. Great. The stakes had just gotten even higher. I snorted, as I thought about it, of course they had. That was the name of the game in gambling.

I also knew that the gambler in me couldn't walk away from a pot of over two hundred and forty thousand dollars, one hundred and twenty would be mine free and clear.

The downside was that after I paid Xavier back the twenty I'd borrowed for this last game, that'd only leave me with sixty, which is how much the game cost. That meant if I lost tomorrow, I'd lose all the money I had. I shrugged, thinking that's probably why they called it gambling. But also knowing that I needed to be able to pay my rent and eat, something that wouldn't happen if tomorrow's game was a bust.

Xavier seemed cocky enough, but hell, he probably had money to spare. I didn't. "Cheer up, darlin'." He fell into place beside me. "We won. Let's say we celebrate."

I swallowed hard as I looked at the games still in process. "I can't celebrate until tomorrow after seven. See me then."

He seemed undaunted. "Your choice."

I sighed and deflated a bit with his easy acceptance. He still looked as good as ever, over six feet tall with shoulder length black hair and a smile that made me want to do things that should probably make me blush. "How about some food?" I asked, stepping closer into his space. He came a few steps closer as well, until we were barely an inch apart. "Maybe you can come up to my room after we celebrate, help me release some of this tension in my shoulders."

He ran a single finger down my face, making me shiver from his touch. "I can damn sure try," he said, voice heavy.

"That's what I like to hear," I said, a little breathless. We'd never had our night together, and everything in me jumped with anticipation.

We followed the attendee to the window, and he verified us, making sure we advanced to the next round. We were given our money, as I didn't feel safe letting the hall keep it.

The hotel rooms came with the tournaments, but we still had to pay for food, drink, and any entertainment we might like. I'd won five hundred from my last game at home, and brought three hundred of that with me to eat and drink. This money I kept separate from the tournament money.

"Where to now, darlin'?" Xavier asked, looking at the throng of people around us.

I thought about it. I was feeling expensive tonight. I hadn't known we wouldn't be able to eat or drink during the game and that had saved me more money than I'd realized.

I could treat myself tonight and still have enough to eat well tomorrow. "How about crab legs, and T-bone steaks? I had no idea they would starve us the whole time we were here."

He grinned. "Oh, now, darlin' that sounds like my kind of meal. There's a steak house down the street. Good food and good service."

"They sell crab legs?" For me, that was a deal breaker. I had to have my crab legs.

He nodded. "Shrimp too. Come on, let's go."

I started to ask him if we were walking or catching a cab. I knew he'd said the place was just down the street, but he didn't say how far, and this road was a couple of miles long.

I didn't get the chance to ask though, because a scream like I'd never heard rang through the hall making me drop to my knees and grab my ears.

I looked around and saw that others looked as pained as I did.

Some tournament players were scrambling by, putting

their money in a safe place and trying to hightail it out of there.

Xavier turned to me, and for the first time since I'd met him, I saw him look truly concerned. "Put your money up and walk away. I'll catch up with you later."

The urgency in his voice left no room for arguments. I started to do as he'd said when the scream sounded again. As howling and painful as the first scream, this one was accompanied by flashing golden lights and a man who looked to be about thirty.

He was slim, almost waif like, and I got the impression that if a strong wind came, it would knock him over. He wasn't dressed appropriately for the weather, and the blue jean shorts and brown T-shirt hung loosely over his five-nine frame. His brown hair was plastered to his head, with sweat or water, I wasn't sure which. His skin looked blistered and was covered with dozens of tiny markings, each which seemed to be on fire and the source of his pain. Some were bleeding, and others were open festering wounds.

I stepped back horrified, not sure of what I was seeing.

He looked at the woman beside him and made to snatch her money. Xavier was on him before I could blink, and I followed right behind.

Xavier reached out to grab him, but the man disappeared. The woman gave Xavier a quick thanks, then hurriedly tucked her money in her pocket and ran out the door.

"What the..." I looked around, but Xavier stood in a crouch, arms out as if waiting for the man to reappear. Mostly everyone else had left, probably figuring they'd get away while they still could. "Maybe we should--"

I didn't get a chance to finish, because that next moment the man appeared again, wailing as he'd done before. With his left hand, he snatched Xavier's money, and with his right he took mine and then disappeared. It all happened in a span of two seconds, and for a moment I was just stunned. "Hey," I said once I registered what had happened. "How did he... How could he... Please tell me they have insurance for this type of thing." It was my last hope, to be honest, anything else was just too painful to think about.

2

The way Xavier dropped his eyes to mine, I already knew the answer, and I felt something in my gut curl up and die. "Nah, Leah. It's up to us to secure our own money. The tournament has guards to protect from the usual threats, but that right there, darlin', ain't no usual threat."

"Well, what is it then?" I snapped. I didn't mean to be short with him, but damnit. I'd come too far, and this wasn't fair. It just wasn't.

Xavier took a seat at one of the now empty tables and bid me to do the same. I sat down slowly, still trying to process that I'd just had eighty thousand slip from my hands.

"You're good with a sword. We should get you one," was all he said.

I closed my eyes and tried not to lose patience. "Xavier." I'd used a sword once or twice the night we'd gone to Pear Town. Xavier had used his transformation power to make it for me out of a stick. Still I had no idea what that had to do with now.

"I'm not joking." He sure sounded serious enough, and

that gave me reason to open my eyes, and really listen to what he had to say.

"If we're going down to Cave Town, we're going to need all the ammunition we can get. You think Pear Town is bad, you don't know bad until you've had to go into Cave Town.

Well, if the dude who'd stolen our money was any indication then I'd say it was pretty bad. I didn't need convincing. "Have you been there?"

He nodded. "A few times."

Of course he had, because he'd been everywhere. "So, it's a fight to get in, and a fight to get out?"

He shook his head. "No. It's not like that. Most people of Cave town won't bother you if you don't bother them. They're a skittish people though, and if they think you're trying to do them harm, or trick them into the daylight, they will hurt you."

"Because daylight is so bad?"

He stood. "Come on, I still have a little cash in my pocket. Let's go have a nice meal and discuss how we're going to get our money back. Tonight."

Damn right tonight, because if we didn't have it by seven tomorrow, we'd just lost the chance of a hundred and twenty thousand each and I'd literally be living on the streets. "Why can't we just go now?" I stood as well. "I want my money back, and I don't see the point in waiting."

"You can't do much on an empty stomach, darlin', and you already said you were hungry. We'll grab something quick. You need to know the history of Cave Town, before going down there."

We grabbed a large thin pepperoni pizza from a nearby parlor, along with two bottles of water. I bit into a slice and closed my eyes in bliss as the hot cheese slid down my throat, and flavorful sauce trickled from my lips. "Hmm," I said around a sigh, it was just the way I liked it. "So, what's the deal with Cave Town?" I asked.

The parlor was packed to the rim and smelled of oregano, garlic, and just a hint of rosemary. It was noisy, though, as kids screamed, and adults talked loudly in order to be heard over the crowd. With a tournament in town, I guessed that was to be expected.

Still, it was a nice, warm, comfortable atmosphere, and under different circumstances, I could see myself having a great time.

Xavier finished the slice he was on and then wiped his face with a napkin. Nice. I liked a man with manners, sometimes anyway. "Cave Town is a well-guarded secret. Most people don't even know it exists."

"But of course, you do," I baited him.

He smiled. "Well, now, darlin', I know a lot of things most people probably don't. You gonna hold it against me?"

Something inside me turned squishy at his candor, and I remembered why I'd wanted him in the first place. That it had been weeks, and I still hadn't gotten him into my bedroom was almost criminal. I cleared my throat, not wanting him to know the effect he had on me. "I won't hold it against you, now tell me what you know."

"Cave Town has been here for thousands of years." He gave me a moment to let that sink in. "The man you just saw, Jonas, he's a drug runner, but he dips into his own product. He has to, to survive."

I picked up another slice and bit into it. "I'm intrigued, go on."

He downed his bottle of water and signaled the waitresses for another. I held up my fingers, letting her know to bring two.

"Did you see his skin? The markings he had?" Xavier asked me.

I thought back to the way the man had screamed out in pain and how his own skin seemed to be working against him. "It looked like they were eating him alive."

The waitress came with our waters and set them before us. We both thanked her and waited until she was out of hearing range to continue.

Xavier bit into another slice. "Have you ever heard of the Council of Thems?"

I thought back on my history lessons. "They ruled thousands of years ago, and could bless you with splendor or despair, depending on how you lived your life?"

"Well, the truth is a little different. They did rule thousands of years ago, and they did hand out punishment, but only in extreme cases. They, however, never made anyone's life more plentiful or joyful."

"So, they were the bad guys then?"

"Nah, darlin', not bad. They mostly stayed out of it and let people live their own lives, but the individuals around them were bad and getting worse every day. A lot of stealing and senseless murders were taking place, and they finally had to step in and bring order back to their part of the world."

That didn't sound good. "What did they do?"

"They cursed them," he said, matter-of-factly. "They rounded up all those who'd committed one or more murders and tainted their skin with their kills. Each mark you saw on Jonas represents a person he's killed and the manner in which he killed them. A knife mark if he stabbed them, a small bottle, if he poisoned them, and so on. In the sunlight, they glow and fester, making sure the person who wears them can feel their victim's death, only amplified."

I sat back with a shudder. "That sounds horrifying."

He took a sip of water. "That's not even the worst of it. Each new generation born is set to bear the marks of their ancestors. So, the curse continues indefinitely."

"Why would they curse children?" I gasped. "That's just… mean," I said for lack of a better word.

He gave me a wry look. "Darlin', do you know of any nice curses?"

"No," I admitted, feeling a bit foolish. "But why punish the children if they've done nothing wrong?"

He shrugged. "That's how they made the curse."

"The light shining in from the ceiling and windows, must have been the reason for his screams."

"The sun is down now. It was almost down when he came, he probably just misjudged. That's why he kept flickering in and out. Jonas has teleportation. He probably just transported back to Cave Town to give himself some relief, before popping back to steal our money."

"And once the mistake in daylight had been made, he had to continue, because he'd already alerted everyone to his presence. If he waited until the sun went down, everyone would've had time to hide."

"Right," Xavier said, clicking a finger at me. "He only does this about once every six months. No one around here knows who he is, but most know to hide their money when he pops up."

I picked up another slice and vowed it would be my last. "You never thought to tell them?"

"No, because then most would go looking for Cave town, and few would make it out alive. Also, not all of the people of Cave Town are bad, some were just born to this curse. How many kids and innocent people will die if the folks here decide to charge into Cave Town?"

"A lot," I admitted. "So, what do we do?"

"Most people don't like Jonas. Remember I told you he was a drug dealer? It's not really drugs though, it's breez. Breez took hundreds of years to develop, and some believe that rogue members of the council of Thems had a hand in it."

"Why?" I asked, not yet understanding what he was trying to tell me.

He held up a few fingers. "Three hours. It gives the person who takes it three hours to go up into the sunlight without the marks attacking their skin."

"Only the Council who made the curse in the first place would be able to create something like that."

He didn't seem to have an opinion either way. "It's what everyone thinks. The thing is, if cornered, if they believe we're there to do them harm, they will attack. Living the way they do has made them bitter and hard. They look at people who live outside of Cave Town as spoilt and privileged. I think we need help going in there."

"Twist," I said, because I'd already been thinking the same thing. Twist was so torn down lately after what had happened with his sister in Pear Town. She'd led him to believe she'd been murdered by me.

For weeks, he'd thought her to be dead, and when he'd finally found out that she wasn't, she'd tried to kill him. That was a hard thing to come back from, especially since I knew how much he still loved her.

I just wanted to give him something to do, something to fight for. Of course, it could also get him killed, so there was that to consider.

"Can you reach him?" Xavier threw some money on the table, and I dug into my purse for my half.

He watched me with a knowing smirk on his face. "Should have known you wouldn't let me treat you."

"Oh, you can treat me," I put down my half of the bill, plus a ten for the waitress as a tip. Xavier left her a twenty. "Just not right now."

His eyes went dark. "I can wait," he said in that low rough voice that I loved.

"Good." His eyes bored into mine, and I could feel his stare all the way to my bones. "Right," I said, clearing my throat, and trying to regain control of myself. "I'll call Twist on the way to get the sword."

3

"Twist said he'd be here in about twenty minutes," I said to Xavier as I hung up the phone. He'd seemed, dare I say it, excited. I'd explained the part about how we might die if we go there, but that didn't seem to faze him in the least.

I liked the way that Twist, Xavier, and I had worked together as a team in Pear Town, and I too was just a little bit excited. I was also frightened, and nervous, but willing to do anything to get my money back.

"Twist lives over three hundred miles away," Xavier pointed out.

"He can travel hundreds of miles in an hour. He said twenty minutes, so..." I let the rest fall away, sure he'd understand.

"Darlin', I don't want to turn on the news and hear about a human tornado that's killed thousands of people."

I gave him a dry look, as we walked through a back alley and down a set of steps that led to another alley, around a corner, and then to another alley. "Where exactly is this sword at?"

"The tornado?"

So, he wanted to talk about that. "Twist knows how to contain his wind to himself alone, sure, if he wanted to release it on an unsuspecting people he could, but as you already know, such an act is punishable by death, so I think we're good. Anyway, I told him what street we were on so he should be waiting for us when we get back."

We walked for about five more minutes, going further and further underground as we went until finally stopping at a small wooden house. Nothing else was around, and the road the house sat on was all dirt and gravel.

It was darker down here than it had been up on the street. Something tapped me on the shoulder, and I jumped until I realized it was just a long tree branch that hadn't been trimmed.

We were surrounded by woods, and the only sound that could be heard were small animals going about their nightly routine. I took a curious glance around, making sure that was the only thing hiding in the bushes.

Xavier didn't seem bothered by any of this if the nonchalant look on his face was any indication. "He doesn't lock the door," he said, pushing it open.

I took another look around at the empty landscape, barren of anything but this house and the trees surrounding it. "Well, when you live miles away from any human contact, I guess you don't have to," I reasoned.

"Nah, it's just too much a hassle for him."

We walked into a dark room where I could faintly make out the outline of a couch and two love seats that would have looked new sixty years ago. It was hot in here, stuffy even. I squinted and figured we were in the living room. From there, we went through a small kitchen that was empty of everything except a stove, refrigerator, and table.

Next, we walked through an opened door that led to a

dimly lit room where a short bald, well, he did have a few gray strands scattered here and there, man sat. He wore a brown wool shirt and brown pants. He looked to be about sixty or seventy, and he didn't really seem all that surprised to see us.

He gave us a knowing look. "Come for a sword, have you?" His voice sounded ancient, like he'd used it for thousands of years and now it was tired and worn, but still expected to work.

The room smelled woodsy, like fresh pine, and on the surface, it was a pleasant enough scent, but there was too much of it here, and it made me want to gag a little.

While my eyes were busy taking everything in, Xavier stood in a relaxed position, as if he'd been here many times before. Well, I reasoned, he'd brought us here, so it was hardly his first time.

The man's skin was wrinkled and gray as if he'd seen far too much sunlight in his lifetime. He sat in a chair, an old black and white TV set played in front of him, yet his eyes stayed on Xavier and me. "Which of you needs a sword?" he asked us.

"I do," Xavier answered quickly.

I wasn't sure what Xavier's game was, but I wasn't having it. "I'll be the one using the sword," I let the man know. "So, I'm the one asking."

Xavier turned to me, his eyes saying I'd fucked up and I swallowed hard because I knew it was too late to take it back now.

"So, both of you then?" The man asked, looking pleased. "The price is, of course, a favor, that you cannot refuse."

My head snapped to Xavier because I didn't like the sound of that. "Can't we just pay you?" I asked, hopefully.

The man sat back in his chair, his eyes roaming over the

simplicity of his home. "What use do I have for money?" He shook his head. "No. A favor or no sword."

I turned to Xavier to get his take on this, but he was suspiciously looking at the wall on the opposite side of the room. Which meant he wanted me to make this decision for myself. Fine. I could do that. If we were going into a place as bad as Pear Town I could use any weapon I could get my hands on. "One favor within reason," I said.

The man's smile brightened as if I'd just gifted him a million dollars. Well, he probably wouldn't smile at that, seeing as he had no use for money, but anyway. "Accepted," he said. He pointed down the hall. "Last door on the left, but first... Let me ask you a few questions."

I stood a little straighter, hoping I was up to the task. "Go ahead."

"Do not answer out loud. Just think about it when you go to pick out your sword."

I looked down the hall, a bit confused. "You're not coming with me?"

He chuckled as if I'd actually said something funny. "Only one person can enter the sword room at a time."

Unless the room was super tiny, I didn't understand that logic, but okay. "So, I can pick any sword I want?" I flexed my hands, anxious to get this over with.

He chuckled again, this time in a way that was almost condescending. "You may pick the sword that most wants to leave with you."

I turned to Xavier again, hoping for some type of guidance, but once again he was looking anywhere but at me. I rolled my shoulders. I could do this. I didn't need his help anyway. "What are your questions?" I asked the man.

"Who are you? What do you do for a living? Who do you love? What are you willing to die for? What are you willing to live for? Where did you come from and where are you going?" When he finished, he pointed down the hall as if telling me to be on my way. I nodded and went in the direction he'd indicated.

I thought about what he'd asked me, as I opened the door to the sword room and stepped inside. Who was I? A card player, a gambler. What did I do for a living? Same answer. Who did I love? That was an easy one, my family.

My brother and sister whom I saw at least twice a week. My brother and sister were both single like me. My brother owned a string of hotels and employed thousands. He often offered me money, but I refused to take a single dime.

He'd told me once when we were kids that he'd have to take care of me when we were older, so I made it my everyday mission to prove him wrong.

I'm not sure he'd meant it in a bad way, as he'd always been protective of my sister and me, but I'd taken it as an insult nonetheless.

My sister was as wild as me, and owned her own fitness center. She'd recently opened a second one in a nearby city, and my family couldn't be prouder of her.

My parents were both spade players, and though they were no longer married, they were still an unstoppable force at the card table. They traveled all around playing cards and stacking up wins, with a few losses here and there.

They never stayed in one place for too long, including in the city where all three of their children lived. Still, it had been them who'd first introduced me to the game, and taught me how to play, so there was that I reasoned.

I thought about this as I took in the massive number of swords in front of me. Some were so small you could barely see the blade, yet others were large enough to fight giants.

I looked around in amazement at the walls covered top to

bottom with shiny metal. I walked from one sword to the next, still thinking about the questions he'd asked.

What was I willing to die for? I would die to protect my family. I would like to think I would die to protect those who couldn't protect themselves, only I wasn't so sure that was true.

It was a nice concept, but if the time came, I wasn't sure I could risk my life for someone I didn't know. I'd like to think that I would, but who really knew the answer to something like that?

What was I willing to live for? My hand gleamed over the metal of the blades, the whole place starting to feel claustro-phobic. I swallowed, a little nervous now and tried to answer the question. I was willing to live for myself, and no one else, and I knew that answer to be true.

Sweat broke out on my face and down my back, making me shiver, as the urge to hurry up and get out of there started to take over.

Where did I come from and where was I going? I thought about growing up the middle of three children, my brother the oldest, my sister the youngest. I thought about how we'd fight and play, then fight, and play some more.

I thought about the first time my parents had sat my siblings and me down at a card table and taught us the rules of the game. I thought about the first time I'd actually won a game, the first time my sister and I had beaten my mom and dad at the table.

More sweat broke out, and my body started to shake as it cried to be free of this blasted room. I walked toward the back, where I saw a faint glow coming from one of the swords. As I went, I thought over the last part of the question.

"Where was I going?" I wanted to continue playing cards.

That was my life, and I couldn't imagine it any other way. I also wanted to get a new car, as my old one had a cracked head, and I'd been told it was better to just replace the damn thing rather than spend thousands to get it fixed.

I'd been thinking more about it and figured if I could win this last pot, then maybe I could put down the deposit on a small house, offer myself a bit of security, something I'd never really had.

My throat closed up, as the glow from the back got bigger. Trying not to panic, I struggled for breath, telling myself that I'd have no trouble making it out of here alive.

I tried to keep that positive thinking going as my skin started to ache and my throat constricted even more, making it that much harder to breathe. Every step I took was painful, and my whole body felt icky and wet with sweat.

Finally, I made it to the spot where the sword shone and gleamed. I looked around, just to make sure, and yup, it was the only one glowing out of the whole bunch.

I took a moment to look at it, my body still shaking from the pain. It was long and slightly curved with a black handle, my full name already written across the metal.

Gasping, I reached out, aiming to run my fingers across my name. Only when I touched it, it nicked me, and a small trickle of blood dripped onto the sword. The blade glowed red and my name along with the blood sunk down into it, causing it to vibrate.

I gasped again and jumped back, shocked, but it wasn't done yet. The blade lifted into the air on its own. My name once again appeared, this time on the hilt. The sword still glowed red but slowly it seemed to settle, the red fading inside the sword. I noticed my name still stayed on the hilt.

Now seized with pain, I slowly reached out and claimed the sword as my own.

It fit into my hand like a glove, and I tightened my grip, liking the feel of my fingers around the steel.

I'd thought the pain would stop once I touched the sword, but if anything, it grew worse. So, this had been what Xavier had tried to save me from? I wish I would have listened and let him go through this. Something told me it wouldn't have been his first time.

My legs felt as if they were on fire, and began to buckle. My vision blurred, and my head became so cloudy that I no longer even knew where the front door was.

The only thing I could see, the only thing that penetrated my now foggy brain, was the sword, which was glowing red again. It pointed up and sideways, so that's the direction I went. Each step was taken in agony, each breath, I thought would be my last. Finally, it stopped glowing and vibrating, and I reached out praying I'd made it to the front of the room.

My hands searched frantically until I found the knob and wrestled the door open. I wanted to run out of there and never look back, but in the state my body was in, it took me a full ten seconds just to get from one side of the door to the other.

Once I was out, it slammed shut with a bang, and suddenly everything became clear again. I was no longer hunched over in pain, in fact, I felt better than I had in a long time, the sword hummed in my hand and my body hummed right along with it. My hair was a mess, and my clothes a little askew, but I suddenly felt like I could take on both Pear Town, and Cave Town combined.

I walked back up the hall, confidence in my step and determination on my face.

Xavier stood in the same spot, but he seemed a little more relaxed as he and the man carried on a conversation about livestock of all things.

I turned to the man, ready to let him have it for not telling me what I was in for, but before I could say anything, he held up one finger and reached behind his chair with the other hand to give me a black leather scabbard for my sword. It had a long strap that would fit nicely around my shoulders. "Anything worth having is worth fighting for, but if you want, pull up a seat, and we can stay here all night talking about it."

I took the gift from him and put it on my back. "Thank you, but we're leaving." I shot Xavier a look letting him know that he could stay or go, at the moment, I didn't really give a damn.

"Don't forget about my favor," I heard the man say as I walked out the door.

I had nothing to say the whole way back onto the street and Xavier didn't push. There were too many conflicting emotions going on inside me, and I didn't quite know how to sort them.

Once we reached the top, I pulled out my phone and saw that I had six missed calls from Twist. Apparently, there'd been no service where we'd come from.

I called him back immediately. Twist was on the same street as us, we just had to walk for a bit. Which is what we'd been doing since we'd left the tournament hall, so it was no biggie.

It took us about six minutes to get to him. He sat up on a bench, feet resting on the seat portion. A street light shined down on him, so it was easy to see the multiple piercings that decorated his ears, lips, eyebrows, and chin. He had one on his tongue too, but since he hadn't started talking, I couldn't see that one yet.

His dark green hair hung loosely around his face, the red highlights on the tips in stark contrast to his olive skin tone. Twist's family was originally from China, but had been here for at least five generations now.

He wore a pair of blue jeans, and a black shirt, with a pair of sneakers. As we approached, he got up and walked over.

"Twist." I pulled him into a hug, which he returned, then kindly pulled away.

"Good to see you again, Xavier." Twist nodded at the other man.

"How you been, Twist?" Xavier asked.

A second of pain crossed Twist's face, but he quickly hid it by rummaging through his bag. "I have verve pills." He held up a small container. "Three in case we need 'em, and other stuff too."

I felt my pants pocket, making sure the two verve pills I'd brought from home were still there. I'd figured if the game went into overtime I might need them to help me stay alert and focused. "Thanks, Twist. I have some already, but the more, the merrier I guess."

Xavier nodded at me, a gleam of approval in his eyes. "Number one rule. Never go to a spades tournament without a little verve to keep you going."

I looked at the time on my phone and saw that it was almost seven. "Okay, so we've got twenty-four hours to get to Cave town, find this Jonas so that we can get our money back, and still make it in time to sit at the final game."

Xavier cleared his throat, a weird look on his face. "Well, darlin', this next part neither of you are going to like, and if you don't want to go any farther, I'll understand."

I stopped cold for a moment. What did he mean? Twist and I had both being willing to enter Pear Town, knowing exactly what we were up against. Xavier knew that, which made his warning all the more worrisome. "What is it?" I took a few steps toward him.

Xavier looked at us both dead on. "Anyone who stays in Cave Town over twenty-four hours will automatically be struck with the same curse as the residents who live there."

4

I had so many questions. "So, let me get this straight," I said, barely able to hide my annoyance. "The scars from all of our kills would be placed on our skin, causing us to burn whenever we hit sunlight."

He nodded as if this was in any way a normal conversation. "Even if you've never killed before, which I know both of you have," he gave Twist and I pointed looks. "It reaches back to the first male and female ancestor that has killed and marks you that way."

"Shamed by the blood." I shook my head, thinking over my options. It was likely I'd have to fight for my life, but I'd never let that stop me from going into Pear Town when someone had cheated me and thought they could escape there, and I wouldn't follow.

I ran a tired hand down my face. This was different, though. A lot different. Anything could happen once we got into Cave Town. Any number of things could prevent us from making it back in time.

Now more tired than I'd been a couple of seconds ago, I thought the situation over. It was a risk, a gamble for sure, but that's who I was. It's what I did every day. I gambled, on everything, so I certainly wasn't about to stop now.

"Also," Xavier said, and I tensed because by now I was convinced he was an evil demon sent from the depths of hell.

"What?" I asked, my voice tight, wondering what he would land on us next.

"Even if the people of Cave Town come to the outside world at night, they're still in a good deal of pain, and it only gets worse the longer they're out and the closer it gets to sunlight."

"It just keeps getting better and better," I said, jaw tight with irritation.

He went on talking as if he hadn't heard me, but from the slight brow raise, I knew that he had. "It's the way the curse was designed. To keep those in Cave Town in Cave Town, giving them a small taste of the world outside only to snatch it right back again. Don't look at me like that, darlin', I didn't enact the curse."

"Yeah, well with you, I never know." I was still a little pissed about him springing this on us all at once.

He grinned, and his eyes lit up, making me soften just a bit.

Twist adjusted the straps on his backpack. "Then we better get a move on." He said it in such a manner-of-fact way that I wasn't sure if he was bothered by the whole thing or not. Maybe he hadn't yet comprehended what it all meant.

He tried to walk forward, but I put a hand on his chest, stopping him. "Twist, you didn't sign up for this. You can go home if you want. Xavier and I will handle this."

He looked horrified that I would even suggest such a thing. "Didn't you both say you'd give me ten percent if you win tomorrow, five percent of what you already have if we get back, but don't make it to the tournament in time?"

I still didn't like it. "Twist look--"

"Uh." He held up a hand, cutting me off before I could say more. "I want that money." He paused for a moment, and I saw a shot of pain slither across his face. "I owe you," he said, his voice low, "both of you. So, just let me do this. I need to do something."

He was gripping the straps on his bag so hard I thought his fingers would pop. His eyes met mine, and something in them told me this was helping him, as much as it was us.

I removed my hand from his chest and looked at Xavier who nodded. "Okay, then," I said, trying to put a little cheer in my voice. "Let's go."

We walked for about ten minutes before coming to a manhole in the street. Xavier used his telekinesis to remove it and then we went down one at a time.

From there it was three tunnels, and four caves, each getting us deeper and deeper and deeper into the earth. The only thing we saw of interest was some scurrying animals and several different species of plants. I took note that the farther down we went, the darker it got.

Xavier had turned a couple of sticks into large flashlights, as well as taken rocks and made us work hats, the kind with the light on top, so we hadn't really had any trouble seeing yet.

We came out of the last cave into an opening. By now we were all tired and thirsty and hungry. Twist had bought some water, but we'd finished off the last of that about twenty minutes ago. You'd think Xavier and I would have stocked up, but we'd been in such a hurry, that we hadn't even bothered.

"We're here," Xavier said.

"Finally," I mumbled. I was tired, irritated, and just ready to find Jonas, get my money, and go. Figuring we might as well get it over with, I walked forward and gasped.

The opening to the cave spread as far as the eye could see. Also, it was so tall that I didn't see an end in sight. "Damn," I said, impressed by the enormity of it all.

"Wow," Twist said, looking about how I felt. "Just, wow."

Xavier pulled a verve pill out of his pocket. "We probably need to take one before we go in, you know, just in case."

I didn't particularly like taking pills dry, but seeing how we'd drunk all the water, I didn't have a choice. I swallowed it down, and Twist and Xavier did the same. "Ready?" I asked.

"No time like the present, darlin'," Xavier said, and together we all three walked into Cave Town.

I'm not sure what I'd expected, probably dirt walls and floors, one large space, people looking half-starved, with their clothes hanging off them.

What I saw was vastly different. Paved streets and side-walks were everywhere. Large brick houses stretched for miles and miles. Each house had neatly tended lawns, which gave me pause until I figured out it was all a part of the curse. "How?" I asked, looking at Xavier.

"Pain and tears, darlin', pain and tears," he said.

Talk about vague. "That's not an answer," I let him know.

He didn't say anything else, and I hadn't expected him to. Up ahead, a big sign read hospital. The building was large, and though it looked like it'd been built some time ago, it still appeared sturdy and from the people walking in and out of it, it was operational.

Across from it was a school, that I could easily imagine fitting at least fifteen hundred to two thousand kids. The bricks looked old but decent and the place seemed to be bustling with activity, as we could hear loud voices, and musical instruments coming from an open window.

Right in front of us was a grocery store. Outside in carts sat apples, oranges, and a host of other fruit. The store was medium-sized, but from what I could see it was clean and not hurting for customers.

Just past the school, was a burger joint with an eating area outside. Its chairs were filled with everything from groups of teenagers, to older soccer moms looking to be on lunch dates. The conversations flowed with ease, and everyone seemed to be enjoying their food.

"How?" I asked again, simply amazed at what I saw.

Xavier gave me a look that said he knew I wasn't going to stop asking, so he'd go ahead and answer. "People wait until it gets dark, or either take the pills, you know the ones that give them three hours of daylight?"

"I remember," I said.

"They go up top, go to school and learn new skills, then come home and put them to use in the community, teach others. Got brick masons, electricians, doctors, so many other professions going back generations." He glanced around, taking in the bustle of activity surrounding us. "They also buy, trade, and work while up top. Money's different here, but they have a decent conversion rate."

"Seems like they're not letting the curse stop them from living productive lives," Twist observed, his body now jumping from the verve.

I was holding myself steady to keep from doing jumping jacks, so I could relate.

"Where do we start?" I asked, resisting the urge to twerk.

A man and woman passed us. Two small children in tow. I watched them with great interest. They looked no different than the families back home, save for the tattoos that covered their bodies.

The man wore tan slacks, with a black sports jacket. The woman had on a brown skirt, with the coat to match. Each child, a boy, and a girl were dressed in jumpsuits with thick winter coats and mittens. They looked happy enough, as they turned the corner, chatting among themselves.

Xavier's eyes scanned the area as if trying to get a sense of direction. "First place we need to look, is Jonas's house."

"Do you know where he lives?" Twist asked.

Xavier took a left and bid us to follow. His body hummed with energy and I could tell the verve was starting to affect him as well. "He'll probably have a house full of people, runners just like him. Jonas likes to make sure that the only place you can buy sunlight, is from him."

"Sounds like most drug dealers," I shrugged.

"Yeah, well, Jonas, is one of the worst I know, so we need to be prepared."

We'd probably walked about five minutes when it really hit me that we were inside a cave. If I didn't know any better, I would say we were on any regular street up top, but no, we were actually walking down a paved road inside of a cave. It was a lot to wrap my mind around.

For the most part, no one paid us any attention. We did get a few stares, but mostly we were left alone. Until we got to Jonas Town that is.

Jonas, it seemed, had made a tiny city inside of Cave Town. In front of us stood a big black spiked gate. It had a sign on it, proudly proclaiming this part of the cave to be Jonas Town.

Large brick houses lined either side of a paved street, but unlike its counterpart, I didn't see any stores, schools, or restaurants, which meant he probably entered into Cave Town to do all his shopping.

The houses were large for the most part and well-kept. No trash littered the streets, the yards were nicely trimmed, and the porches held nice patio furniture. If I didn't know any better I would think I was in a regular middle-class neighborhood in the suburbs.

Except I could almost feel the menace in the air. Cave Town had felt warm and inviting, whereas Jonas Town seemed cold and threatening.

There was only one street, but it was long, and as far as my eyes could see, filled with houses on either side. Everything else was grass and dirt. No weeds though, as it looked like someone ran a mower through here every day.

I shook my head. They were inside a cave, but I believed the curse allowed them to do many things that would normally be off limits to ones living in a cave. Like having grass with no sunlight, or not dying from the gas fumes of a lawnmower.

These people had tried to make something out of the hand they'd been dealt, yet here Jonas was, trying to make their lives even more miserable. "What an asshole," I said, looking at the large black fence that stretched around the whole of Jonas's small town. There didn't seem to be an opening.

Twist used his wind to propel himself a few feet off the ground. "How do we get in?"

I raised my hand and used my TK to fly the gates apart. Immediately two guys and a woman appeared. For some reason, I got the distinct impression that they'd been waiting in the shadows for someone to stroll through uninvited.

We walked in anyway, as the verve in our systems was practically begging for a fight.

The woman was tall and slender. She had red curly hair that flowed down her back, her skin was a sort of cream color, and she had on brown boots, jeans, and a brown sweater. Her face was hard and severe, and her eyes said she meant business.

One of the men was also tall. He had purplish blue hair, and wore a navy blue sweat suit, and had on black sneakers.

The other guy was of medium height, bald headed, and had a massive chest, broad shoulders, and huge arms. He looked like he'd lifted weights every day since birth, and the sneer on his face said he was ready to put those massive muscles to use.

All three of them had tattoo marks covering the entirety of their faces.

We walked right up to them. It was three on three, so I figured we were okay.

"What business ya got here?" the tall man asked.

"We're looking for Jonas," Xavier answered.

"Well, he ain't here," the woman bit out.

"Then we'll wait," I said, calling all attention to myself.

The medium height man gathered his weight, and his chest stuck out just a bit more. "Not here you won't." He then spat on the ground right by my feet, missing me by mere inches.

Xavier's hands began to turn in a set of complicated motions. "Really wish you hadn't done that, but since you did…" He slung his hands out, and all three of them turned into frogs and wasted no time hopping away.

Xavier looked at Twist and me. "They'll be fine in a couple of hours," he assured us as if we didn't already know that.

In here, one house in particular stood out. As large as any mansion, its blue brick matched that of the mailbox and walkway. The columns were blue, while the awning was white and blue striped. The yard too was huge, and recently cut from the smell of fresh grass that tickled my nose.

It looked like a house a state governor might live in with his or her family and I caught myself straining to find the row of flower beds that had to be planted somewhere on the property.

As we got closer, I noticed there were no flowers, but there was a group of about eight people sitting on the porch, talking, and laughing. They hadn't noticed us yet, which was a good thing.

"Let me guess, Jonas's house." Twist was looking in the same direction as myself.

Xavier nodded.

We were all three watching when a man burst out the front door. He stood about six feet and was a bit on the heavy side. He had a young woman, who looked to be about twenty, twenty-one with him.

Skin a shade or two lighter than my own, she had black wavy hair that flowed down her back and she wore a pair of jeans with a white button up shirt, no coat.

Her arms were twisted behind her back, his meaty hands holding them in place. Because of the placement of her arms, she was bent almost to the ground, her tattooed and scarred face twisted in pain.

"Caught her out in the field, trying to steal sunlight," the man said to the others on the porch. "Jonas will have to make an example out of her for this."

Protectiveness rose in my chest as I watched the scene play out, and I knew I wouldn't be leaving here without a fight. I needed more information, though. I turned to Xavier. "Explain."

"Remember, I told you hundreds of years ago, someone developed a drug that allowed Cave Town people to be in direct sunlight for three hours?

I gave him a tired look. "No one can remember where it originated, so probably that was the council as well? Yeah, I remember, what about it?"

Before he could answer the woman being held down

screamed, and the people on the porch all began to talk at once.

I flexed my hands, ready for the coming battle.

Xavier talked quickly. He too seemed anxious to get into the mix of things. "Well, it's only one ingredient, a sunlight-colored plant. Once it hardens, it's cut into small pills. All you need is a small piece to start a whole field growing."

By now the man had pushed the woman to her knees, and Twist had begun to rise in the air, his anger as palpable as my own. "So basically, everyone can have it in their backyard?"

"Everyone did have it in their backyard, until Jonas, either by fear, death, or complete take-over, got the baddest, meanest, willing to do anything residents here on his side. They ripped all sunlight from the ground and planted it here, in Jonas town. Now, if residents want to go up top, they have to pay Jonas to do it."

I looked back at the house and saw that the woman's face was now pressed to the porch, her hands still twisted behind her back. One look at her though, and I could tell she was plotting her escape.

Her eyes were dark storms, and her hardened jaw, and tightened brow told me that she wasn't going down without a fight. "So, she was just trying to steal back what was rightfully hers, and everybody else's?" I asked.

Xavier's hands vibrated, and I could tell he was barely holding himself back. The verve in our systems made it almost impossible to resist the lure of the fight. "He has people that guard the fields and the gates twenty-four hours a day."

Well, we'd taken out the ones that minded the gate so...

The woman's eyes darkened even more, and then her hair began to grow until it was down her back and draping off the porch.

The man holding her either didn't notice or thought it a

simple response to her fear, but whatever his lack of judgment, he paid for it with his life.

The woman's hair stood bone straight on top of her head, pulsating with the power it must have held. One thick strand wrapped around the man's neck and began to squeeze.

Turning purple, he choked and gasped, clawing at his neck, trying unsuccessfully to break free. So strong was her hair, that it rose him in the air, still wrapped around his neck, while his legs, dangled and kicked to be free.

The others, as soon as they noticed, leapt to attack, and she wrapped hair around each one of their throats as well.

I watched in horrified amazement, as her hair sizzled and crackled with yellow and silver energy. She leaned her head to the side, and a final pop sounded, breaking every single neck ensnared in her locks.

Never batting an eye, she dropped them, then slowly came back to her feet. Her hair had now shrunken to just below her chin, and her movements looked slow and painful.

We didn't have time to reach her before an alarm sounded, and more people came running out of the house, as well as some of the other houses in Jonas Town.

The woman looked terrified and tried to run, but ended up falling over instead. Apparently, her earlier attack had weakened her. "We have to help," I said, but Twist was already in the air, wind whipping and turning as he landed on the porch beside her.

Xavier and I rushed forward, taking out every man and woman that challenged us.

The woman was on her knees now, looking as if she was struggling to stay upright. A heavy-set guy with a mohawk ran straight toward her, his hands popping with energy.

I used my telekinesis to sling him away, and he turned into a bird, mid-air and flew off.

I looked to Xavier, who winked at me before we both got back into the fight.

Soon we'd cleared the porch, but they were still coming from the street. I saw Twist give the woman a verve pill, and with only slight hesitation, she decided to take it.

Twist gathered her in his arms, and flew to where Xavier and I were still fighting, using his wind to knock back everyone in his path.

He touched down in front of us, and the woman leapt away from him and onto her own two feet. "Join hands," she commanded, and we did so without question.

Then, just like that, we were no longer in Jonas Town, but in a wet tunnel that smelled dusty and old.

"How the..." I looked around to make sure my team was still intact. Satisfied that we'd all made it, I turned to the woman. "So, you teleport, just like Jonas."

With the verve in her system, she stood a little taller, and her hair had already grown back to the length it was when we'd first saw her. "If you mean my cousin Jonas then yes, it kind of runs in the family. I'm Celeste, by the way."

My eyes bulged as I stared at her. I looked to Xavier and Twist and saw they were just as surprised as I was. "Your cousin? Then why would he--"

She dropped to her knees and began digging through the dirt of the tunnel floor. "Because he's a greedy asshole who never saw a dollar he didn't like." Blue cloth appeared under her hand, and she unfolded it to reveal a small tin box. She stood with the box in her hand and a wary expression on her face. "Now, I've got to go through that all over again. Thanks for the pill. Verve, is it? I've heard of it, but never got a chance to try it."

"You're welcome, I'm Twist and this is Xavier and Leah. Now why do you have to go back."

Celeste clutched the box tighter. "Because it's not right,

what Jonas is doing. Everyone should have sunlight, and no one should have to pay for it, but Jonas ripped up everything, even the roots. So now we all have to get it from him, and of course, pay whatever fee he sets for that day."

"Can't you just teleport in, get a vine and start to replant it?"

She blinked at me. "I tried that, just now. You saw. Jonas has people patrolling day and night." She shook her head in a self-defeating way. "I just wasn't fast enough."

A bat flew by, and I ducked, wondering what else loomed in these tunnels. "Well, maybe with our help, you can be," I said softly.

She cradled the box closer to her, and I began to wonder just what she had inside that thing. "It won't matter. He'll just find us and take it back. We've tried that before. It gets us nowhere, besides sunlight won't work unless it has breez sprinkled on it every thirty minutes. It's what hardens it and the ingredients in the breez mixed with the planet is what allows us to be in the sunlight."

Xavier walked about, the verve in his system making it impossible for him to stay still. "Yeah, I've heard of that stuff. It's got a whole lot of uses, hard as hell to get now too, used to be a lot easier."

Celeste kicked a rock from in front of her. It made a swishing sound as it sailed through the air, and then promptly disappeared from sight. "Yeah, that's because of Michael. He did to Gate City, what Jonas did to Cave Town. Probably where Jonas first got the idea." She mumbled that last part.

Twist was keeping himself a few feet off the ground, a small bit of wind whipping at his feet. "What did he do?"

"All sales of breez must go through Michael now. You know, it didn't use to be that way." She let out a small sigh. "But he's just as greedy as Jonas and meaner too. Jonas is only allowed to bring two men with him when he goes to Gate City. Every time they come back, they're bloodied and bruised. Sometimes the men with Jonas don't come back at all." She stopped talking, and her eyes began to water. "This last time was the worst though, Jonas could barely walk."

She wiped her eyes, and at first, I thought it was concern for her cousin, but as she talked on, I realized that it was something else entirely. "This last time Jonas cut Ron Taylor's ear off, just because he could. To prove he was still in control, after being hurt so bad by Michael and his men. Ron is fifteen years old!" She wiped a hand down her face, and her eyes turned stormy with rage. "And everyone just stood and watched."

I wanted to comfort her, but didn't know how. "So, you decided now was the time to strike out?" I asked.

She nodded, rage still controlling her features. "After that, we all knew it was time. People couldn't just bury their heads in the sand anymore. The time had come to do something." She stopped talking, and a strange look crossed her face. "Why are you here? I didn't think to ask before, but not many people know about Cave Town. How do you?" She didn't seem scared, more like intrigued.

"Jonas stole our money," Xavier said, "and we aim to get it back. Plus, I've been here a time or two."

She thought it over. "So, we can help each other then?"

"What do you have planned?" I asked.

She opened the box, and my eyes widened as I saw that it was filled to the brim with money. "This is from up top. We have people here who work there you know. We've been saving for years. We're not sure how much breez costs, but we hope that three hundred thousand will be enough."

I looked at the box again, my voice filled with dismay. "You have three hundred grand in there?"

She licked her bottom lip, suddenly looking unsure.

"Well, we've heard it was a few hundred thousand. If he charges more, then we'll just have to save a little longer." Her chin rose stubbornly in the air, and I knew that whatever it took, she'd make sure that it was done.

"So how can we help?" I asked, ready to make a move or do something.

"Go as my back up. I'll secure the sale of breez, and you can get your money back from Jonas. It's a win for everyone." She sounded as if she was trying to convince herself as much as us.

"You still won't have a plant sample," I pointed out.

"Then I'll get one," she said through gritted teeth, looking at me as if she wished I'd stop with the questions.

"Can you get the breez from anywhere else? So you don't have to go deal with this Michael?"

Xavier answered for her. "Only one place breez grows, darlin'," he said looking at me. "That's in Gate City, two hundred miles away."

"Two hund--" I looked at her for confirmation, and she nodded.

"We have seekers here. They've searched high and low. It's all in Gate City." She chuckled, but it was bitter and without humor. "I'm sure the council had a good laugh at that. All a part of their dumb curse no doubt. We can have three hours of sunlight, but we must somehow make it two hundred miles, without dying from pain to get the necessary ingredients."

"Probably got their jollies off on that one," Twist said, sounding sympathetic.

She shrugged. "Well, some say my great, great, great, well you get the picture, grandfather was a good man. They say he'd only killed to protect his wife and children. Maybe making the breez hundreds of miles away was because it would be only my family who could get it." Her fists curled at her sides. "Well, I hope they're happy because Jonas has taken this to a whole new level. No one in my own family dares to challenge him," she sneered. "He'd probably kill us just as easy as anyone else."

"Let's go," Twist said from his spot in the air. "We know what we have to do, so let's just get this over with before our time runs out, and we're stuck down here forever."

5

Celeste landed us in Gate town in the blink of an eye and I hoped we would be able to do this quickly and leave.

"At least we don't have to worry about that stupid curse now." The relief in Twist's voice matched my own, but it only took one look at Xavier and Celeste's less than enthusiastic faces to know something was wrong.

"What?" I asked, sure I wasn't going to like the answer.

Xavier pulled no punches. "Well, darlin', the thing about that curse is, you have to leave out the same way you entered, within twenty-four hours."

I could literally feel the blood drain from my face. "And you tell me this now?" My voice was full of accusations, which was exactly how I meant it.

"When would you had liked me to tell you?" He made it sound like it was my fault that I hadn't asked.

"How about before we first went to Cave Town?"

His face softened. "Sorry, darlin'. You're right. I just didn't know any other way to leave, so I didn't think it would be a problem."

I couldn't stay mad at him, not when he was looking at me with those deep soulful eyes. "Whatever," I said, and charged ahead, to hide the look that said I'd already forgiven him.

It was night here, which was a good thing. Streetlights lit up the sidewalk though, so it was easy to see where we were going. I looked to Celeste, and though her marks were visible, they were not burning and festering. At least not yet, anyway.

Gate City wasn't that much different from my own city. We must have been in downtown, because many storefronts lined the streets, from donut shops to stores selling street apparel.

Stoplights were on almost every corner, and most people wore jeans or sweats, with a few "suit-and-tie types" as well.

We walked for about ten minutes until we saw a body of water in the back of a house. At first, I thought it to be a swimming pool, but the green color and the tiny yellow crystals floating on top gave me pause.

"Breez," Celeste said pointing to the water, her voice full of excitement and her eyes shining with victory. "Let's go see if they'll sell us some."

She took off before I could stop her, and Xavier and I passed an uneasy glance between us. If this guy was as bad as she'd said he was, he probably had most people here scared to death. I highly doubted they'd be willing to sell anything without his permission. Nevertheless, we followed her to the front door.

The lady who answered was of medium height and had her brown hair done up in a ponytail. She had on a red and black checkered shirt, with white jeans to match. "Hi," she said cautiously, as if not sure she could trust us yet.

Celeste held out her free hand, and the woman shook it.

"Hey, ma'am, we're here about the breez in your backyard. We'd like to buy some."

"Oh." The woman smiled as if everything was alright now. She opened the door wide and backed up a little to let us in.

"Well, that was easier than I thought it would be," Twist mumbled under his breath.

I agreed, and a sinking feeling settled in the pit of my stomach, thinking it was a little too good to be true. The house appeared nice and cozy. It was clean, and smelled of lemon furniture polish and vinegar.

The couch and two love seats were modern and a deep chocolate, that matched the walls and carpet perfectly. A brown wood table sat a few feet in front of them. Pictures of her and two kids hung throughout the room, and they all seemed happy enough.

"Let me grab my pen." She made to go down the hall then stopped and turned at the last minute. "I'm sorry, would you like tea or coffee, maybe some lemonade?"

"No," Celeste said speaking for us all. "We want to get back before it gets too late." I started to raise an eyebrow at her until I realized she was just anxious to get back before the sun rose.

Celeste watched the lady go and then let out a startled gasp once the woman was out of sight. "I was so determined to get here, I didn't remember to bring something to put the breez in." She thought about it for a second. "Maybe they have barrels that we can buy," she said, perking up at the thought.

"Don't worry," I said, smiling at Xavier, as if he was actually mine and I had something to be proud of. "He can take any stick or rock and transform it into a boat if we need to. You'll just have to hurry and distribute it. Transformation only lasts a couple of hours."

"That's plenty of time," she said, rubbing her arm as a

pained looked crossed her face. It would only get worse, so we really did need to hurry and go. "We already have secret pits built, bigger than most pools. All we need is the supply." She seemed to have it all worked out.

The lady came back up the hall, with a manila folder and a pen, as promised. "How many gallons will you be needing, and I just need to take a quick look at your paperwork."

Celeste folded in on herself as if she'd been sucker punched. "Paperwork?"

The woman looked taken aback, and then her eyes widened in horror. "You're trying to get me killed." She backed up against the wall as if we were actually attacking her. "I can sell you nothing until you pay, and Mr. Michael puts his stamp on it." She grabbed the bottom of her shirt, twisting it in her hand. "All sales must go through Michael." She made a run for the door as if we were chasing her and opened it wide. "Leave, and never come back. It's not like we get a part of the sale anyway. Michael's headquarters are three streets over." She ushered us out and then slammed the door in our faces.

Celeste stared at the closed door for a minute and then stiffly walked away, her eyes rapidly blinking as if to stave off the tears threating to fall.

"Come, on," Twist said, looking back at the house as if he couldn't believe what had just happened. "They can't all be like that. Let's try somewhere else, okay?"

His voice was low and comforting, and he got a big smile from her as an award. "Okay," she said, moving a lot slower than when we'd first arrived.

We walked to the next street over, and this time a short man with glasses opened the door.

Celeste cleared her throat and made an effort to stand a little taller. "We'd like to buy--"

"Where are your papers?" The man asked, cutting her off.

"I was hoping--"

"No papers, no sale." He too slammed the door.

"Well, shit," I said, looking at the rest of the houses on the street.

Celeste was almost limping now, and I wondered if another verve pill would help, because of the curse, probably not, but it wouldn't hurt to try.

We walked onto the next street, and I stopped abruptly, causing the others to stop as well. "Hey, Twist give her another pill. See if that will help."

She smiled gratefully at him and then swallowed it down dry. After a second she shook her head. "Nothing like when I took it the first time, but you can't easily get around a curse, right?"

Well, at least she had the verve in her, I reasoned. Even if it didn't slow down the curse, if trouble came, she would hopefully be protected from getting hurt too bad. I pushed hair out of my face. Theoretically, that's how verve was supposed to work anyway, who knew how it interacted with the curse.

The more we walked, the more Celeste's shoulders began to slump, her eyes quickly losing the hopeful look she'd had when we'd first arrived.

"Let's try one more house," Twist said. He moved a little closer to her but was still careful to keep his distance and give her space.

"It won't do no good." A voice said from a set of bushes to our right. Stunned, we all whipped that way. Celeste put her hands up as if expecting an attack. Xavier went into a fighter stance, his body practically buzzing. Twist rose two feet off the ground, wind nipping at his heels, and I held my arms out, ready for whatever came next.

A woman with short brown hair, wearing beige cargo pants, and a tan jacket, stepped out onto the street. She looked rough, like she'd been digging through the dirt and grime all day, and had only stopped when she'd heard us talking. "You can try ten more houses and it ain't gonna help you none. No breez gets sold without Michael's approval. How you gonna work around that?"

As she talked, more people came out, looking every bit as rugged as she did. They stood together watching her as if awaiting her command.

She pointed to a blue and white clapboard house. "Mrs. Ginny lives there. Everybody's favorite granny. The kids love her and a lot of us adults do too. A sweeter lady never walked the earth. Now go see what happens when you ask her to sell to you with no papers."

"Who are you?" I asked because there was a lot of them, and I'd stopped counting at fifty.

She waved a hand toward her crew. "We are the people of Gate City, and unless you want a fight with Michael and his crew, you better run." She paused, probably making sure we were listening. "Or hide."

Energy popped from me as I stepped forward. "We run from no one, and we don't hide, we find."

She smiled and nodded as if that had been the answer she'd wanted. She leaned her head toward the blue and white house. "I'm Melvina. Go do your thing, we'll wait."

I looked to Twist because Celeste was in no condition to make it up those steps.

"Why's everyone so scared?" I asked as Twist lifted off the ground and floated up to the house.

Melvina's brows furrowed. "I would have thought it was obvious. Michael has this whole town on lock. Anyone who disobeys his orders are killed on the spot." She pointed to Mrs. Ginny's house, and I looked up in time to see the door slam in Twist's face.

At this point, I wasn't even surprised.

She waited until he touched back down before speaking again. "There are at least four of his men guarding each spot where breez grows, including the three houses you visited tonight."

I cursed under my breath. We hadn't seen anyone, but of course they'd be out back where the breez was, not in the house, with us. No wonder these residents had been so scared. I cursed again, hoping we hadn't gotten them in any trouble.

A rope mark on Celeste's neck, as well as a footprint on her hand, began to glow and fester. She sucked in a breath, and I knew whatever we needed to do, we had to do it fast. "It's where Jonas got the idea from," she said, looking around. "He turned our town into this. How unoriginal."

Well, I was glad she could still joke, but I was convinced she was right. Jonas probably came here, got beaten to a pulp, saw how Michael ran this place, with fear and bullying, and figured he'd do the same. Either to boost his ego, after being handled so harshly by Michael, or because he was envious of the control and power the other man had.

A woman, a little on the heavy side, with a red mohawk, stepped up beside the first lady. "I can hear them coming." She pointed down the road.

Melvina's whole body went stiff. "Gin here can hear for miles. If she says Michael and his men are coming, then they're coming. His people at the three houses you visited no doubt called it in."

I looked to Celeste, whose teeth were clenched as a tattoo of boxing gloves, and one of a long sword lit up a small part of her face, causing a yellow glow that hissed and burned.

"Will Michael sell to us?" I asked Melvina.

She thought about it. "Depends whether he thinks you'll be repeat customers or not. If he thinks you're going to keep bringing him money every couple of months, then yeah, he'll sell, gotta keep the cash flowing, right?" She sounded disgusted.

"What about one-time customers?" Though I was sure Cave Town would have to buy again, especially if they all set up sunlight gardens, I didn't know when, and I wondered if it made a difference.

She chuckled and looked at me as if I was too naïve to breathe. "Why would he sell to one-time customers when he can just take their money and kill them? They are no use to him if they're never bringing him cash again."

"Getting closer," Gin said, letting us know that Michael's men were almost on us.

Xavier, who'd been strangely quiet through all this, finally stepped forward. "Are you prepared to fight?" His eyes roamed over her and her crew.

Melvina looked at the men and women who stood beside her. "Nah, we're not ready. Need to strengthen our numbers." She thought about it for a second, then relented. "But if you plan on throwing down tonight, I guess we'll have to join ya." She held up a fist, and her crew began to disappear back into the bushes. "We'll see you there. Remember Gin can hear everything, so we'll know when it's time."

Michael's men were on the street with us now, a few more steps and they'd be right in front of us.

Xavier put a hand on my arm. "We don't have to do this tonight. If he's willing to sell to us, then we need to get Celeste and the breez back to safety before anything pops off."

The sun had started to rise, and Celeste's skin was now lit up and bubbling every place she had a scar. She was well covered, but her clothes couldn't hide what was happening. Her body stayed rigid, her eyes focused ahead as she waited for us to make a decision.

"Okay," I said.

Xavier and I both looked to Twist who nodded. "Good." Xavier walked a few feet in front of me and Twist. "We only fight if we have to."

As Michael's men got closer, I saw that there were eight of them, four men and four women. "Easy now," I reminded Xavier, Twist, and Celeste. "We want to go with them, remember? We don't want to fight. Let's just secure the purchase of breez and worry about the rest later."

Celeste gasped in pain, and Twist wrapped an arm around her waist and lifted her and himself a bit off the ground. That way all her weight was on him, but you'd have to look really hard to see that he was floating in the air.

"What do we have here?" A short man with a close cut asked. He stood beside a woman, who was slightly taller, and a little more muscular. The rest stayed in the back and let these two do the talking.

Xavier was the first to speak. "We want to buy breez. Tried a few houses. They all said we needed to see Michael. Are you him?"

Instead of answering, the man's eyes set on Celeste. He pointed to her and looked at the girl beside him. She raised a brow and then addressed us. "Yeah, we'll take you to Michael. Let him decide what to do with ya."

The sun was out in full force now, and I felt an itching to get going. The last thing we needed was to become stuck in Gate City and not able to make it through Cave Town's entrance in time to avoid the clock.

Michael's people surrounded us. Some walking behind, some in front and some right beside us. I looked to Celeste. The tattoos on her face were fully lit now, and she had her teeth clenched, her hands in fists, as if she was doing everything she could not to cry out.

Could she even teleport us back to Cave Town in the condition she was in? If she couldn't, even if we made it out of here alive, there was no guarantee we could make it back to Cave Town in time. Not if we had to find an alternate means of travel anyway.

I let out a heavy breath, as I realized that our fates may have already been sealed, and there was nothing we could do about it.

6

The house we entered was so huge it took up half the block. It was red brick, and two large lion statues sat on either side of the walkway leading up to the porch.

A brown metal fence surrounded the house, and the yard had so much patio furniture that I lost count of design and color. It looked eccentric, like someone was just spending money because they had it and hadn't figured out just quite what to do with it yet.

We were led to a large room with multiple floor-to-ceiling windows. The sunlight in here was almost blinding, and it didn't take long to figure out why. On his knees, with a man and woman both covered in marks, was Jonas, the guy who'd stolen my money.

The room was a sterile white and felt cold and detached. The only thing in it was a large silver table that sat in the middle of the floor, with about twenty silver chairs around it.

A man stood in front of the table. He was tall and dark with brown hair that reached to his ears. He had a long scar running down the side of his face, and his brown eyes bored into us as we were pushed into the room.

Twist kept his arm around Celeste, neither of their feet touching the ground, though at this point she was trembling.

On the table sat a pile of money and I shot Xavier a look to let him know that we would not be leaving without our winnings.

"You see," the man said, Michael, I presumed. "That's the thing I don't understand." He walked to where Jonas and the others were on their knees shaking and moaning in pain. "Why do you need so much breez and why does your skin burn like that when it hits sunlight."

His eyes landed on us, and he took in Celeste. "Ah, maybe you can tell me since you seem to be struck with the same affliction." He turned to the woman who'd spoken to us earlier and had helped bring us here. "Are these the ones trying to buy the breez?"

She nodded.

"So maybe you can tell me, then," he pointed at Celeste. "Since no matter what I do, I can't get it out of him." He stepped back and without warning bought a hard foot down on Jonas's face. The man screamed out in pain and toppled over. One of Michael's people was quick to set him back up.

Michael looked at Celeste. "I charge two hundred and fifty thousand for five thousand gallons. A fair price I think. You know breez develops here naturally. Once the minerals in our soil, mix with the sunlight and those special yellow rocks, all it takes is a good rain, and voila, another breez pool forms. The supply is never ending, and neither is the cash flow."

The yellow rocks he spoke of probably were the council's doing, but why they'd decided to put it over two hundred miles away from Cave Town was anybody's guess. Unless this was the only place that had the right kind of soil, that is.

"I'll take five thousand gallons," Celeste said, her voice barely above a whisper.

I knew she was in pain, but she had two verve pills inside of her. So hopefully if a fight broke out, the verve in her system would protect her.

Michael's eyes turned predatory. "And when will you be back for more?"

"Soon... Soon... As I can," she answered through the pain.

He walked closer, and I saw Twist tense. I needed him to keep his cool until we could figure out where this was going. I walked up beside him and put a hand on his arm.

Michael never took his eyes off Celeste. "I don't know what that means. Will you be back in six months, or will it be two years? See because if you don't know, that means you're probably not coming back at all." He looked from her to Jonas. "See him, I know he's coming back, he always does. But you." He pointed to Celeste. "I'm not so sure about. So why should I let you live, when I can just take your money and not lose a drop of breez?"

Celeste's face turned hard, her eyes furious and challenging. "Try it, and I'll kill you where you stand," she gritted out.

Jonas's head snapped in her direction, and his eyes went wide. Apparently, he hadn't noticed us until now. "Cousin... What... What are you doing here?"

"Getting... Out... From under your... Hold," she ground out, each word seeming harder than the first.

Jonas hissed as the sunlight grew a little brighter, damn near blinding us all. Celeste's whole body shook, and Twist's grip on her waist tightened.

Jonas looked at his cousin. "Wanted... Wanted... I wanted to pro... To protect... You all from... this."

Celeste sneered at him. "No. You... Wanted... To be this." She pointed to Michael. "Not... On my watch."

Michael clapped his hands and laughed. "Ah, so it's a family thing." He pointed to the four Cave Town residents in the room. "This disease must run in your bloodline. I get it now, breez is the only thing that helps." He looked to Xavier, Twist, and myself. "The trusted neighbors and friends, I see."

No, he really didn't see, but we'd let him think what he wanted.

"The price just went up," he said. "Five hundred thousand, for three gallons."

"We won't be paying that." Xavier stepped forward, and Michael's men moved in, blocking Xavier from getting too close to their fearless leader.

Twist and I came to stand on either side of Xavier.

Michael shooed his men away and stepped forward, his face mere inches from Xavier's. "See, that's where you're wrong. I make the rules around here. No one else."

Xavier never blinked an eye, and his voice went deathly low. "Give us a fair price, and we'll pay it."

Michael stepped even closer. "The price is what I say it is."

Xavier chuckled, and it was the most dangerous thing I'd ever heard. "If you don't get out of my face right now, I'll have you hopping out of here instead of walking."

"You'll do--" a whip of hair flew out and wrapped around Michael's neck choking him. His crew surrounded us, as he wheezed and hissed clawing at the hair trying to get free.

I looked to Celeste and saw that she was on her knees shaking. Her skin glowed brightly as it festered and popped, giving the impression that it was eating her alive.

I gasped, as I knew the pain had to be unbearable.

Still fighting, she slung Michael in the air, her hair still wrapped tightly around his neck. She then slammed him down, in front of her. "I... Bow... To... No one... Not anymore... Fair price."

He held a hand up, telling his people to stay away. "Fair price?" she asked and loosened her hold a little so that he could answer.

He swallowed hard, and then his eyes turned to granite. "Get 'em!"

I used my TK to fly the money, my money, mine and Xavier's, to me and stuffed it in my jacket, all the while ducking a fist aimed toward my head.

When I looked down, I saw frogs and mice running around and knew Xavier was doing his thing.

Twist was up in the air, and he had three of Michael's people with him. He twisted and turned them head over body until I could see their eyes detach from their heads, and their limbs start to break off into pieces.

Celeste still had Michael down on the ground. She straddled his hips, choking him. Sweat dripped from her face, as she grunted and clenched her jaw tight.

Michael himself was almost blue now. His eyes rolled to the back of his head, and all the fight seemed to had left him.

His people kept coming though, and I flung every one of them against the pristine walls, making them hit the floor unmoving.

Finally, Celeste unwrapped her hair from his neck and slowly stood. "A... Fair... Price," she said, breathing hard, her chest rising and falling with effort.

Coming shakily to his feet, and taking large gulps of air, while rubbing a few fingers over his throat, he struck out, and electric light flew out of his hand and hit her dead in the chest, knocking her back. I gasped before I remembered that she had the verve in her system and it would protect her. At least I hoped it would anyway.

Michael turned from her after that, probably thinking he'd finished her off. He slid a hand under the table, and a loud horn sounded.

I jerked my head toward the door, but I could already hear footsteps headed our way.

He pushed another button, and the blinds opened fully,

letting even more sunlight in. Celeste, Jonas, and the others screamed in pain, the sounds harsh and unnatural.

More men entered the room, and Twist whirled in the air toward Michael, knocking the other man to the floor. Twist felt around until he found whatever button Michael had used to control the blinds, then pressed it until they slammed completely shut.

Now the only light came from the chandeliers hanging from the ceiling.

Celeste leapt to her feet, as did Jonas and the two people with him. Jonas hit the man right in front of him, and the man and woman he was with jumped into the crowd.

More of Michael's people stormed the room carrying, knives, swords, and bats.

Celeste's hair went in all directions as she began wrapping them by the throat and waist.

"I'm going to get the others," Twist shouted. I had no idea who he was talking about, but he left in a whirlwind as Melvina and her crew fought their way inside.

A man with a sword raised high in the air came at me, and I instinctually pulled mine out and blocked the hit. The sword seemed to move as if it had a mind of its own. The red glow was back, and it guided me across the floor, taking down everyone in my path.

Xavier pulled two quarters out of his pocket, turned them into two curved knives and began cutting as well. One man came at him and tried to hit him with a bat. Xavier stepped back, crossed his arms, and brought the knives down across the man's face leaving him with a bloody smile and a scream.

Melvina had Michael on the ground, her fist pounding into him as she yelled out her grievances. Jonas tried to get a lick in, but she slung him across the room and went back to the task at hand.

I gripped my sword tight and felt a connection that

reached through to my body and to my soul. This thing had been made for me, there was no other explanation.

Five of Michael's crew advanced on me at once, and a woman with short bobbed hair knocked my weapon away. Before I fully realized what had happened, they were on me.

A man about six feet tall laced his hands together and brought one huge fist down on my face. It knocked the wind out of me, and I dropped to the floor. The pain was biting, and I knew that the verve was starting to wear off.

I tried to come to a stand, but a woman, tall and slim, straddled my hips, her fist raining down on my face as the others kicked and stomped.

I felt every blow, every damn one of them, and my body shook and rocked as the pain rippled through me leaving no part untouched.

"Now," she screamed, as she raised her sword, and the others raised theirs as well. All aimed at different parts of my body, but the lady who sat on top of me had hers headed straight for my face.

I screamed and tried to use my TK to fly them away, but I was too weak, and only managed to throw them back a few feet. They were back on me in a second.

Damnit! I needed another verve pill, and I also needed my sword. Shit. Where the fuck was my sword?

I could see my attacker's blades shining from the light overhead as they raised them. I took a deep breath and tried to prepare myself for what I knew was about to happen.

In one last ditch effort, I tried to use my TK again, refusing to just lay there and die. I didn't have time to do anything else, before blood splattered across my face and all five of my attackers' heads rolled to the floor, their bodies dropping as well.

Startled, I looked up to see my sword in mid-air, bloody and glowing in front of me. I got to my feet, sore and bruised, and held out my hand, no TK involved. The sword flew right into it, hot and pulsating as if waiting for me to make the next move.

Twist blasted back into the room, a trail of men and women with him, too many to count, but no doubt more than thirty. Still up in the air, he released his hands, directing his wind to slam them to the floor. They hit hard, some of them already bleeding and missing limbs. "Those who guard the breez, all that I could find, anyway," he said.

Melvina stood with her hand wrapped around Michael's throat. "Call your men off and agree to step down, and there doesn't have to be any more bloodshed tonight."

He had one eye swollen shut, and the other looked as if it would be joining soon. His face was black, blue, and puffy, and his lips were cracked open and bleeding. "This." he stopped and took in a breath. "This is my town."

Her hand squeezed his neck, and I heard the bone pop around his throat, as his eyes went wide, and he dropped to the floor. "This town belongs to no one," she said, spitting where he now lay unmoving.

Gin and the others cheered, and I looked around and noticed that the only ones still breathing were Melvina's crew and my own.

Celeste stood over Jonas's unmoving body. He'd been run through with a sword, the man and woman that he'd come with were also dead. "He was bad, and he did bad things, but he was still family," Celeste said, her voice breaking. "I'll see to it that he gets a proper burial back home. See to it that all three of them do."

Twist and Xavier stood side by side, checking each other for bruises. They were full of them, the both of them, and I wondered why they even bothered.

Twist's ear was bleeding, and he had cuts up and down

his arms and neck. His clothes were halfway off him, his shirt ripped to shreds, his jacket completely gone.

Xavier still had his coat on, but it too was torn and looked as if it'd seen better days. His face hosted multiple marks and small bleeds, and he had a gash over his right eye. I could feel my face starting to swell and figured I looked as bad as they did.

Melvina, who now walked with a limp, held out her hand to Celeste. "We'll have to vote on it, the whole city, not just a few members, but as of today, I'm willing to sell you five thousand gallons, for five thousand dollars."

Celeste seemed skeptical. "Who gets the money?" she asked, probably not wanting to replace one bad person for another. From what I'd witnessed so far though, I thought that Melvina would do alright.

"Whichever house you choose will get ninety percent. The other ten will go into the city coffers. If you choose one of the spots in the wilderness, then it all goes into the city coffers."

Celeste thought about it for a minute and then held out her hand. "Five thousand gallons for five thousand dollars. I hope you've got a lot of barrels."

7

I nstead of using barrels, Xavier had produced a big swimming pool to hold all the liquid.

Our first priority when landing back in Cave Town was to get the liquid into something real that could hold it for longer than a couple of hours.

Celeste transported us to an open field, where a hole big enough to hold a swimming pool had been built. "It's three times too small," she said, looking from the actual swimming pool to the hole in the ground.

I smiled at her and nudged Xavier. "We can fix that." Using our combined telekinesis, we cleared away enough earth to form a hole twice as big as the swimming pool holding the breez.

We also used our combined powers to float the pool over and land it inside. "Now, when the transmuted pool disappears your breez will be safe."

She thanked us, but then her eyes turned sad, as she looked over to where Jonas and his two associates lay. "You know my grandparents never stopped believing in him.

Never stopped thinking he'd be the little boy they'd watched grow into a man."

She sniffed, and her voice broke a little as she talked. "This is going to break their hearts." She wrung her hands nervously as if psyching herself up for what had to be done. "I have to tell them, but I can't let them see him like this. I have to get him to a funeral home, and we have to take down the rest of his crew."

Twist gave her arm a slight squeeze. "You deal with your family, we'll clean up Jonas Town."

I expected an argument from her, but she simply nodded. "Okay."

We stayed outside while Celeste went into a large brick-red house. I assumed that some of her family lived there.

"I can't believe they have funeral homes here," I said, looking from Twist to Xavier.

Twist ignored me, and Xavier wrapped a warm arm around my neck and pulled me close. "I'd say they have a little of everything here, darlin'."

Celeste came back out, looking down the street. "I called for help while I was inside, and alerted the jails that they'll be having a few new residents. All that are left alive anyway."

A man walked up, tall and thin. "Celeste." His voice was filled with both desperation and relief. He wrapped her in his arms and then kissed her fully on the lips. "We've been so worried about you. Everyone's been worried."

She hugged him tight and then eased out of his embrace. "I'm fine, Kemp, just tired." She pointed to us. "Thanks to them. They helped me a lot. Now I need you to go with them, and help take down the rest of Jonas's crew while I break the news of his death to the rest of my family."

She looked at the watch on her wrist. "If it's not done by a quarter to seven then just head back here, and we'll have to find another way. They have to be out of here by seven."

He nodded and turned to us. "You ready to go?"

"Wait." She placed three trinkets in his hand. "Show this as proof that Jonas and the others have fallen."

We made it to Jonas Town in record time, and it was exactly as we'd left it.

I ripped the newly built gates apart with one swipe of my hand. "Okay, we don't have time to be nice. Twist, do your thing."

He rose in the air and began to twirl, swiping up every human that came in his path.

"Xavier be ready," I told him.

He smiled and pulled a bunch of coins from his pocket and tossed them in the air. "Already ahead of you, darlin'." Midway down, the money transformed to ropes, and cuffs.

Kemp looked doubtful. "That won't hold them for long."

"Best hurry, then," Xavier said.

Twist came back, with about fifty people caught up in his wind. Xavier threw the ropes in the air and began to wrap their arms behind their backs.

Kemp took a few steps forward. "Allow me..."

A slight gust of wind hit me across the face, and then it was just myself, Xavier, and Twist standing there. "Did he just..."

"Yes, I did," he said, popping back up. "We have a prison, built a long time ago, but it still works to hold in magic. Some of them are guiltier than others, but they'll each get their fair day in court."

I pulled out my phone and saw that it was six-fifty. "We have to go," I shouted, knowing that there was no way we could make it to the gate in ten minutes.

"Oh, don't worry about that," Kemp said.

I felt another rush of air, and my lungs seemed ready to burst. When it stopped, I realized we were outside the entrance to Cave Town.

I breathed a sigh of relief, and saw Xavier and Twist, taking deep gulps, of air. Well, that was probably just from the super speed, I reasoned.

Xavier pulled me to him and wrapped his arms around my waist. "Now, aren't you glad you ate before coming here?"

I pulled away and looked at him. "Yeah, there's that, and there's the little point of my sword, dude, what the fuck?"

He grinned slyly. "Nice ain't it?"

Before I could answer, Celeste came flying around the corner. "You haven't left yet," she said breathlessly.

She gave us each a hug. "Thank you so much.

"No problem." Twist smiled at her.

"Where to?" she asked, her hands at her side waiting.

I looked at my phone. "Guys, we have one minute to make it to the tournament in time. It'll take longer than that to explain where it's at."

Celest put a hand to my head. "You don't have to explain. Just think real hard about where you want to be, and I'll get you there."

I wrapped fingers around Xavier's shoulder, and he touched Twist on the arm. One second we were standing outside of Cave Town and the next we were in the tournament hall, in front of the check-in window, loud noises all around us.

Everyone who passed gave us a wide berth, and some even held their noses. I couldn't really blame them. What a sight we must have been, covered in blood and dirt, our clothes hanging half off, and our hair in disarray. "Doesn't matter what they think if we win the game." I popped a verve pill and Twist did the same.

"All set," Xavier came back to us, and I saw him slip a pill in his mouth as well.

8

W e won by three points, and the hall extended our rooms for three more nights, offering Twist accommodations as well. He accepted and Xavier and I paid him his money. At first, he wouldn't take it, but finally, we wore him down.

Twist dipped a chicken wing into his ranch dressing and bit into it. "You know, you guys should call me again the next time you'd like to bring down a couple of evil towns. I think we're getting quite good at it. No charge next time of course. I had fun." He chewed what was in his mouth and washed it down with a swig of beer.

Xavier smiled at him. "Yeah, well, it was a good time, now wasn't it?"

I rolled my eyes. We all sat around a table at a restaurant near the tournament. We'd showered and changed, so we at least now looked presentable to the world.

"Twist, about Celeste," I said, bringing up something I knew I shouldn't. "For a minute, there, I thought you two, might, you know."

He held up a hand. "Let me stop you right there. Not my type."

"Oh," I answered, scolding myself for reading too much into every single interaction.

A tall guy with a close cut, wearing brown jeans and a white jacket walked by. Twist's eyes lingered, as the man took a seat at the bar and ordered a drink.

I watched Twist with interest as he licked his lips and his eyes became hooded.

"Oh," I said with a little more enthusiasm this time, finally understanding what he meant. "That reminds me." I leaned over, my hand on Xavier's face as I brushed my lips against his.

It started off chaste and then quickly heated up. His mouth was soft, tender, and inviting. He tasted like chicken and beer, and I wanted to eat him up right there in the restaurant, but I knew better.

Reluctantly I pulled away and came to my feet. "Twist, you have your room key, right?"

He looked at me and nodded. "Don't worry about me, Leah, I'm fine." He looked back toward the bar where the man in the white jacket still sat.

"Good," I said, holding out my hand to Xavier. "Because I'm ready to go to bed and I don't plan on sleeping alone."

CURSED BREATH

I turned the light off in my bedroom and picked up my purse. Giving a final look around my apartment, I grabbed my keys and walked out the door. It was still hard sometimes, adjusting to the fact that this place and all the things in it actually belonged to me.

Back in my own universe I'd been homeless for several years. I'd lost my job at the mill, lost both my parents to illness a few years before that, and had pretty much given up on life. I hadn't cared when my home, car, and everything else I owned had been taken away from me.

At first, living on the streets had been a cold comfort to all that I'd lost. Then after a year or so, it was just cold.

I hadn't met many friends. It's hard to trust anyone in the streets and that's a hard lesson to learn.

Yet there'd been one man who'd wormed his way in and I'd almost seen him as a fun uncle of sorts. Ed. He'd never really been homeless like he'd led me to believe.

He'd tricked me, trapped me in his world, an alternate universe, Siana, so that he in his wife, Renee, could sell me to the highest bidder, at their annual people ball. The whole universe participated in this as far as I could tell.

The Sianas have a special energy power and not every being's body can sustain it. The Sianas would kidnap those of us who had the right body type to hold that power, then sell us as glorified bodyguards and body slaves to those beings who wanted the protection of someone with Siana's powers.

They'd messed up when they'd given us this power because I'd met friends there and together we'd fought back and brought the whole universe to its knees.

Lia had been taken just like the rest of us, but she'd actually been an undercover agent investigating them. She'd offered those of us who'd survived a job with her organization, The Coalition of Interplanetary Crimes. She'd also offered us a place to call home.

I hadn't had anything waiting for me back on my world. My parents had been my only family and they were both gone. So, I'd stayed here and decided to make a life for myself and help others, who'd been hurt like I had.

I'd been on Plex three months now, and so far, things were going well. We'd trained for the first month and a half, plus somehow still managed to squeeze three missions in. I felt like we got better every time we went out, but knew we still had a long way to go.

The last universe we'd investigated, Uglle, would drug its visitors and hold them captive, until they'd given up all of their banking information.

They'd then erase the victim's memories so that they had no clue where all their money had gone.

They all had one thing in common though. All had visited Uglle before they'd lost all their cash and that's how Uglle had first gotten on our radar.

We'd gone in undercover and been able to bring the wrong doers to justice.

A warm feeling washed over me because I really did feel pride in my work. Every time I helped bring someone to justice, I felt as if I was striking back against Ed, Renee, and all of Siana.

I also liked the sense of accomplishment earning a paycheck brought me. Back home, I'd given up all hopes of becoming productive a member of society again. A small smile formed on my lips. It was nice, being able to prove one's self wrong sometimes.

I walked down the sidewalk, the night air providing a pleasant breeze to accompany me. I was on my way to meet Andrew, his brother Lincoln, and their friend Gerell. All had been with me on Siana, and all had fought back and helped to win our freedom.

I'd been very happy when all three had decided to stay here on Plex and join the coalition as well. It wasn't an easy job. We'd been back from our last mission about five days and had done nothing but train from sun up to sun down since then.

Tonight, we'd decided, was all about relaxing and having a good time. Something we hadn't done much of since we'd been here. I, for one, was eager to get more of a foothold in this new world.

A couple with a little boy passed me, and I smiled and waved. The people here were friendly for the most part, really not that much different from my home world.

I saw a small bit of silver on the sidewalk as I walked and figured Andrew and the others were already there. That's the thing about the power the Siana's had given us. Silver sparks leaked out no matter what we did, which kind of made it hard to hide from anyone really.

We'd trained with these new powers enough to know that they didn't exactly work the same for all of us. Each of us had abilities unique only to ourselves, which came in handy when out on a mission.

I pushed open the doors of the restaurant, and my stomach churned as the smell of marinara sauce and garlic hit my nose. It was a good scent and one I could stand around and smell all day.

Gerell, Andrew, and Lincoln sat it the back, and from the looks of it, they hadn't ordered yet.

"Check Please" was a restaurant that served a little of everything and had food from each of our home worlds, which was why we enjoyed eating here so much.

The atmosphere was quite nice too. It was a family friendly place, evident by the many couples who sat with children from the age of newborn to teenager.

The walls were covered in pictures of guests, family members, and art from people around town. The floors were wooden, but more of a red and green color. The tables had red and white linen on them which the curtains matched perfectly. It was noisy and crowded, yet everyone seemed to be having a good time.

"Kerry. We waited for you," Gerell said as soon as I reached the table. His tone told me he thought I should have gotten here a little sooner.

"Why didn't ya'll order drinks?" They didn't need me to do that. I was sorry for being late, but come on.

The place was warm, so I made sure to take my coat off before sitting. I sat beside Andrew. Andrew was tall, over six feet and all hard muscles and abs. Though he sported a bald head, I could tell from his brownish-blue eyebrows what color his hair was.

Andrew was smart, at least I thought so anyway, and he handled himself with a confidence and sureness that was hard not to admire.

Across from us sat Lincoln and Gerell. Lincoln looked a

lot like his brother, though one was a little lighter brown than the other. But like Andrew, he too was tall, about five feet eight. Lincoln had a small blueish brown patch of hair right above his forehead, the rest was shaved, which I thought gave him a sort of punk-rock look. He didn't agree.

Gerell was full of muscles like the brothers. About five feet six, he had black curly hair and skin a shade or two lighter than the brothers, more like my own. Gerell looked like someone you'd expect to see still riding his skateboard at twenty-five and enjoying every minute of it.

Right now, he was busy cocking a thumb at the waitress as she walked by. "We asked her to come back in five."

A red and gray laminated menu sat in front of my chair, but I made no move to grab it. "I already know what I want."

"What?" Andrew asked, a twinkle in his eye. When he looked at me like that, like he was interested in what I had to say, like what I had to say mattered, it sent shivers down my spine. It'd been a long time since anyone thought I was worthy of anything, yet Andrew hit me with that look on a daily basis. It was a pleasant feeling.

Another whiff of the marinara sauce filled my nostrils, and I smiled, loving the smell. "Lasagna." It had always been one of my favorites and living here hadn't changed that.

Andrew chuckled. "You promised to show me how to make that one, right?" He looked to his brother and Gerell. "You take a bunch of food, pile it on top of each other, pour a thick red sauce over it, and then coat it in cheese." He shuddered, a look of pure distaste on his face. "It sounds horrible."

Lincoln picked up his menu and peered at it. "It really does sound dreadful. Were you forced to eat it as a child or something?"

I shook my head, trying not to laugh. "Stop being dramatic. It's good, you'll see."

Lincoln's eyes widened at the mere prospect. "No, I will

not." He raised the menu over his face as if that would protect him from me and my lasagna.

Gerell laughed and pulled it down. "You're ridiculous."

The waitress came back, and we gave her our orders.

Gerell held up an arm and made a muscle. "I feel like I'm in better shape than I've ever been." Lincoln reached over and felt it, his eyebrows raising as if he agreed. "My mom thinks so anyway," Gerell went on.

Hearing him say that and watching the three of them interact really warmed my heart. Lia had seen to it that we were each given guidtags, the little devices that made it possible for us to open a portal whenever we needed to.

I knew that Gerell, Lincoln, and Andrew often went to their home worlds to spend time with their families, and had even brought some of them here for a visit a couple of times. I thought that was wonderful, though the same couldn't be said for me.

I had no family left on my home world. The only person I'd had was Ed, and he'd betrayed me, so just the thought of going back home, left a sour taste in my mouth.

Not that I'd written it off completely. It's where my parents had lived and died, and a part of it would always be with me, but Lia's world was where I lived now, and I was more than happy to call it home.

Our food arrived, and we chatted easily about everything and nothing. It felt good to have friends, to go out for a night on the town and to know that I had a nice safe home to go back to.

I forked off a piece of lasagna and noticed the suspicious look Lincoln gave it. "It's not going to bite you." I laughed, sliding some in my mouth and enjoying the tingle of the sauce and the richness of the cheese. Hmm. I looked up to see Lincoln still eyeing it doubtfully. "You're ridiculous, you know that? Eat your steak before it gets cold."

As the night wound down, we each prepared to go home and get a good night's sleep so that we'd be ready for training in the morning.

That changed when all four of our phones beeped a text message, halfway through dessert.

"Lia," I said, looking at it. "We have a mission."

2

W e spent the next day in briefings, learning everything we could about the world we were about to enter.

My eyes grew wide as I looked the information over. Thousands of people from many different universes went missing every five years, and it was the coalition's opinion that this world, Lakvec, had something to do with it. "What do you think they're doing with them?" I asked Lincoln, who sat beside me, doing his own reading. "Why do they need so many people?" I shuddered to even think about it, especially after some of the stuff we'd seen.

Lincoln sat with his legs propped up on the table in front of him, pencil twirling in his hand. "Well, we know what the Siana needed us for, so maybe something along those lines?"

I always cringed when I remembered what the Sianas had had in store for us, and I couldn't be happier that we'd put an end to it. I often wondered at the many who'd come before us, but was able to take comfort in the fact that the coalition had infiltrated all worlds known to be associated with Siana, and brought thousands of people home.

Lia stood, pacing, going over her own set of notes. Her short pink hair was spiked and shiny, and I'd learned that she wore it like that most days. "This won't be like before," she said, making all eyes snap her way. "We won't go in under cover. Our data analyst says it would be too risky. So, we'll be going in an official capacity. Think you can handle that?"

I chewed a bit on my bottom lip as I thought about it. Up until now, we'd always gone in undercover. Getting in people's faces and demanding they tell me all they know wasn't something I'd ever been good at.

On the other hand, as far as we knew, people's lives were in danger, maybe even thousands of people, so, personal feelings aside, I had to give it a try.

Gerell sat on the table, a laid-back look on his face. "I think I can do it. I mean, I tell Andrew and Lincoln what to do all the time, and they don't mind."

Andrew pretended to look annoyed. "Jury's still out on that one, but yeah, I think we'll be okay."

"See?" Gerell said as if this validated everything.

Lincoln rolled his eyes at both of them, while Lia continued to go over her notes, a small smile on her lips.

A warm feeling spread through me as I realized how much more at ease we were now. No longer trapped in that awful place, full personalities had come to life and started to flourish, something that could have never happened during our time on Siana.

Lia picked up her bag and went to the door. "We leave in an hour."

Lakvec was a cold, dark place. We'd portaled in during the middle of the day, yet the sun stayed hidden behind a massive amount of clouds.

The wind was strong enough to blow my hair back, and make my clothes flap around me. I shivered, just a bit, but knew I'd spent many winters without so much as a coat, so I could definitely handle this.

"Looks like hell," Gerell said, looking around.

"Worse than hell," Lincoln agreed.

The city seemed pretty busy, with cars and trucks going up and down the street, people walking briskly on the side-walk, going in and out of shops and storefronts.

Blue and red seemed the norm here, as most vehicles and dwellings appeared to be in that color. It kind of looked like a skilled builder had come through and used a bunch of colorful Legos to make a town.

Andrew's eyes scanned our surroundings. "Maybe the blue spices things up a bit," he offered.

I looked at a corner blue building with a red porch and blue shutters. "Does this look spiced up to you?" I asked drily.

He laughed, and we kept walking.

So far everyone seemed friendly enough, as many people's eyes lit up with welcome as we passed them. A few even stopped to ask us where we were going and if we needed help.

"They seem mighty eager," I said as a feeling of dread washed over me. Renee and Ed too had been helpful and eager.

Lia must have been thinking the same. "Something they have in common with the Sienas, remember." She said it as if she needed to remind us of what we'd been through there. Probably her roundabout way of telling us to stay on our guard. "The data analysts think we should check on a guy named, Morgan. His name comes up dozens of times."

I checked my icater to see if we had an address for him. "Says here he's five miles away." Before we'd left home, the tech guys had matched our GPS to this world, which I thought was beyond cool.

Gerell reached into his bag and pulled out a small blue shell, about the size of a quarter. "Well, I just got these shoes, I'm not walking."

"Why would you bring brand new shoes with you on a mission?" Andrew asked.

"It was either wear them here or wear them to training. Not like we go anywhere else," he mumbled.

"We were just out last night," Andrew pointed out.

"Hey." Lia held up her hand, stopping both men from going any further. "I know it feels like lately all you've done is work and train, but trust me it'll pay off in the end."

Gerell gave her a "whatever" look. "Still not walking." He pushed the button on the side of the shell, and it became a small disk-shaped floating device, that looked almost like a frisbee, only a little bigger. On Siana, they'd been called soarers, but in Lia's world they were called escalates.

"Five miles *is* a long way to walk," I said, pulling out my own green shell.

Lia must have decided it was a lost cause because after a few seconds she pulled out her orange one. "You guys are so extra. You do ten times this in training."

Andrew pushed the button on his black one, a look on his face that said he didn't care either way. That was fine for him, but I was with Gerell. Who knew what we'd come up against today. It was probably better to save our energy while we could.

Unlike the soarers on Siana, our feet didn't sink into the escalates. Instead, metal straps buckled around them, keeping us in place.

I stepped on it without fear, having used it enough times to know I would be safe. As always, I marveled at the technology on Plex. There was a shell for just about everything, and they certainly came in handy on missions.

Lincoln twirled the small gray shell in his hand, his eyes never leaving Gerell. "What if I feel like running instead?"

Gerell gave him a quizzical look. "Then run, Linc, but my ass is staying on this escalate. You do what you want."

Lincoln shook his head, a hidden smile on his face. "You make me sick." He stepped on the disk and floated over to Gerell until they were only inches apart. "You know that? Sick."

Gerell huffed as if he was annoyed but we could all see the fondness in his eyes. "Babe, if you wanted a kiss all you had to do was ask. There's no need for all of this."

"Shut up," Lincoln said, before leaning over and giving the other man a peck on the lips.

"Focus." Lia clapped her hands to put all attention on her. "What's going on here is serious." She pointed between Gerell and Lincoln. "Anything else is best left for later." Not waiting for a response, she stepped on her escalate and looked over the navigation route.

Unlike the soarers of Siana, these didn't fly themselves, they came with a small steering knob that we'd actually had to learn to drive.

I'd driven it enough times to understand that it wasn't that much different from steering a car, in fact, in some ways it was easier. "Lead the way," I said, falling in line beside Andrew.

He typed in the route. "Seems like we're the only ones here riding these things."

He was right, the people of this world all seemed to be driving cars or trucks, but I didn't think it mattered. "We're not undercover this time, so…"

He raised an eyebrow. "Our first time coming in an official capacity. We'll see how that goes."

We arrived at a large black metal house set about twenty feet from the road. We'd stopped seeing overlapping blue and red right after we'd passed the city limits, which was a relief, to be honest. I loved the colors blue and red but seeing them every few feet, had been a little overwhelming.

Gerell's eyes went wide as he took in the large structure in front of us. "Okay, that's got to be over two hundred steps," he said, pointing to the metal stairs leading up to the front porch.

Lincoln gave him an amused look, his eyes full of merriment. "Then float your ass up there and stop complaining." With that, he took off through the air, and we all followed.

Once we reached the top, we put our escalates up, and Lia knocked on the door.

We only had to wait a second before a tall, heavyset man answered. His eyes lit up with surprise and a bit of excitement when he saw us, which made me a little nervous. He seemed thrilled we were there, which immediately put me on my guard. "Right this way," he said, stepping back so we could enter the house.

Unease gripped me, but I swallowed hard, telling myself I could do this.

Andrew too looked unsure. "Anyone else get the feeling that he was expecting us?" he asked as the man stood back waiting for us to enter.

Lia answered in a fierce whisper. "Keep your guard up. Already I don't like the vibe here."

We walked into a living room with black and silver furniture placed throughout. It almost looked like someone had raided a steel factory.

Two metallic sofas sat on opposite ends of the room, with iron end tables beside each. No pictures hung on the wall, which themselves looked to be made of steel.

The whole place felt cold and unattached, and I shivered a bit as we followed the man down the hall.

He led us outside to a screened in deck. Out here, the chairs, though made of iron, at least had cushions. Two were lounge chairs, the other a patio loveseat. They sat facing the rolls of hills and mechanical flowers that seemed to make up the backyard.

The porch itself was regular concrete, which was a little surprising, to me anyway. The whole deck was enclosed in charcoal fiberglass, with holes small enough to keep out insects, but just wide enough to let a small breeze in.

Pillows of different shapes and sizes littered the porch, and there was a small bar set up in the corner.

On one of the lounge chairs sat a man with shades on, and a drink in his hand. There was no sun out, so I wondered what he was trying to protect his eyes from. I looked to Andrew and raised a brow, making him shrug because he didn't know any more than I did at this point.

The man wore a loose blue shirt, with blue pants to match. He looked relaxed when we'd first walked out, but seemed to perk up the moment he realized he had company.

His voice sounded like sweetened honey when he spoke. "James, what have you brought me?" He stood and removed his glasses, his red eyes sparkling with excitement as he took us in. "What am I to do with them, James?" He looked absolutely delighted, and I felt my blood turn to ice. What the hell did he think he was ready to do with us?

James answered in a voice loaded with secrets. "Probably offer them something to drink, since they're our guests, Morgan."

That stopped him cold, and he turned to look at James. "Guest? They're... Oh, well excuse my manners, but why are you in my house?" His eyes turned hard and accusing as all pleasure left his face.

I blinked, shocked at the sudden change.

Lia stiffened slightly before taking a few steps forward. "Five thousand people go missing every year. As far as we can tell they all end up here and somehow your name keeps popping up. What do you have to say about that?"

He gave her an appraising look. "Your business, Miss…"

"Name's Lia, and it's my business because I'm with the coalition investigating their disappearances."

He sized her up a little more, then turned to James, his eyes once again filled with excitement. James, gave him a small nod, a secretive grin on his face.

Beside me, Andrew bristled and step forward until he stood shoulder to shoulder with Lia.

I think we all felt the sting of that little exchange and went on guard.

"You know what," Morgan said, once again becoming friendly and easygoing. "I left my manners somewhere in a bottle upstairs. Terrible of me to behave this way. Have you traveled far? Are you hungry? Need a place to stay? I'd be more than happy to offer my hospitality for the length of your visit."

Lincoln's face was hard, not trusting this abrupt change any more than the rest of us. "We need answers about the missing people, and then we'll be on our way. No hospitality needed."

Morgan snapped his fingers. "Ask me what you want, but first let's have a drink."

Lia shook her head. "We didn't come here to drink."

His eyebrows rose, and he looked truly taken aback. "Why did you come to my house then? Uninvited, I may add."

Gerell looked at Morgan with a narrowing gaze. "Just what kind of drink are you offering us?"

Something dark and dangerous passed through Morgan's eyes, but it was quickly covered up with a smile. "Why whatever you'd like of course. I try to keep a little of everything on hand."

He played perfect host well, but behind his flippant manner, I saw nothing but intelligence and cunning. A small shiver went through me as I wondered just what he had planned for us.

"May I use your bathroom," I asked, knowing it was a good way for me to get a look around.

He knew it too, because his eyes bored into mine almost like a challenge. "Down the hall, third door on the right," he said in a clipped tone.

Lia narrowed her eyes as if she didn't trust anything about this place. "Lincoln go with her," she said, before turning her attention back to Morgan.

The walls of the hallway were blank and made of the same material as the rest of the house. "Why metal?" Lincoln asked as we arrived at the door that led to the bathroom.

I'd wondered the same thing. "You think it has something to do with what's going on?" I asked him.

He took a look around. "I don't know. I'll check out the first couple of rooms, you check out the last couple."

Nodding, I turned the knob and walked inside. The bathroom was just that, a bathroom. The only thing strange was how big it was. The only other bathrooms I'd seen this large had been inside of locker rooms.

The tub was easily the size of the above ground swimming pool my parents used to have in their backyard.

I sighed as I thought about it. I'd lost that as well. Unable to pay the taxes and insurance on the property, all that my parents had worked for had gone down the drain along with everything else I'd owned.

A deep pain tried to settle in my chest, but I shooed it away, determined to focus on the mission at hand. The bathroom, unlike the rest of the house, was pure black and white marble. The sink was so large I was sure it could double as a tub if need be.

The bathroom looked newly cleaned and smelled of fresh lemon and citrus. Still on my guard, I walked further into the room and noticed five black toilets lined against the wall beside the sink. Across from them, were ten urinals. "Why so many?" I asked the empty room.

A crackling and popping sound caught my attention, and I turned toward the tub/pool, whatever it was. The thing was solid black marble and filled with what I assumed was water, though it was so thick and black, I doubted it. Blue electricity shot up from it, causing me to jump back and wonder what the hell was in there.

"Something best left for when I'm not alone," I mumbled, taking a few steps back.

I looked past the toilet area and saw a couple of linen closets. I searched through each one, but found nothing but towels, soap, and wash cloths. Lots of them. "Why so many?" I wondered again.

Figuring I'd been gone long enough, I took one last look around, trying to soak up as much as I could. When I turned the knob, to step back in the hallway, James was there, staring intently at the door.

3

"**F**ind everything you need?" he asked, his eyes holding a small knowing glint.

Well two could play that game. "Yes, thank you," I said, without batting an eye.

"Where's your friend?" He looked behind me as if expecting Lincoln to pop up out of thin air.

I cocked a thumb at the door. "He's still using it."

His eyes went to slits, but the smile never left his face. "Of course."

I expected him to leave after that, but he just stood there, unblinking, and staring at me.

"You know, I think I will have that drink after all." I raised my voice when I said it, hoping that Lincoln what take the hint.

We walked back onto the front porch, where a silver table was set up with multiple beverages.

The frustrated look on Lia's face told me that Morgan hadn't told them anything, and this visit was a lost cause, because it was clear he'd say only what he wanted to.

James looked at me. "What would you like to drink, dear?

I'm sorry I didn't get your name."

Gerell only took a second to read the situation. "That's because she didn't give it, and sorry about the drink, but we have to go."

"Leaving so soon?" Lincoln walked back onto the porch, wiping his hands on his pants as if he'd just washed them and they were still wet.

Morgan looked both disappointed and exceedingly excited. "I hope you'll be sticking around for a while?"

Andrew gave him a fake smile. "I'm sure we'll see you again. We're not going anywhere until this investigation is over and we have the answers we need."

Morgan held a coffee cup in his hand. "Well, I'll be sure to say hello, if we meet on the street."

Closing the door behind us, I took a deep breath and tried to shake off the feeling of wrongness that emanated from that house.

Gerell hopped back on his escalate. "Well, I don't know about the rest of you, but I can use a drink after that."

I think we all agreed.

We decided to have lunch in the park, so as to get a better feel for the people around us. The data analyst had advised not to partake of any of the food or drink here, so the kitchen at the coalition was on standby.

Tom, and Katie, both of whom we'd met on Siana, had been chefs on their home world, and both had opted to earn a paycheck with the coalition doing what they loved most.

They were still agents. They just put their talents to use where they would be best appreciated. They'd made us sandwich lunches, and had them on call for whenever we opened the portal wanting food.

Sitting at one of the many picnic tables in the park, Lia placed a platter filled with turkey and ham sandwiches in the middle of the table.

Andrew had gone with her, and he passed out bottles of water and chips, along with napkins.

"Not exactly the drink I had in mind," Gerell said, taking the water from Andrew's outstretched hand.

"Yet, here we are." Andrew gave the last bottle to his brother, then took a seat beside me at the table. "Hey, Kerry. Notice anything yet?"

I looked around. It didn't look too much different from the parks back home. It was well kept, as nothing looked old or even chipped or dented. Three slides were placed at different ends of the park. A couple of swing sets took up space in front of a jungle gym, and a sandbox was spread out in front of a climbing pole. Carefree children ran and played, while parents sat on benches, talking to each other or reading.

Andrew took a big bite of his sandwich. "You know, I never saw one kid on Siana. What do you think that was about?"

I popped a few chips in my mouth and thought about it. "Maybe they hid them away until we left? I don't know."

A ball rolled over to us, and a small boy of about eight ran up to get it. Lincoln picked it up and handed it to him. The little boy's eyes raked us over and a small smile formed on his lips. "Mom, Dad come look what I found!" he said, pointing at us. Ball tucked securely under his arm, he ran to his parents.

A couple sitting on a bench a few feet away looked up as he approached. The woman leaned over and whispered something in his ear. His shoulders sagged, then after a second he turned on his heels and ran back to play kickball with his friends.

Lia guzzled some of her water. "Well, that was awkward."

"No more awkward than James and Morgan," I said.

She nodded. "Yeah, that's what bothers me. Everyone we

meet is giving us that same glinted eye look."

We wondered around town for a bit longer soaking in as much information as we could, and trying to make some headway. Everyone was really nice, but no one was talking about the missing people and some of them had to know something.

No way did five thousand beings come here every couple of years and no one noticed. Especially when the people being captured were all from different worlds and had dissimilar appearances and customs.

I opened my shell pack, aiming to take out the one that would offer me shelter in the empty field we'd decided to spend the night in, but Lia stopped me.

"I don't think we should separate. I'm not sure it's safe. Just a feeling I have." She pulled out a yellow shell and pressed the button, making it open up to a green cod house, big enough to sleep eight.

We each had private shell housing that slept two to four, but each senior coalition agent also had ones that slept anywhere from eight to twenty, depending on the need.

"Okay." I put my shell away, kind of happy that I wouldn't be going at it alone tonight. Something about this place really frightened me.

I didn't know if it was the way people stared when we walked past or the way their eyes would light up from our mere presence. Whatever it was, it creeped me out enough that sharing shelter for tonight seemed like an excellent idea.

The house, which looked like a super large mushroom, appeared to be made of clay when you first looked at it. I knew from experience, though that the material was tough and sturdy.

The first room of the house was a large living room, with a fully functional kitchen off to the right. Two bathrooms sat at the end of the hallway. Four bedrooms were on the right side of the hall, and four were on the left.

There were no pictures on the walls, nothing to make it personal. Yet, the furniture was modern and well taken care of. The living room held three large yellow couches, and two recliners. The kitchen held a refrigerator, stove, microwave, a set of cabinets, a sink, and a large square wooden table big enough to seat ten. It was spotless in there, as Lia always kept things clean and tidy.

Each bedroom was exactly the same, with a wooden bed, dresser, and nightstand. Every door had locks on it, though. So, there was that.

Gerell plopped down on one of the couches. "Does anybody else get the feeling that we're in a large fish bowl?"

Andrew sat on an opposite sofa. "I get the feeling that they want something from us. I just can't figure out what it is." He sounded frustrated.

Lia sat beside me on the couch, while Lincoln sat in one of the recliners. "Well, we better figure out what they want, and then figure out how not to give it to them," Lincoln said.

Lia removed her shoes and put them on the side of the couch. "Another name that keeps popping up is Anna Bringman. Tomorrow we'll go there. Hopefully, we can get more out of her than we did James and Morgan. I mean what the heck was that about?"

We all laughed and agreed that talking with those two had indeed been a strange experience.

As the night wound down and we each retired to our separate bedrooms, I still felt one hundred percent better here with these people than I had the last couple of years out on my own, and that in itself, was something to be thankful for.

4

The next morning, Andrew and Lincoln portaled to the coalition to get us breakfast, and we ate it at the table in the kitchen. After that, we exited the house and Lia punched in a code that turned it back into a shell. As long as no one was inside, the house closed with no problem. If something as small as even a bird were in there, the house would not close.

That done, we went on our way, with me hoping that we'd conclude our business today and not have to come back.

Anna Bringman lived in a two-story brown house. The yard hosted about a million blue and red lights, and the porch had patio furniture of the same color. While not new, it was clean, without blemish, and easy to see that it was well-taken care of.

Wind chimes in every variety hung from the rafters, and a red jug that seemed to be continuously overflowing with milk sat on a blue table.

I tapped Andrew and tilted my head toward it. He looked,

brows furrowed, which I took to mean he didn't know its purpose any more than I did.

"It's the kaleidoscope of life," a woman sitting in a red rocking chair, about three feet from the table said, looking at us with knowing grins.

I almost flinched but was able to get control of my emotions before I did. I hadn't seen her there and looking at the others, neither had they.

She had pale skin, paler than anything I'd ever seen and her brown hair was tied back in a messy ponytail. She looked to be about forty, and when she stood, her blue dress reached the floor. "Like life," she walked over to the table with the milk and ran her hand over the top of it, "this jug is never-ending, always full." She turned toward us. "Milk curdles your stomach, life curdles your heart. What can I help you with today?"

I blinked, not sure if she was serious or not, but willing to roll with it.

Lia took a step forward. "Ma'am, we just wanted to ask you a few questions. If…"

"I don't talk to people looming over me." Anna sat back down and waved a hand to indicate that we were welcome to sit as well.

"What we wanted--" Lia started again, but once again Anna cut her off.

"Yes, yes, I know all about what you want." Her eyes took us in, and I could see a small glow to them. "Morgan told me all about it. You somehow think that every five years, we kidnap thousands of people and hide them where?" she asked, her hands waving around as if challenging us to produce said people out of thin air. "Where?" she repeated.

Andrew gave her a hard look, condescension lacing his voice when he spoke. "Have you seen anything strange?"

She pursed her lips in a way that seemed to imply that the

only strange things she'd seen lately were us. "No," she answered, giving each of us a measured look that said the opposite. Maybe she really did think we were strange. Maybe we were, to her anyway.

"Would you tell us if you had?" Gerell asked.

Her eyes lit up again, and she let out a small chuckle. "Would you tell anyone if you were involved in the disappearance of thousands of people?"

He stared at her jaw tight as if waiting for a real answer.

Her eyes squinted into calculating slits. "No. I wouldn't tell you. Who in their right mind would?"

Lia pulled out her handheld com and began to type. "Well, I guess we can't cross you off the list then?"

Anna smiled, and I had the distinct impression of a shark rising from the water. "I've been as nice as I'm going to be. You're free to leave now."

She walked past us and into the house, shutting the door behind her.

Lincoln watched her go. "Is it just me, or are she and Morgan begging to be caught?"

Lia thought about it. "They're drawing us to them. The question is why."

We left not knowing the answer, but sure that both Morgan and Anna were acting suspicious for a reason.

Lia decided we should split up and stay in touch through our coms. Each of us took a different street, and our goal was to wander into shops and businesses, gathering what information we could.

The reason was that maybe we'd be less intimidating as one person rather than a whole team.

I walked for a while, my head starting to spin a little. I'd first noticed it last night, but I'd put it down to lack of sleep and being on a new mission. My heart beat triple time, as sweat poured down my face, and now I wasn't so sure what was making me feel this way.

I ended up having to lean up against a building, trying to catch my breath. I was a little hot with myself. This was our first mission in an official capacity, and I didn't want to mess it up.

The previous missions had been undercover assignments, but somehow this one felt more real. Yet here I was, up against a wall barely able to breathe, an elite detective I was not.

People passed me by, most of them smiling with bright eyes, but none stopped to ask if I was okay.

I made it to an outside deli, and took a seat, hoping the rest would recharge me. Out of my backpack, I took the shell that held the cooler with my drinks in it. Taking out water, I put the shell back and rolled the cold bottle around on my face. It felt like heaven, but I wondered what had come over me.

No one seemed to notice my distress, which was a good thing I guessed. A waiter came over to take my order, and I shooed him away. "Feeling kind of sluggish here, guys," I said into my com after the man was out of hearing range.

"I'm sitting on a rock by the lake," Lia answered, her voice panting. "I can't seem to catch my breath."

"Dizzy more like it," Gerell said, his words sounding short and forced.

"I feel like I did that time Lincoln and I party hopped for three days straight," Andrew said. He tried to chuckle, but it just came out gagged and restrained.

"Feels worse than that, bro," Lincoln said, not sounding much better.

"Everybody meet back up at the park. We stick together

until we can figure out what's going on," Lia said, sounding as if she was gasping for air.

I drank my water down in one gulp, unable to stop myself. Yet I was still thirsty for more, and hungry too. I felt as if I hadn't eaten in weeks, and my stomach growled its protest as I got up from the table.

My steps were shaky at best, so I figured I'd use my escalate instead of trying to walk.

I waited until I was a few feet from the deli and then leaned up against a tree to catch my breath. I needed to get my pack off my back so that I could get the right shell out, but even that seemed like too much of an effort. "I'm coming," I said into my com. "Just give me a moment."

"I'm pretty sure you may have to rethink that," a strange voice said.

I looked up to see four women standing in front of me. One with black hair that reached almost to her waist. Another was blond with a close cut. One woman had red hair done up in a bun, and the last one had blue spiked hair piled on top of her head, but the sides were shaved close.

All four were decently dressed, looked clean, and had flawless skin. I could easily assume they were on break from work, or maybe they'd just come from the beauty parlor.

The one with the blue hair spoke again. "Did you think you were better than us?" she asked, in a curious voice.

I looked at her and was shocked to see that she really expected an answer. "Better than who?" I asked. I came up from the wall, gathering what strength I could to hold myself steady. Sweat dripped down my face, and my mouth felt dry, my vision blurry.

The one with the black hair held out her hand. "Come with us. It's time now. Time to go home where you belong."

"No." I tried to step back and stumbled, nearly falling to

the ground. "No," I said again, this time into my coms. "Need help, guys. People are here, four of them."

The ladies came forward, and I staggered back, trying to get away. Something in my gut twisted and cold fear gripped me. I felt helpless, a feeling I swore I'd never feel again after leaving Ed and Renee's. Yet here I was, and I wasn't sure I could survive going through this again.

"We're not going to hurt you," the blond one said. At least I think it was the blond one, by now my vision was so blurry, I could only make out shape and color.

All four advanced on me, coming forward, and I tried to fight them off, but I was in no shape to defend myself.

"Stop waving your arms around like that. You're going to hurt yourself," one of them said. I think it was the one with black hair.

"We don't want you hurt. We want you safe and happy like us. Come on now, stop fighting. He'll take care of you. He takes care of everything."

By this point, I was only slightly alert. I could feel myself being lifted in the air, my hands swinging at my side. "Being taking away," I mumbled into my com, leaving sparks of silver everywhere so that they'd know where to find me.

"We're coming to get you," I heard Lia whisper into my com. She sounded about as out of breath as I felt. "Just hold on."

I think I must have dozed at some point because a small hand tapped me on the shoulder and stood me upright. My legs buckled immediately and one of them, not sure which, put her arm around my waist to support me.

The one with the blue hair waved a hand at the huge house before me. I could see that it was big and that there was a small bridge we had to cross to get to it, but I couldn't make out much else. "Look at your new home. Have you ever lived in something this big? This is going to be so much better for you."

"No." I tried to step away, but my legs folded again. "I don't, I don't want--"

"Let her go." I looked up to see Lia and the rest of my team floating on their escalates in front of me. They all looked like they were on the verge of throwing up and from their wobbly appearance, I was sure the only thing keeping them up were the straps.

The one with the blue hair was the first to speak. "Ah, we've been waiting for you."

Lia or one of them must have looked shocked going by what the red head said next. "Did you think we didn't know that she was talking to you the whole time, or leaving a trail so that you could find her?"

"You are all invited here as guests," the one with the black hair said. "But as for Kerry, she stays. This is her home now."

Lincoln came forward a bit, I could tell it was him because of the color of his escalate. "We're not leaving here without her." Yup, definitely Lincoln's voice, hard as stone when he's mad.

"You're more than welcome to stay," one of the women said.

I could see my team's colorful escalates close in around me.

"At least let me carry her, she's too weak to walk." That was Andrew.

He lifted me in his arms at the same time one of the women launched at me, trying to stop him. "Now," he screamed, and a portal opened sucking us through, but not before I saw the flash of silver energy so like my own, coming from the one with the black hair and the one with the blue.

5

I awoke on a bed in the coalition. From what I could tell, they'd put me in the decontamination department. My head felt a little better, but I was still thirsty and very hungry. "What happened?" I asked the agent in front of me looking over my chart.

She was a short lady who looked to be about thirty-five. She had brown hair curled tight to her head and carried an air of assertiveness around her as she went about her work.

"In layman terms, you're suffering from a severe lack of energy." She paused for a second. "All of you are. We've boosted you as much as we can, but you really need to eat something and take a few days off to rest."

I nodded my agreement, and a tray with a covered dish was placed in front of me. "Where are the others?" I asked as I took the lid off to see what I had. Beef, one of my favorites.

"They're in their own rooms, getting treatment as well. We were able to open a portal and pull you back just in time, so everyone is okay."

I bit my bottom lip, as a shiver ran through me. I'd almost

been taken again. Just the thought of being held captive in another place like Siana made me want to hurl.

I sighed, and tried to get a grip on my emotions because I knew in a few days we'd have to go back.

On my plate, I had pot roast with onions, potatoes, carrots, and gravy. On the side, I had a honey butter biscuit and broccoli and cheese casserole. I was so hungry that I don't even think I tasted the food as I wolfed it down. To drink, I had ice cold milk and water. I tossed them both back and then asked for more of everything.

I ate my second helping a little slower, thinking about all that had happened so far. We were a new team, not as trained as others, and I wondered if Lia would have done better with a group that had more experience.

I put a carrot in my mouth and thought about that house, the lake, and the women that had tried to kidnap me. What did they want? I really wanted to know.

Two of them had had the power of Siana. I'd been woozy, but I knew what I'd seen. I bit into a forkful of my casserole. It was nice and cheesy like I liked and had sharp cheddar and spring cheese in it. Spring cheese was something new I'd discovered when I'd first gotten here. It tasted like a mix between pepper jack and mozzarella, but not quite.

My mind floated back to the women who'd had the Siana powers. We'd always figured that a few people had escaped as soon as the fighting had begun. Some Siana residences probably, but also some who'd come to bid at the auction.

I took a drink of water, my hunger finally sated. Even if the coalition had records of all the worlds suspected to be involved in the auctions, I was willing to bet they didn't know all of them, or at least didn't know where to find them all, as I was sure some of the participants had gone to ground. Which made this even harder, I thought, as I came to my feet and stretched.

"When can I go home?" I asked the lady who'd been standing over me. She was busy looking through another chart now, but turned back around as soon as I spoke.

"Now if you want. All of your numbers look good. Just check back in a few days. We need to make sure you're okay before you go back out there."

I nodded and grabbed my coat, putting it on. I could have taken a bath at the coalition, but the only thing I wanted right now was the comfort of my own home. So much weighed on my mind, and to be honest, I didn't want to talk to anyone right now.

When I got to my apartment, I took a long hot bath, scenting the water with rose and jasmine. The combination was a sweet mix of memories that reminded me of the lazy days of my childhood.

Family barbecues, playing double dutch, hopscotch, and dodgeball were a norm growing up, and I sometimes longed for those carefree times when not having my favorite dessert at dinner was my biggest problem.

Over the next two days, the only thing I did was eat, sleep, and talk with my therapist. I had a lot of feelings going on and needed a positive way to express them without hurting myself or those around me. I didn't want to mess up on a mission and cost someone their lives.

That right there was one of my biggest fears, that one day I'd screw up and it would lead to the death of one of my team mates. I let out a sigh because I just didn't think I'd be able to handle that if it ever did happen.

We'd come close those last few minutes on Lakvec, and it just drove home the point that each and every time we went out there, we put ourselves at risk. Not a pretty thought when you considered I had to go back in another day or so.

My third day back, we met at the club house to regroup. The clubhouse was a place away from the coalition. It had four bedrooms, a couple of bathrooms, a meeting area, a boardroom, and a kitchen. It was made for brainstorming a mission, and ideal for when we had to stay up going over a case and it was too late to go home.

Today we sat in the meeting area, which really was just the living room, as it had couches, chairs, and a whiteboard. The whole place was cozy and contemporary. The walls were a nice calming brown, while the carpet was plush, and of the same color.

A coffee table sat in the middle of the floor. Deep-seated brown couches sat in front of it, with the recliner on one end of the room and the whiteboard on the other.

The smell of fresh coffee floated from the kitchen, and Andrew came in carrying a tray with cups for everyone. He placed it on the table, then went to get a tray of muffins.

This was the first time I'd seen any of them since Lakvec, but from what I could tell, they all seemed to be back to their old selves.

Gerell picked up his coffee, sipped it and then gave Andrew a sour look. "I like mine dark, as you well know. You do this on purpose, I believe. Making it so I can barely stand to drink it."

Andrew picked up one of the muffins and bit into it, blueberry by the smell. "Kerry likes her coffee light. Lia and Lincoln like theirs medium. This is a compromise." He picked up his cup and inhaled like it was the best thing he'd ever smelled. "It's not all about you, you know."

"You can make two pots." Gerell held his coffee in one hand, his muffin in the other. "It's not that hard. I do it all the time."

"That's because you're the only one who requires something different."

"You're an asshole," Gerell replied, taking a sip of his coffee anyway, while Lincoln looked on in amusement.

"Anyway," Lia said, calling our attention back to the task at hand. "They had Siana powers, those women. Did anybody else notice that?"

Lincoln picked up a muffin and tossed it around in his hand. "I saw, wasn't sure at first, but yeah that's what I saw." He continued to throw the sweet bread back and forward until Gerell tapped him on the arm.

"Don't play with your food," the other man said. "That's just nasty."

Lincoln gave him a challenging look and then shoved the whole thing into his mouth at once. Gerell raised an eyebrow at him, and I turned my head, leaving them to their silent communication, as I was used to this by now.

"We need to go back in with a plan," Andrew said. "Now that we know somewhat what we're dealing with, we can better combat it."

Lincoln let out a small chuckle. "We don't know shit, bro. What is it that you think we know?"

"We know that they have the power to make us sick. Either that or there's something in the air or the trees doing it."

Lia shook her head, she'd tucked her feet under her, and her cup rested on her lap, her right hand holding it. "It's not that. The coalition would never send us to a place that was unsafe health wise. No, it has to be something else, and we don't have time to figure it out. The higher ups want this case closed by tomorrow, no excuses."

"What's the hurry?" I asked, thinking our continued safety should be more important.

"Because the five years starts two days after tomorrow,

and thousands more people will go missing unless we stop it now."

That hit me hard in the chest and strengthened my resolve to get back there as soon as possible. If I could save anyone from going through what I had, I'd do everything in my power to make it so.

Gerell continued sipping on the coffee that he obviously didn't hate as much as he thought. "We need to find out whose house that was they were trying to take Kerry to. That may answer a lot of our questions."

"I agree," Lincoln said. "Except we have no way of doing that until we go back. It's not information that we have on hand."

Lia put her cup on a coaster atop the coffee table, and placed a small throw pillow in her lap, holding it tight. "Whoever it is, it's not Anna, and it's not Morgan. I think this person is on a whole other level."

I thought back to the moment the women had taken me and shuddered. They kept saying it was time for me to go home now. "The whole place is just creepy and strange."

We talked for another couple of hours, tossing around ideas before we were all struggling to keep our eyes open.

I stood and went for my coat after we'd officially called it a night. Gerell and Lincoln slunk off to the bedroom they shared, and Lia did the same.

Andrew grabbed his coat. "I understand the need to be surrounded by your own stuff, familiarity. I'll walk you home. If you want me to," he offered.

I smiled warmly at him because the truth was, I was always happy in his company. On the way to my apartment, we talked about some of our neighbors, a couple of our favorite TV shows, and just about anything but the mission, we'd already said all there was to say about that tonight.

When we got to my door, he paused, looking across the

street at the three-bedroom duplex he shared with Gerell and his brother. "Can you stay?" I asked, not ready to say goodbye. "I've been alone the last couple of nights, and I don't want that right now."

He stared at me for a second, his eyes burning holes into my own. "I don't have a problem with that," he said, his voice thick and husky.

He'd stayed before. Sometimes he slept in my spare room and other times we simply shared a bed. Tonight, I was in the mood for sharing. I went into my bathroom and changed into a set of thick cotton pajamas, and he used my spare room to put on a t-shirt and pair of sweatpants. He kept a few clothes at my place, for occasions just like this one.

Once under the covers, his strong arms wrapped around me, pulling me close, and making me feel warm and protected. I snuggled into his embrace and found myself able to truly relax for the first time since I'd been back. We stayed that way for the rest of the night.

6

———

The first thing we did upon arriving back on Lakvec was storm the house the four women had been trying to take me to. We teleported right inside, sticking together and clearing each room as a group.

Nothing.

The whole place was empty. Not a scrap of paper, or piece of furniture remained.

"What do we do now?" I asked. We stood in an empty living room, looking around as if a clue was just going to pop out at any moment.

"I think we need to go back to Morgan's," Lincoln said. "That dude knew a lot more than he let on."

Lia agreed. "Yeah, but something tells me he's not going to be so nice this time around."

"We'll never find out if we don't go," Gerell said, walking toward the door.

"Okay, but what's the game plan?" I asked before we got a little too ahead of ourselves.

Andrew tapped a finger to his chin. "On the information

that we have, I say our best bet is to just bust up in there," he finally answered.

Lia only took a minute to contemplate this before giving the okay. "No matter what, we stay on our guard, and at the least sign of trouble, we regroup and get out of there. Understood?"

Morgan's house looked as quiet as it had the first time we'd been there, but I didn't trust that we were alone.

When we got to the front door, we saw that it was already partly open. "It's a trap," I whispered, though I was sure the others already knew this.

We walked softly inside, careful feet taking us down the long, dark hallway. When we got to the door that led to the back porch, Lia stopped and called us to attention. "I hate to do this, but I think two of us need to at least check outside, while the rest of us continue looking in here. If anyone disagrees or thinks we should just stay together, then that's what we'll do."

"No, I think it's a good idea. No one seems to be here so far, and we'll cover more ground that way," Lincoln said.

She looked to Andrew, Lincoln, and myself for confirmation and we all nodded our agreement. "Okay, Gerell, you're with me. We'll check outside. The rest of you go ahead and clear the house and then we can figure out what to do from there."

We went from room to room finding nothing, until finally coming to the bathroom. I remembered how huge it had been and knew it had enough nooks and crannies for someone to hide if they wanted to.

Not wanting to talk too loudly, I pointed to it and indicated that I'd be going inside. The brothers backed me up, and together we took careful steps into the room.

On first look, it seemed empty, and not all that different than when we'd been here a couple of days before. We walked fully inside, and Lincoln checked over by the toilet stools, while Andrew checked the closets.

I walked past the tub, aiming to get a look around the huge crackling thing when someone sprung out of it and tried to pull me under. I yelped and jumped back as Morgan, completely naked, came fully out of the water.

I gasped when I saw him. His skin popped and sizzled, just like the water. He smiled at me, a wicked grin, and threw his head back in ecstasy as if being in the tub was the most enjoyable thing in the world to him.

From the corner of my eye, I saw James hop down from the ceiling and tackle Andrew to the floor. I knew Andrew could handle his own so I turned all my attention to Morgan, blasting him with my powers as hard as I could.

He laughed as a silver spark hit him square in the chest, and his eyes and skin glowed, even more. Something wasn't right. That should have knocked him off his feet, he shouldn't be…

I didn't have time to finish that thought before another body popped up, this one a woman. She had black hair, long lashes, and she too was naked. Her eyes popped with energy and she focused her attention on Lincoln.

She floated out of the tub, headed straight toward him. He stopped what he'd been doing and tried to blow her back with an energy blast. This only made her laugh, and like Morgan, she seemed to grow stronger by it. "They're eating the energy," I yelled out. "Fighting them with it won't work."

As I said before, we all had a unique power because of what the Sianas had done to us. Mine was taking the energy we had and using it to drain other people of theirs. Which is what I expected the people of this world had been doing to us the whole time we'd been here. It was the reason we'd felt so weak and sick, I was sure of it.

I took a step back as Morgan came closer, a savage look on his face. "So full, so powerful. You three are like a forgotten gift from the once great Siana, sending us the last of its sacred offerings."

I didn't want to hear that shit. I raised my hands, one toward him, and the other toward the lady Lincoln currently fought with.

Though he looked just a bit weakened, Andrew seemed to be holding his own, throwing jabs and knocking James off his feet every chance he got.

I took a deep breath, my hands trembling and my mind filled with thoughts of how this could all go wrong. I needed to focus, so I tried breathing through my nose and out of my mouth.

It helped, and I found their chi, the source of their energy and concentrated on stripping it apart and dismantling it.

At first nothing, then Morgan grabbed his stomach at the same time that his legs buckled. He dropped to the floor squirming and crying out in pain.

I heard the woman cry out as well, and turned to see her grappling on the floor, clutching at her chest and looking very much like a fish out of water.

Sweat dripped down my back, and my arms started to tremble. "I don't know how much longer I can hold it, guys. Let's get out of here."

By now, Morgan and the woman were starting to shrivel up like grapes left in the sun too long.

My shout alerted James to what was going on, and it only took a second for him to assess the situation and take off running my way. Lincoln hit him with a left before he even got close, and the three of us bolted out the door and straight into the four women from before.

"Now you didn't think--" The one with the red hair started, and I raised my hands and stripped all four of them of their energy.

The one with the red hair looked mostly shocked, but soon all four were on the floor writhing in pain. I didn't have time to drain them like I had Morgan and the lady, but it was enough to let us escape.

Lincoln, Andrew, and I ran outside and into the back yard. It was empty, no Lia or Gerell in sight. "Guys, where are you? This place is crawling with people so be careful," I said into my com.

Silence.

I looked to Lincoln and Andrew, who looked as worried as I felt. "Gerell come in," Lincoln said, hand on his com. "Gerell, dammit, this is not the time to play games. Where the fuck are you?"

Nothing.

My heart shook with fear as I thought of all the horrible things that could have happened to them. Together the three of us went running toward the front, where Anna stood with a knife to Gerell's throat.

She had him on his knees in front of her, a curved blade biting into his skin. Blood trickled down his throat, but the look on his face wasn't one of fear. Instead, he looked wrathful, and his eyes held promises, that I knew if released, he planned on keeping.

Beside me, Lincoln took in a sharp inhale of breath, and his body went rigid with fury as he watched the knife cut deeper and deeper into Gerell's skin. They locked eyes and began doing that silent communication thing that they did sometimes.

Lia was still standing, but a tall dude with a shaved head

had his arm around her throat and a knife to her face. She didn't look scared either. If anything, she seemed to be calculating her next move.

I didn't waste time warning either of them. I just held up my hands and began to drain Anna, and the man holding Lia.

As soon as I did, their grip on my team members loosened, allowing both Gerell and Lia to break free. Anna fell to her knees, and Gerell snatched the knife from her, at the same time that Lia elbowed the dude holding her, and grabbed that knife as well.

Soon we were all four back to back. "Don't fight them with energy, it only makes them stronger," I said.

"Yeah, figured that out the hard way," Lia answered.

"So, what do we do?" I asked. "We can't leave. Not with thousands of lives on the line."

"I think it's time to call for backup," she said, but before she could move, a loud boom sounded, and something ripped at my insides, pulling every ounce of strength I had out of me. I dropped to the ground, and the rest of my team did as well, looking as pained as I felt.

My whole body was loose and uneven. I felt as if all of my internal organs had stopped working, and then a face loomed over me and called my name.

I looked up into the eyes of a person I thought I'd never see again, and the victorious grin on that evil face made what was left of my insides want to curl up and die. "Hello, Kerry. I think we've got some catching up to do."

7

When I came to, I found myself in a sitting position, something tight around both my arms. My mouth felt dry, and my skin icky and wet. My eyes were bleary, but slowly everything came into focus. I was at a dinner table, with a mountain of food in front of me.

To my right, I could see Lia, Gerell, and Lincoln. To my left was Andrew. They each had thick metal bracelets around their arms, and I looked down and noticed that I did as well. "What... is... this," I asked, my words sluggish and groggy.

From what I could tell, we were in a dining hall of some sorts. The place was huge. Black carpet-like material lined the walls, while the floors were plain granite.

Guards in red and blue uniforms stood in front of and behind us, letting me know that it wouldn't be easy to break out of here. They had large fat sticks in their hands that seemed to glow with energy, and I shivered, thinking of what those things would do if they hit one of us.

The dinner table could probably fit fifty, and the feast laid before us stretched the entire length. Behind me I saw men and women, from many different worlds laying around, sitting about, and basically chilling.

One woman with silver hair and a light silver face had gills on her neck and was busy reading on an electronic reading device. Every couple of minutes she would smile and laugh as she turned the page.

A man with red hair sat watching TV, his six eyes paying rapid attention to the screen. Another man with black hair sat beside him, a mobile tray in front of him, hard at work on what I thought was a model car.

Another woman with short dark hair sat on the floor playing with a small brown animal that looked like a cross between a dog and a small cat.

I turned back around as the awful voice that I'd been dreading called my name. "You know, I feel as if you already belong to me," Charles said. His black hair hung loosely at his shoulders. He was as tall as I remembered and still muscular and well built, with orange-blue eyes that bored into mine.

"You don't own me," I choked out, all the hurt and anger from that blasted ball coming back in a rush. Especially since this was the man Ed and Renee had tried so hard to auction me off to. "You don't own me," I repeated through gritted and slurred teeth.

He picked up a glass of something purple and took a delicate sip. "I'm not the monster you make me out to be, Kerry." He said my name as if we were old acquaintances, and that only served to piss me off more.

He sliced off a piece of meat, steak from what I could tell, and carefully placed it in his mouth, closing his eyes to savor the flavor. "Hmm," he said, wiping his lips with a nearby napkin. "This is most excellent. Eat your food." He pointed to the plate in front of me. It was piled high with a little of everything, and my stomach went queasy at the sight of it. "It'll build up your energy."

"Which is what you need, and the reason you tried to buy me in the first place," I guessed.

He smiled as he cut into another piece of meat. "I need it to live. Just as you need food to survive."

"What about the rest of them?" I asked. "Morgan? Anna? James?"

"All natives of Lakvec need energy to survive, no different from me." He took another sip of his drink and then set the glass aside. "Tell me, Kerry, why is it okay for you to eat the cow placed before you, something that offers you nutrition and keeps you alive, and it's not okay for me to do the same? Would you rather we just die out? My whole world, many of whom are children?"

"You can find a different energy source," Lia said, looking like she'd finally got her bearings. "You cannot kidnap people and force them into your service. You can't think that's okay?"

His brows rose in a way that said he was truly offended. "Most of these people I bought from Siana. I bid fairly, just as everyone else who was there did. Others our scouters found. Some were living on the streets, others were simply unhappy.

"We offer them a safe, warm place to live, with all the food they can eat, and never-ending entertainment. Whatever they want, whatever they like, I acquire it for them. We are all happy here," he finished, sounding affronted that someone would dare question his motives.

"I was kidnapped and then almost auctioned off. I agreed with none of it. How is that okay?"

He folded his napkin and put it to the side. "I have no knowledge of this. You destroyed Siana, which is where I got most of my people from, and now you sit and judge me for daring to be hungry. Are you really that much of a selfish girl?"

"So, the thousand that go missing every five years is simply your people filling their coffers?" Lia asked.

His grin was worse than a Lion's. "Everyone needs variety, surely you know this. Too long with the same thing and it starts to get boring, predictable, and unexciting." His eyes shifted to the people in the living room. "But they are all happy. No harm has been done to them, and they are welcome to stay as long as they want."

"Then what? You kill them?" I asked. I wouldn't be surprised if the answer was yes, and of course, it would be for their own good.

He pursed his lips. "No. They can leave my house, get a home here on Lakvec, even start a family if they want."

"But they can never go home?" I asked, already knowing the answer.

"None of the people we get have the power to open portals, Kerry, and neither would you if you didn't have your guidtag. Something we, of course, had to take from you. But still, my people are happy and healthy, as you can see for yourself."

"These people are fucking brainwashed," Gerell said, finally coming to life. "You've convinced them that they're happy and they believe you because they have nothing left. You've taken it all."

Charles picked up his fork. "We have an arrangement. Just because you don't like it, doesn't mean it's wrong." He waved a hand at the people in the room behind us. "They have no complaints."

"Yeah, well." Gerell raised his hand to attack, probably figuring we'd gained enough energy back to take Charles and his guards down. Only nothing happened. He blinked, looking a little shocked and tried again. Still nothing.

Telling myself not to panic, I tried something small, like leaving a few sparks on the table. Nothing. My heart started pounding, and I swallowed hard trying to remain grounded. Up until now, I'd thought we were just playing his game to find out enough information to take him down.

The thought that we may actually not be able to leave hadn't crossed my mind. I looked around and realized I had no idea where we were.

The coalition would come for us, but we had to be able to tell them where to look. I was more than sure he'd probably disabled our coms, and our GPS tracking devices before we even left Morgan's. "Shit," I said under my breath.

I looked to Charles, who had a sly grin on his face. He seemed to be enjoying himself immensely. "What did you do?" I asked through gritted teeth.

He took in a forkful of some green leafy vegetable and smiled. "The silver cuffs on your wrist are called nullers. They stop you from accessing your powers. This is not needed in those who come willingly, but with you five I think you'll be wearing those for a while yet. Now eat, build up your energy. That is after all why you're here."

He waved a hand across the table. "All food here on Lakvec gives the highest amount of energy boost available. Without a good helping of energy, you are no use to me."

At least we now knew why everyone's eyes had lightened when they'd seen us. Because of the powers given to us by the Sianas we were practically a buffet of energy.

Which is probably why we'd been so tired after that first day. Everywhere we went people had no doubt siphoned off a little here and there.

Morgan and Anna had probably had a field day as we had been with them the longest.

Cold fury gripped my heart, and I held a piece of chicken to my mouth and bit into it, tearing the meat off with my teeth and chewing harshly.

Andrew's eyes met mine, and I tried to convey that I was alright and knew what I was doing.

His expression settled, and he cut off a piece of meat and started to eat as well. Catching on, Lia, Lincoln, and Gerell did the same. They wouldn't poison us, not if they wanted to feed from us, and the added energy would do us good when it was time to escape.

Charles had been right. I felt an energy boost after the first bite, and the more I ate, the better I felt.

He watched me, a pleased look in his eyes. "You know, Ed and Renee told me how accommodating you were. I'm happy to see that I was right in choosing you. Keep up in this vein, and in six months or so, you may even see your nuller removed."

I wanted to rip his face off and break every person in here free, and I was going to do it, power, or no power. We would not be going down without a fight.

The coalition had made us train from sun up to sun down for situations just like this one. We'd been taught how to get out of almost any trap, and now I planned on putting those techniques to the test.

I finished the first plate of food and started on another one. All the dishes were plastic as were the silverware. Charles had taken no chance in giving us something that we could use as a weapon.

I guessed he assumed the guards would keep us in line or intimidate us. He couldn't have been more wrong. What he saw as a tool of oppression, I saw as a means of freedom.

I drank down a full cup of the purple liquid. I didn't know what it was, but it tasted like beer mixed with Kool-Aid. No matter the name, it provided energy like nothing else. The smug and satisfied look on Charles's face every time I took a sip, informed me that he really thought he'd have a feast of energy tonight.

Finishing his meal, he pushed his plate aside. "You have plans, I know." He looked at me when he talked. "I'm sure you figure you'll gather your energy and fight your way out of here, but," he waved his hand at the men guarding us. "You have no power, and there are more where they came from. There is nothing for you to do but serve me as you ought, and in exchange, you'll be well taken care off."

My stomach clenched, and the same rage I'd felt at Ed and Renee was now directed at him. He wanted to break us. To have us like the people in the living room, mindless to our own needs and serving his without question.

He thought he owned me because he'd once bid on me at an auction. Now he thought of me as his property, a thing to play with. My hands shook with rage. I'd gotten myself out of this situation before, and I'd be damned if I'd go back.

Charles clasped his hands in front of him, a self-satisfied grin on his face. "You know…"

I jumped up as quick as lightning onto the table. Dishes rattled and shook under my feet, but I didn't care. Kicking the guy in front of me, I snatched his stick and used it to deliver a smack right to Charles's face.

He'd had a chance to siphon some of my energy in the process and had been standing with an outstretched hand when I'd hit him.

When I'd jumped, my team had jumped as well, disabling the men, and taking their sticks. Charles pushed a button on the table, and a loud alarm blasted in our ears. The people in the living room disappeared as more armed men stormed the room.

I tried to hold on, but I was losing strength fast, as Charles seemed to be sucking in as much as he could. I used the stick like I'd been taught in training and hit him in his face three times without pause. I then hit his stomach, side, and finally his legs all in quick succession.

He let out an "ugg," sound as he dropped to the ground, holding his face which was bloodied and bruised.

I came back to the floor, as two of his guards came for me, one on my right, the other on my left. Not even thinking about it, I ducked and quickly moved out of the way, so they would hit each other. I then used my stick to smash them both in the face repeatedly.

They fell to the ground, and I hit the next two as well. Lia was better with the stick than any of us, and she twirled it like a baton, taking down anyone in her path.

Gerell stood on the table, using sticks and legs to defend himself, while Lincoln stood on the floor in front of him, bashing and stopping anyone that came close.

Andrew had three men lying by his feet when he saw me and came to my side, knocking two men back with his stick in the process. "You good?" he asked me.

"Yeah, I'm good."

Charles came shakily to his feet, his hand outstretched as if to take more energy from us. I jumped on the table again, stick in my hand, and flipped through the air, landing behind him. With a speed that I knew came from Siana, I brought the stick to his neck and began to choke him with it.

He struggled, for a bit, his hands waving about, but I waited until he went limp, and I was sure he'd passed out, before letting go.

Lia took out two more men, then reached into her mouth, to the side of her jaw and pulled out a guidtag. I blinked at her, and she shrugged in a way that said, "always be prepared."

Coalition guards must have been on standby since we'd lost contact, because the moment she opened the portal, enough came through to take down Charles's whole house in a matter of seconds.

We told them about the people being held against their

will, and they were gathered up as well. Once things calmed down a bit, I took a seat at the table and poured myself some of the purple liquid, out of one of the only jugs still remaining upright.

Andrew, who had a bruised face, and was missing a shirt, raised an eyebrow at me, but Lia joined me in a cup. "What?" she asked, her face bleeding a little by her cheek, along with scratches and blue marks on her neck.

Lincoln and Gerell also looked haggard and bruised, but not enough that they couldn't give me and Lia wary looks because of the cups in our hands. Lia took a sip of hers, and I gulped mine as well, instantly feeling better.

Lia came to her feet, cup still in hand. "Oh, stop looking at us like we've poisoned the well." She snorted. "This is the quickest way to get our energy back."

Gerell snatched up a cup. "Well then, I guess we can all drink to that."

8

The nuller cuffs were removed the moment we stepped back onto Plex, and I immediately tested my powers, thankful to see that they still worked.

My skin was a little raw at my wrist where the cuffs had bitten into them, but the medics rubbed them down with cream, instantly making them feel better.

We were sent to the decontamination chamber after that and stayed there until we were given the all clear. The events of Lakvec had left me a little rattled. This was my fourth mission now, though the first where I hadn't been under-cover, and I was getting a little better at shaking it off and moving on.

I didn't know if that was a good thing or not, but for the moment, it's where I was.

Charles had tried to break me, the same way that Renee and Ed had, and I'd showed all three that I wasn't as weak as they'd apparently thought me to be.

I felt better now, had more confidence in myself and my actions. Not that I didn't still have moments of doubts which

I saw as a good thing because it helped to ground me and keep me focused.

The coalition searched out other worlds like Lakvecs and found that they had plants, vegetables, and animal meat sources that provided them with tremendous sources of energy.

Upon research, it was discovered that the Lakvec too had this native to their land. Somewhere through the years, they must have decided that it was better to get it from a human source so that's what they'd been doing since.

Anna, Morgan, the four women, and a few others had been found at Morgan's house, still so drained they could barely move. James had been in the process of packing, trying to make his escape. The coalition had had no problem rounding them all up.

Special coalitions within the interplanetary network had been called to help deal with the thousands of people who had been held there over the years. Like they'd done with us, they were offered help in getting set up back on their home worlds, and any aid and assistance they may need, at the expense of the Lakvec, of course.

Charles had been taken into custody. He'd slipped away before the coalition could get him back on Siana, but he wasn't going anywhere now.

He still insisted that he'd done nothing wrong, but the only person listening to him now was himself.

I wiped my hands on the dishtowel thrown over my shoulder and put it aside. We were at the guys house, Lia and me, and I'd decided to show them all how to make lasagna.

"You know these come precut, right?" Gerell said, slicing onions, tears running down his face.

I smiled and continued chopping the fresh parsley and basil, something I refused to eat spaghetti or lasagna without.

"Okay, set the pot to boil," I told Lia, who was in charge of the noodles.

Gerell finished the onions, and started on the green peppers, while Lincoln smashed and chopped up the garlic. "Why do we have to go through all this?" Gerell asked, still complaining. "We can get sauce in a jar."

Andrew lit a pan on low and looked at the other man. "You know, I've come to the conclusion that you're not happy unless you have something to complain about."

"Just put a *little* olive oil in," I warned Andrew.

Lincoln picked up the red bottle of wine I'd picked out. "Eating processed foods will kill you quicker than anything else, you should be happy to eat healthy for a change."

Gerell snorted. "This is not healthy."

Lincoln would not be deterred. "If you calculate…"

"No one's calculating anything," Lia said, placing the top on the pot of water to bring it to a boil faster. "I swear, you two." She shook her head, but in a good-humored sort of way.

Andrew had the bottle of olive oil gripped tightly in his hand as he pointed it at his brother. "And you, you're too pessimistic, about everything."

Lincoln looked truly shocked. "I mean, I don't know how you came to that conclusion, Andrew. I'm one of the most upbeat people I know." He looked at Gerell. "Isn't that right?"

Gerell carefully kept his head down, still chopping. After a few seconds, he turned to Lincoln with a smile. "If you say so, Linc," he answered, before leaning over for a quick kiss.

Once the food was done, we all settled in front of the TV to look at some new movie that had just come to Plex.

Andrew and I sat together on the couch. Lia sat in the

recliner, and Gerell and Lincoln huddled together on the floor.

"This is pretty good," Andrew said after taking his fifth mouthful.

"Yeah, nowhere near as toxic as I thought it would be when you first told us about it," Lincoln said.

Lia rolled her eyes, and Gerell just kept eating like he hadn't heard anything at all.

I looked at them and smiled, feeling happy, safe, and more than ready to take on our next challenge.

A CURSED SUCCUBUS

1

"You know they're following us, right?" Ninia asked.

I downed my shot of curltoe and smiled. This was the third bar we'd been to tonight, and the third time we'd seen the two guys.

One was a snake, tall with black hair and green eyes. He looked like he could take on about ten opponents at once and not break a sweat. The other was wolf, also tall, with red hair and yellow eyes. He had that shifty look about him that made you want to take your drink with you when you got up to use the bathroom. They sat halfway in the back now, pretending to watch a turtle wrestling match on the TV.

"Yeah, well, got a woman sitting a few tables up, she's been on our tails tonight too." The woman was a phoenix of average height. Her eyes were green and her black hair was in a ponytail down her back.

She looked like she'd ripped your face off if you tried to sit beside her and most kept their distance. Right now, she was playing with her phone, checking out the menu, and doing everything she could to keep from looking our way.

The sports bar we were in had big screen TVs lined up on

the wall every few inches, so that no matter where a customer sat, they had a good view. The bar was in the middle of the floor, with plenty of tables and chairs surrounding it. Another bar was outside, and people played games of horseshoes and name the power out there.

It was noisy, so much so that the owners kept the TVs on mute because no one could hear them anyway. The place smelled of alcohol, burgers, and wings, which is what most people ordered when they came here.

Still, it was a nice atmosphere, which usually put me at ease after I'd had a rough day hunting down murderers and thieves. I worked for the government agency Skit, as did Ninia. Our job was stopping mystical beings like ourselves from intruding on the human population. Something the First Families took very seriously.

The First Families were those whose iron fist had ruled us since the beginning of all things. Each country had them, and all laws that governed the magical community went through them.

On a whim, they could sink you into despair or favor you with wealth and prosperity. Their word was final, and no one dared to challenge them.

Ninia set her drink down on the bar. "Peeped out that phoenix some time ago. What do you think this is about?"

I was about to answer when two bears walked up. Both tall, one with a mustache and curly brown hair, the other with a close cut. They were both medium-built and looked to be in their late thirties, early forties.

"You drink that shit?" the one with the mustache asked, pointing to our curltoe drinks.

Curltoe was a hundred times more potent than moonshine, or what those around here called bootleg. Humans couldn't drink it. It would either kill them or drive them completely insane.

In rare cases when it didn't, it still kept them inebriated for more than a week. A lot of magical folks were wary of it too, and with good reason.

I signaled the bartender for another. "Drink it every chance I get."

They smiled, and I looked to Ninia, who raised a brow, which usually meant she was down for whatever.

See that's the thing about Succubi, we needed sex every night, no exceptions. We couldn't think or function properly without it and if we went too long, our bodies would start to break down until there was nothing left.

Since all of our normal partners were off limits for the next couple of days, these bears would do very nicely.

Lin and Boya were the two men in my life. Lin was an incubus, while Boya was a dranghum, which meant he was descended from dragons. All three of us loved hard together and apart. The thing was, I didn't want to wear Boya out. Sometimes I felt as if he needed a break from me.

On the other hand, Lin and I could only be intimate once a month. Sex between Incubi and Succubi was too damn destabilizing if it happened more than that. Two high voltage entities coming together often canceled each other out, that was the case with Lin and me.

Lin and Boya were agents as well, Boya being my partner. Ninia was partners with Steva, who had black panther DNA. She usually satisfied herself with him or with her sometimes partner Iscca, who like Boya, was also a dranghum.

All of us lived together, along with twenty other agents. That in itself was an experience.

"What do your plans look like tonight?" Ninia asked. We didn't need to flirt or be coy, these guys knew we were Succubi, and most likely knew exactly what we wanted from them.

"Whatever you want," the one without the close-cut said, positioning himself in front of me.

My pulse quickened with thoughts of later. Bears had an excellent sense of smell, which made them wonderful lovers. You couldn't hide your desires from them, and sometimes they knew what you wanted even before you did. I motioned him closer at the same time my damn phone started to ring.

The name that popped up had me groaning. "Hello, Chief." I looked to Ninia and rolled my eyes. She looked amused but didn't say anything. "Need you and Ninia to wrap up a case," the chief said.

"Do you know where Ninia is?" I asked cautiously. I didn't want to ruin her fun if I didn't have to. No reason we should both be pulled away.

The chief's voice was chastising. "Boya already told me you two were together. We don't have time for games, Kia."

I sighed and promised to give my partner an extra hard thumping once I got home. "What do we have?"

I was listening to the Chief when I heard Ninia's voice in my head. *Is that the chief?*

Yes.

Shit.

Tell me about it.

"Private residence. The owners, Mr. and Mrs. Harris just called in an attack. Couple of teenagers with yellow glowing eyes. Might be Misha and Mitch, didn't want to bring Lin in on this either way." Everything in me stopped for a minute.

Misha and Mitch were twenty-year-old twins and for two years, Lin had dated their father Kevin. He'd broken up with him a few years ago, but he'd never fully detangled himself from the twins.

He loved them and only wanted what was best where they were concerned. They were from a Samg family. Samgs were human families who'd aided and supported the supernatural community for thousands of years and were paid handsomely for their help.

The twins had gotten involved with Rome, an incubus who also had absorber powers. This power was rare, but it basically meant he could take powers from any being and transfer it to another, shaping up his own Frankenstein.

He'd waged war against the First Families and used the twins to help carry out his plan by infusing them with a lot of power their bodies had never been meant to handle.

We'd stopped them, for now anyway, but the twins had left with him the night it'd all gone down and been missing for the last three months. We'd had no idea where they were or if they were even okay, and Lin had just about gone out of his mind with worry. I couldn't wait to let him know that they were at least alive.

"Well, I'm not keeping it from him, chief. You should know better than that. Lin and I don't have secrets."

His voice said he expected as much but still didn't like it. "At least find out what's going on before you go running your mouth. Now take down the address."

I keyed the location into my phone, now anxious to get there and pick up any sign of the twins that I could. I might not have been as close to them as Lin, but I still cared about them and their safety mattered to me.

I turned to my new friend. "Catch up with you guys later?"

He held out his hand, and I placed my phone in it. He keyed his number in and gave it back. "Call us when you're done. We'll be here."

The air was a little frigid and hit us the moment we stepped out the door. There was a light drizzle, so we walked as quickly as we could to get to the car.

Ninia opened the passenger door and got in. "As always he has impeccable timing." Her voice held a scold, and I couldn't help but agree. The chief was a grade A blocker when it came to us satisfying our succubus needs.

I turned over the engine and pointed the car toward the address in Spray Town. "It was just an attack. Hopefully, we can take their statements and be done with it." I was trying to be optimistic, but I think we both knew the night was shot.

The house was a modest blue clapboard that sat in one of the most rundown parts of town. Not violent, but it wasn't overly friendly either. On the wooden porch steps was a woman of frog descent and a man of turtle.

They sat huddled together, the man wiping sweat from his face and the woman smoking on a raw. Raw were what some mystical creatures used to get high. I didn't use it myself, but I did know a few agents who did.

It was legal, so that wasn't a problem, but just like curltoe, it was a little too potent to be allowed in Morse town where most of the humans lived.

"Want to tell us what went on here?" Ninia asked as we walked up.

The woman, Mrs. Harris, I presumed, took a long drag off her smoke and then pushed green hair out of her face. "A boy and girl looked to be about nineteen or so. They both had the same type black hair and yellow eyes, probably could pass for brother and sister. Might've been for all we know."

Ninia and I locked eyes for a minute because that did sound a lot like Misha and Mitch. I licked my lips, wondering if this was their way of reaching out to us. "Do you know what they wanted?"

Mr. Harris shook his head. "They just barged in and tore the place apart. Didn't say much, just tossed us across the room every time we tried to move."

I blinked. Were they looking for something or trying to get my, or Lin's attention? The fact that they had yellow eyes meant they were still under Rome's spell. Which meant I couldn't be sure of anything they did. Rome kept his people on a tight leash, especially Mitch and Misha.

"Do you know what they were looking for?" I asked, hoping to gain some type of insight into what the twins had been thinking. That is if it even was them.

The woman wiped tears from her face and lay her head on her husband's shoulder. "No, but for the last couple of days, we've been feeling like we're being watched, you know?" I looked up at the two rocking chairs on the porch and the small table that sat between them. The furniture looked freshly painted and the porch though wood, was sturdy and strong.

These people took pride in their home, and someone had invaded that, invaded them. It pissed me off every time I dealt with a case like this, but I had to remember that the twins were not themselves. Rome had infected them, put them under his incubus spell and then hit them with so much power that at this point they probably didn't even remember their own names.

"Know what they might want with you?" Whether they'd been watched or not was anybody's guess. Sometimes in cases like this, the paranoia took over, and we had to weed through what was real and what was imagined.

"Nah," the man answered, his voice a little broken. "We don't know nothing. We don't ever bother nobody. Ain't got no problems. Everyone on this street, we all get along great."

I sighed and walked past them and up the steps. "Mine if we take a look inside?"

Mrs. Harris waved an approving hand toward the door and Ninia and I went in and spread out. The home only had one level, so she took the front of the house, and I took the back. The place had been ransacked as if the perpetrators had been in a hurry to find whatever it was they were looking for.

I kicked a throw pillow out of my way and wondered just what Rome was up to now.

It had been three months since the incident at the warehouses and still no sign of him. The First Families had put their best skills to finding him. The fact that they hadn't, spoke to his abilities and foresight.

The back door had been left swinging open, and I wondered if the intruders had entered or exited this way. I walked out, aiming to search the backyard, but as soon as my feet hit the porch, the tattoo on the side of my neck that identified me as a member of one of the First Families lit up and began to buzz. I could see a golden glow from the side of my eye, and the buzz was something that ricocheted through my whole body.

I felt a tingling sensation, then my blood began to pound as if something or someone were trying to break free. I swallowed hard and tried not to panic, but the truth was I was scared.

This was... I'd never felt anything like it before, and for a moment I wondered if I was being singled out by the First Families. But no, something was pulling me, calling me to the back of the yard, over by the fence.

I walked as if in a trance, my feet seeming to have a mind of their own. Once I'd went about five feet, I dropped to the ground and begin to dig.

Doing it with my hands was taking too long, so I used telekinesis to clear the dirt away until I'd made a small hole. Inside of it was a medium silver baton.

The glow from it matched my neck, and without thinking, I reached out and picked it up. It was hot to the touch, and once I grabbed it, I couldn't let go.

The buzz sounded even louder now, as something blazed from the baton and onto my skin, burrowing underneath. I let out a quick breath of air, as confusion clouded my mind. Something was inside me, and I had no idea what it was.

My heart sped to triple time as my whole body lit up with that same golden light. I didn't have time to think or wonder before I heard a long wailing banshee cry. It was excruciatingly loud and sent pain rippling through me. I dropped to my knees and heard the sweet intoxicating song of a siren.

The sound tormented my ears, calling me to it, and I held up my hands reaching out, only to see fire shoot from my palms, no different than Boya's and Iscca's.

I tried to call for help, but my tongue was thick, the sound dying in my throat. Then I heard both the scream of the banshee and the song of the siren, and my heart started to pound even more as something in me shattered and broke.

I couldn't close my ears, couldn't drown them out, and I was sure I'd go crazy if it didn't stop soon. Fire engulfed me and raised me in the air. I shivered, fear marking my every feature. I didn't know what was happening to me and my thin grip on reality was steadily slipping. I didn't know how much longer I could hold on.

Ninia! I mentally screamed and prayed I still had enough power to reach out to her.

After only a few seconds, the back door flew open and she came running out, phone gripped tightly in her palm. Something in me calmed a bit at the sight of her. Ninia would know what to do. I was sure of it. "I'm calling Lin, Boya, and the chief." Her hands shook as she tried to punch in the numbers.

I had to stop her. I didn't want anyone else getting hurt. *No! Just the boss, at least until we find out what this is.*

She nodded, and I closed my eyes as all signs of the banshee, siren, and dragon disappeared. Relief shuddered through me, and slowly I came back to the ground.

I used a shaky hand to wipe sweat from my brow, but still managed to hold on to the rod.

"Ninia." I gasped, my mind replaying what had just happened. "I think I just found the fifth soulbar."

She slowly lowered the phone from her ear and then turned to me dread written all over her face. She looked at the item in my hand and frowned. "You didn't… You touched it!" Her voice took on a slightly panicked tone. "Kia… Shit."

"Touched what?" I could hear the chief from the other end of the phone.

"The fifth soulbar. Kia just found it." She sounded and looked as dazed as I felt.

The chief let out a strong intake of breath, and then his words became heavy and rushed. "Don't touch it! Find something made of silk and frog's spit to wrap it in. I'm calling the first families. Don't move from that spot until you hear back from me!"

Ninia swallowed hard. "Okay, Chief." She hung up the phone and turned to me. "What the fuck are we going to do?"

I couldn't answer. I didn't know what to say. My pulse raced with well-founded fear as I thought of what the First Families would do to me once they found out I'd touched it.

The fifth soulbar had been hidden for centuries. The other four rested with the First Families and were the source of their enormous power. All four bars were unique, yet had some of the same characteristics. Each held the cry of the banshee, the song of the siren, the sex of the succubus, the fire of the dragon and so on.

My body wasn't meant to hold such power, yet the fact that I had First Family blood meant that the rod hadn't known any better. There was a ceremony to go through, and a body had to be made ready before taking on such power.

I bit my bottom lip until I tasted blood. I'd fucked up good this time. The damn thing had called out to me, and I'd answered. My mind worked in rapid fire speed trying to find a solution.

There had to be some way I could get this power out of me before the First Families found out, because if they knew they'd probably kill me and take the power as their own.

Ninia paced back and forth, biting on a thumbnail, as she too tried to see a way out of this. Her phone rang, causing a slight jump before she answered. "Chief," she mouthed to me before saying, "hello."

She listened for a minute, her face unreadable. When she hung up, I saw the trepidation in her eyes before she said a word. "Riverwalk has a special guest. One who'll be there for two more days. Until then the place is on lockdown, and no one is allowed in or out. Thursday evening at six, you're to take the soulbar there. You are not to let it out of your sight until then. If you do, then you will be killed. If any harm comes to the soulbar while in your possession, you will be killed."

She stopped for a moment giving me time to process. "If you touch the soulbar, either accidentally or intentionally you will be killed." She closed her eyes slowly. Then opened them wide, a determined look on her face. "No! I rebuke that. I send that shit back to the ethers." She stopped talking for a minute and seemed to be concentrating. When she spoke again, I could tell from the slight grin on her face that she'd come up with something. "We'll go see Drem. He can fix this, he knows how to fix everything."

Hope rose in my chest like a beacon, my lips trying their best to turn up into a smile. Drem was a wizard and had charms and spells for just about any situation. He didn't come cheap though, and money wasn't his number one currency. Still, as long as I stayed breathing, it didn't matter.

"Okay," I said, still cautious that it could go all wrong. "Let's go see Drem."

She held up a finger. "First." She reached out, using her powers to call something to her. I didn't know what until a silk scarf flew into her hand. "Guy three houses down likes to be blindfolded in the bedroom." She reached back toward the Harris house, and soon frog spit covered the silk. She handed it over to me. "Wrap it up and conceal it. We'll go see Drem now."

Fingers trembling, I took the scarf from her and folded the baton up in the silk that would neutralize it, while enzymes in the frog spit trapped the power inside the soulbar until it was ready to be used.

Once it was covered completely, I stuffed it into the waist of my pants for safe keeping.

I'd only walked about two feet when fire shot out of my mouth, burning the bushes in the backyard and the side of the Harris's house. I tried to close my mouth, but the flame forced it open, laying waste to everything in sight. Smoke filtered up my throat and out of my ears and mouth. It tasted like charcoal hot dogs left on the grill too long.

Ninia ran to where the water hose lay in the yard, searching desperately for the spigot.

The flame died out and once again the banshee took over. I fell to my knees and tried to cover my ears as a sound worse than a hundred scratched chalkboards overloaded my system. Blood leaked from my ears and nose, and I figured if I had to listen to that damn scream one more time, I'd rip my own vocal cords out.

Ninia fell to one knee as the call of the banshee grew louder. She put her hands to her ears but quickly took them down once the Harris's house began to flame. She struggled with keeping the hose in her hand while fighting off the howl of the banshee.

It stopped as quickly as it'd started and when I sat up, I saw both Harrises getting off the ground. Apparently, they'd been affected as well. I saw Mrs. Harris call for help. While Mr. Harris took the hose from Ninia and began putting the fire out.

Ninia explained that the department would pay for the damages as I took my time coming to my feet. I was almost scared to breathe since I wasn't sure what activated the small bit of soulbar power inside me. I didn't think I could go through it all again. So, I'd try my best to stay calm and not overload my system.

Once steady on my feet, I stood in a daze watching the fire die out around me. I would have helped, but I was too scared of what would happen if I tried.

Ninia's voice was soft in my ear as she wrapped an arm around my waist. "Come on. Let's get you to the car."

I held onto her, afraid I'd completely implode if I didn't.

She eased me gingerly onto the passenger side and buckled my seat belt for me. "Stay right here, I'm going to finish up with the Harris's, and I'll be right back."

I lay back in my seat and tried to shake the fuzziness from my brain. I don't remember Ninia coming back to the car, but at some point, I became aware that we were moving. I felt hungover, like I hadn't had sex in a month and barely had the power to stand. If this was what it took to rule as a member of a first family, then those in Riverwalk could have it.

I wanted nothing to do with that shit.

Ninia kept up a steady chatter, but I was only able to make out a word here or there. She was trying. I'd give her that.

We drove for about ten minutes before I started to feel better. The haze lifted like a blanket, and suddenly things were clear again.

Ninia turned down a private driveway, leading to a single

house. It was surrounded by acres of land and set miles back from the highway.

I looked around, wondering what a wizard needed with so much land, then remembered that Drem liked excess and space, lots of space.

The driveway was long and curved at unexpected angles, making it feel as if we were in bumper cars.

Ninia pulled to the front of the house and parked. "Wait right here. I'll go and see if he's home."

I shook my head. It was my fate on the line here. I wouldn't let her do all the work. "No. No. I can go. I'll be okay. I feel... I feel better now."

I got out and was able to stand on my own, which was at least a little improvement.

She still looked doubtful but nodded anyway. "Okay."

The house was one of Drem's creations, and it was said that he'd built it with a magic potion, a spell, and the wave of his hand. I grimaced looking at the huge thing, thinking he'd probably started that rumor himself.

It was said to have over three hundred rooms, ten kitchens and so many tunnels and secret hideouts that even Drem himself forgot some of them.

The steps leading up to the front door numbered well over two hundred, and the house itself was made out of adobe. It was blue and orange and almost looked like something a child would create out of dough and clay.

Not wanting to waste time walking, we simply floated to the top.

Whelm, a man of about four feet, with a large head, and eyes that would look more at home on a lizard, was on the porch the moment we landed. "Looking for Drem?" he asked before either of us could say a word.

Ninia strained her neck trying to see past him and into

the house. "It's urgent." I could read the nervousness on her, and that was making me jumpy as well.

Ninia usually kept a cool head, so if she was worried, then I was double worried. She closed her eyes, and I did the same, both of us searching for Drem's unique energy signal. "He's not here," she finally announced, putting words to what I, myself had just figured out.

Whelm shook his head. "He has business with the First Families. He'll be back in two days." Then he disappeared right in front of us, not saying another word.

"Great," I said, feeling liked I'd just been sucker punched. The First Families had said they had a guest, but somehow, I didn't think they'd meant Drem. As I thought about it, I realized they'd probably meant someone else, as Drem was there all the time.

"Two days is when you have to take the soulbar in," Ninia said as we touched down in front of the car. "Maybe he'll finish early and come home," she reasoned. I didn't believe it, and she probably didn't either. Neither of us wanted to face the truth, that I was probably fucked three ways from Sunday.

We'd ridden halfway down the driveway when my phone rang. I looked at the name and felt a cold chill go over me as I cautiously brought it to my ear. "Hel... Hello," I said, hating the way my voice quivered when I spoke.

"Kia." My grandmother's cool voice echoed over the phone. "You have recovered the fifth soulbar." She paused as if she was telling me something I didn't know and was giving me time to let it sink in. "You do your family here in River-walk proud tonight."

I sucked in a hard breath and tried to stop my hand from trembling. She was proud? Of me? I didn't even know what that meant. It was something I'd never experienced before, and I wasn't sure I trusted it now.

Her silken voice broke me out of my reverie. "You do your bloodline proud, my child, Kia. This has positive ramifications for us all."

I gripped the phone tight, not sure if she'd included my mother in that or not. I wanted to ask, but dared not. I didn't see or talk to my mother often, and I told myself that that was okay. That I was okay with it. She had to know, though. If my grandmother was calling me, surely, she'd called my mom first and told her.

"Your mother sends her regards," she said as if reading my mind. "She's as proud of you as I am."

I took in a ragged breath, refusing to give in to the tears. They were proud of me? It was hard to believe, and thinking about how bad I'd messed up by touching the soulbar, I knew it wouldn't last long.

The line clicked while I was still thinking, and I slowly put the phone down, not sure what to make of the conversation. My family were a sore subject for me, and I tried not to think about them if I didn't have to.

Ninia kept her eyes on the road, but reached out and laced her fingers with mine. Energy flowed from her to me as she offered what comfort she could.

Grateful for the effort, I gave her hand a tight squeeze, and stared out the window, thinking about my grandmother's call. Maybe this could have been the start of something for us. Maybe we could have started to heal the relationship that had been broken years ago, only...

Rage clouded my eyes, and I held my other hand tight in my lap to keep from lashing out. If only I hadn't touched the damn soulbar! If only I'd truly earned the respect they were now throwing my way. This, this right here would only make things a hundred times worse between us. No way it couldn't.

By the time we reached the end of Drem's three-mile driveway, I'd had time to collect myself.

We made a turn to get back on the highway and saw three figures blocking our way.

"Great," Ninia said, sounding as tired as I felt.

We got out to see what the problem was and I couldn't say I was surprised to see that it was the two men and woman who'd been following us back at the bar.

Ninia flexed her hands, and her unique succubus scent filled the air. Oh? So, she wanted to play it like that? I held out my hands and released my pheromones.

The smell drifted over to our would-be attackers, and I could tell from the droop of their eyes to the silly smile on their faces, the moment they fell prey.

Ninia rapidly changed appearances, representing what each of them desired the most sexually and imprinting it in their mind. "Why have you been following us?" she asked playfully as if she was telling a dirty joke and wanted to be coy about it.

I reached into their darkest fantasies, and presented myself as a redhead, with glowing green eyes for the one with snake DNA.

His long tongue flicked back and forward and his eyes glazed over with love and admiration.

"What do you want," I asked, as softly as one would a familiar lover.

He flicked his tongue even more, and I wondered if he'd lost the ability to speak.

Ninia had the phoenix and wolf on their knees. The phoenix had her feathers spread out, while the wolf bared his neck.

Ninia looked like herself again, but they still saw that which they desired the most. "Tell me why you're following us?" she said as if asking them if they wanted a back rub.

Keeping his neck available, the wolf was the first to answer. "To get the soulbar. Rome needs it."

I closed my eyes, wishing he hadn't said that name. Rome was hell to deal with, and in my current state, I wasn't sure I could.

Ninia cursed under her breath, and I figured she was thinking the same thing. Rome had been quiet for too long, and we shouldn't have been surprised that he'd resurfaced. I just wished he hadn't dragged the twins into this. "Where is he?" Ninia asked.

Heat roared through my body, and before he could answer, I fell to my knees, a banshee scream erupting from my lips.

The bloodcurdling sound dropped everyone to the ground including our would-be attackers.

My throat felt like it had been raked over burning hot coals for a week. My neck muscles stretched in ways they were never meant to, and the pain from that left me reeling.

Gratefully it didn't last as long this time and once I stopped screaming the others came quickly to their feet.

I tried to get up too, but suddenly my body felt as if it'd lost all density. I slithered on the ground like a snake, then hissed, and stuck out a long forked tongue, that hadn't been there before.

My eyes only saw street and concrete, but I could hear talking from above.

"She has the power of the soulbar," the phoenix said as I continued to slither around.

"Rome won't like this," the snake sounded anxious.

"She touched it," said the gravelly voice of the wolf. "She touched it and…"

He didn't finish his sentence. The next thing I heard was a growl, and then Ninia was on the ground. I couldn't see her clearly, but the scent of blood exploded through the air, and I knew she'd been hurt.

My body began to shake again, and this time I could feel wings start to form on my back, the wings of a phoenix no doubt.

"Get it now while they're both down," the snake shouted.

I tried to move, but the wings were still forming, making my body rigid and unyielding. I couldn't lose the soulbar. If I did, I was dead. I knew that with absolute certainty.

I tried to fight it as the wolf's eyes zeroed in on the indent of my pants where I'd placed the soulbar. He smiled in victory, and my heart shuddered as I realized I was about to lose everything.

He turned to his friends, his tone sharp and hard. "Bring me the cloth." Within seconds, the snake handed him a silk cloth, dripping in frog spit. He wrapped it around his hand and as easy as popping the top on a soda can, reached down and plucked the soulbar from my possession.

Inwardly I screamed, but outwardly there was nothing I could do. Something in me died in that moment, and the fact that I couldn't move, couldn't cry out, left me feeling useless and alone.

The wolf's eyes flashed bright yellow, and he smiled at me. "Pleasure doing business with you, ma'am," he said as he and his crew got in their car and drove away.

I watched helplessly as they disappeared down the road, my body once again twisting and turning. This time I ended up on all fours, a howl escaping from my lips as the call of the wolf ripped from my throat. "Lin!" I mentally called out as my vision began to blur and I felt myself getting light-headed. "Lin!"

2

The first thing I noticed upon waking, was that I was not alone. Familiar voices filled the air, and the smell of coffee and honey had me opening my eyes wide.

I took a deep breath because it smelled like home and there was no other place I wanted to be at the moment. I relaxed back on the couch, glad I wasn't alone. Thinking about it, I realized I'd been set up and the twins had been the bait.

Rome must have figured out the soulbar was there. He had bet on me taking the case because of the personal connection with Mitch and Misha. Who else would the chief give it to? Certainly not Lin who was too close to the whole thing.

No, it had to be me, and Rome had known that. He couldn't get the soulbar himself because it would only reveal itself to a member of one of the First Families. He could have dug in that same spot for days and never found it.

Still, once it had been unearthed, it was anyone's game. I looked up, figuring the others had probably already figured this out.

Boya and Lin stood in front of the TV, caught in a conversation that had Lin's brows furrowed, and Boya using a lot of hand gestures. It looked serious, and I wondered if it was about the soulbar.

Lin was a tall man with light brown skin. He wore a shaved head and his broad chest and clearly defined muscles made it clear that he worked out daily.

At five feet eight, Boya wasn't short, but he wasn't as tall as Lin's six feet three either. Boya had brown hair, that reached just below his chin, and it was curly enough, without being too curly, but still thick and full. Also, he was pale in the winter and sported a nice tan in the summer.

Ninia sat on the opposite couch from me. Her skin was a little darker than mine. Where I was a shade beyond walnut, she was a more beautiful ebony. She stood about five feet seven and her short spiked red hair, perfectly complimented the red in her eyes.

Right now, her shirt was ripped at her belly, and an angry wound was slowly closing. Steva sat beside her holding her hand. Steva was about the same complexion as me. He had jet black hair and emerald green eyes and stood about five feet nine.

Iscca rested in the recliner, looking around, his green eyes going wide, once he noticed I was awake. Iscca was about five feet even, and had the same skin tones as Boya.

His hair was black, but he kept it bald so you couldn't tell. He wore earrings in his nose that he liked to change out every few days. "I don't even know what to call you now." He grinned at me.

When I didn't smile back, he cleared his throat in a self-chastising way. "I know, too soon." He still had a big grin on his face, though.

I was saved from saying anything as the others in the room began to crowd around me. I pressed back into the couch and noticed that my phoenix wings were now gone. I stuck out my tongue and saw that it too was back to normal. "How did we get here?" I asked Ninia.

"You called me," Lin said, his voice low and throaty as he looked down at me. "Sensed out where you were at and we came for you."

I nodded my thanks as Steva handed me a cup of coffee. I took a sip, thinking this was exactly what I needed. The flavor was sweet with just a tinge of bitter, and it caused a relaxing warmness to spread through me. "How much do you know?"

"Ninia filled us in," Lin answered. "Rome used you and the twins to get the soulbar."

I nodded, glad I didn't have to explain. To give them a better idea of what we were up against, I changed my appearance to look like that of the phoenix, then the wolf, then the snake. "This is who we're looking for, but they're working for Rome."

"Ninia already showed us," Iscca said. "But good of you to reinforce."

Steva growled at him. "Shut up, Iscca."

Iscca let out a pouting breath of air. "Just trying to lighten the mood so it's not all doom and gloom."

Boya sat down beside me and laced his hand with mine. I smiled at him, glad for the comfort. "Well, the mood could use a little lightening. I'm just saying."

Steva looked from Boya to Iscca. "See, this is why you two are not allowed to work together."

Lin's eyes crinkled, and his lips turned up into a smile when he heard me laugh. "It's a welcoming sound," he said, staring at me. I squeezed Boya's hand harder and stared back at Lin, completely opening myself to him, letting him see all that had happened.

"Okay," Ninia said, throwing her hands in the air. "Later

for that. Right now, we need to figure out how to get the soulbar back and how to keep the First Families from finding out it was ever missing."

The First Families. My chest tightened as I thought of how my grandmother had sounded on the phone. She'd said that she was proud of me, that my mother was proud of me. I let out a weary breath. I didn't even know such a thing was possible, me gaining their approval. I still wasn't sure I had.

My gut twisted and I could see the look on their faces when they discovered I'd lost the soulbar. Suddenly the only thing I wanted was to be left alone. I removed my hand from Boya's and stood.

From behind me, warm hands wrapped around my waist and lifted me bridal style. Lin, he felt familiar and right, and if I could've disappeared into his chest, I would have.

He didn't say anything, just carried me up the steps and into his room, placing me on the bed.

I fell back on the sheets, glad to be away from the others. I needed…time.

Lin straddled my hips, sliding warm fingers across my face. "I know you're hurt." He sighed and shook his head. "I don't want to diminish that. Parental approval, we all crave it." He looked at me, his eyes saying he'd do anything to take my pain away. I blinked rapidly trying to stop the tears from falling.

He used the tip of his thumb and swiped them to the side. "I'll always love you." He leaned down and kissed my tears away. I sighed deeply, loving his touch. "It's not the same. I know that." He kissed me again. "You can't change them, and you don't need to change. Perfect the way you are. Any change has to be because you want it, not to please someone whose love you'll probably never have. Don't twist yourself into knots like that, Kia."

I nodded, wishing like hell we could be together tonight

and not have to wait weeks for what came naturally to both of us. "You always know what to say." He got off me and I pulled the covers up and snuggled into them. Hey, just because we couldn't have sex, didn't mean we couldn't sleep in the same bed.

Still on his knees in front of me, Lin smiled and then pointed his head toward the door. I bit my bottom lip trying to hold in a grin. Boya was out there... waiting. I knew he just wanted to make sure I was alright, but he'd probably stay out there all night if we didn't say anything.

"Let him in," I said.

Len waved his hand, flying the door open. Boya sat on the floor, arms wrapped around his legs, rocking back and forth. He jumped up when he heard the hinges squeak, an unsure look on his face. Len held his hand out, and Boya hurried in, shutting the door behind him.

"Okay?" he asked me, a small bit of smoke coming from his nose and mouth.

It had been a long day, and right now I was just tired. "Let's talk about it tomorrow."

He smiled, and climbed into the bed, giving Lin a kiss as he did so. "Hey."

Lin kissed him back. "Hey." Boya got under the covers and wrapped his warm body around my cold one. Lin came up behind him and did the same.

I closed my eyes and finally allowed myself to believe that maybe I would make it out of this unscathed after all.

By six that next morning we'd already left Klemn, the name of the house we lived in. We'd only gotten about three hours of sleep, but it'd been enough. It had to be.

Ninia and I changed back into the snake, phoenix, and

wolf so that Boya and the others could take pictures, making them easier to identify.

Ninia and Steva went to check in with a couple of wolves they knew, while Lin and Iscca went to flash the picture of the snake around. Boya and I took the phoenix.

Boya had a phoenix contact, Katarina. "She know that we're coming?" I asked as we got in the car and buckled in.

The crooked grin on his face was answer enough. "Element of surprise, Kia. Element of surprise."

The address was in Spray Town, it was where most magical and mystical beings like myself and Boya lived.

We pulled up to a regular sized yellow clapboard with white shutters and a yard the size and shape of a postage stamp. Because it was cold this time of year, the grass was dead, but it wasn't hard to tell that everything here was well-kept.

The porch held a blue rocking chair, with a pillow on the seat, plus two more chairs. Windchimes and birdhouses hung from the rafters, with two bird baths set up on the side of the house.

We got out of the car, and I raised my eyebrow at Boya. "This is nice."

He looked toward the door. "She's got her charms. Now let's go see what she knows."

We walked up the steps, but before we could knock, the door swung open and the phoenix stepped outside. "Katarina," she said, letting me know her name. She was about six feet tall, slim, and had red hair that flowed down her back in waves. When she looked at me, I saw that her red eyes held knowledge and intelligence.

"Nice to meet you," I said. Instead of showing her a picture, I transformed into the phoenix that had attacked me. "Know this woman?"

She looked me over, an assessing look on her face. "What

would the succubus say if I asked her to rat out one of her kind?" She tilted her head to the side. "What would she say?" She sounded as if she really wanted to know the answer.

I got the feeling that she respected straightforwardness, so that's what I tried to give her. "It would depend on who it was and what they'd done. Do you know what she's done?"

She clicked her teeth, and blue, red, and green feathers ruffled up behind her, a clear sign that she was irritated. "I don't think it matters," she said, looking more at Boya then at me.

Boya nodded as if he'd expected as much. "The First Families are not going to let this one go, Katarina. They're going to strike hard and fast." He hooked his thumbs into the buckle of his pants. "Just being honest here."

Her breath had quickened when he'd mentioned the First Families, and her whole demeanor changed. She looked frightened. "All I know," she said, glancing around nervously, as if she expected a member of the First Families to jump out and attack. "The blue and gray phoenix feather on her neck marks her as part of the clan, Yaya."

Some symbols are easier to identify than others, but if it's one of your own species then nine times out of ten, you knew it on sight. "Okay," I said, glad we were finally getting somewhere. "Where can I find this clan?"

She shrugged, and her feathers moved up with the motion. "Some hang out on East. You'll find some over on Fifth." She huffed. "I don't know, do you know where every Succubi clan hangs out?"

"No," I admitted, glad she'd been able to tell us that much. "We'll let you know if we have any more questions."

"What do you think?" I asked Boya once we got back in the car.

He looked back to where she no longer stood on the

porch. "I think we scared her. Doesn't mean she's telling us everything, but we scared her all right."

I started the engine and turned it toward East Street. It was in an upper middle-class neighborhood, and over two miles long. "You want to split up?" I asked, figuring we'd cover more ground that way.

He gave me a hard look as we exited the car, and I got the distinct feeling he didn't want to say what he was about to. "Sure you'll be okay on your own?"

I gritted my teeth. "I can take care of myself." The last thing I needed was him and the others looking over my shoulders every five minutes. I didn't think I could handle that.

He smiled, but it didn't quite reach his eyes. "I'm not trying to infantilize you, babe, but this is some serious shit. The First Families--"

I stepped closer to him and put my fingers over his lips. "I'm scared enough," I said my voice barely above a whisper. "I need you to be you."

He sighed and closed his eyes, pulling me into his arms. I lay my head on his chest, so glad that it only took a few words for him to know what I needed.

After a couple of seconds, he pulled away. "Let me fly above and see how things look. We can better understand what we're dealing with that way."

I nodded, and he kissed my head before taking off. My stomach clenched as I walked down the street, eyes sharp for anything out of the ordinary. I heard sounds coming from a few houses in front of me and decided I'd walk that way.

I figured if the phoenix I was looking for lived or hung in this neighborhood, changing into her now could give me a slight advantage.

I transformed quickly, and instead of looking as if I was

searching, I walked in a manner that said I knew where I was going.

I'd probably only made it about twenty feet when I came across another phoenix. She looked to be in her mid-twenties and had on oil-stained blue jeans, with a blue sweater and white coat.

Her black hair was pinned up into a bun, and her wings were nowhere in sight. She had glasses on her face though, red, purple, green, and blue. Phoenixes loved bright colors and showed them off whenever they got the chance.

She stood under the hood of a light green sports car tinkering with something. When she heard me approach, she stopped and turned my way.

I smiled slightly. I didn't want to give away too much, and I didn't know if her and the phoenix I was impersonating were friends or not.

She didn't really acknowledge my presence, but I saw her eyes glance about three houses up.

I guess we weren't friends then, so I kept walking, right to the house she'd unknowingly indicated.

Boya flew down and joined me where I was paused at the front steps, not quite ready to go up them yet. "Nice disguise," he said. "I didn't see much." He wrapped his coat tighter around him. "It's a cold day, not many people out."

"I know." I pointed to the woman still under the hood of the car. "When she saw me, her eyes strayed this way…"

He looked the two-story red brick house over. "So, let's go see if you live here, babe."

Before we could make it to the top of the steps, the front door flew open, and a tall woman, with blue, green, and yellow feathers came storming out. "That's how we do it now, then, huh?"

She was looking at me and ignoring Boya completely. "You've been gone for three frigging days, and no one knows what the beak is going on. Have you been at the bottoms this whole time?"

The bottoms was a place where some magical creatures went to drink, gamble, get high, or do anything else they wanted kept away from 'polite society.' She sighed, her eyes resigned and sad. "Have you eaten, then?"

I shook my head, my voice changing into that of the phoenix. "I'm not hungry."

She nodded and then looked at Boya. "And who is this, Shia? Is he with Rome? Have you come home to stay or is this just another stop through?"

I didn't want to oversell myself. So, I knew I couldn't go inside. "Just wanted you to know I was okay." I went back one step, letting her see that my intention was to leave. "You'll hear from me soon." I went down another step.

She rolled her eyes as if she'd expected nothing less and then put her hand on the door ready to go back inside. "Well, I'd better. It's not right, making us worry like this." We waited until she closed the door, before making our escape.

"I think we need to compare notes with the others," I said once we were back in the car and driving away.

Boya pulled out his phone. "Good. 'Cause I'm starving. Let's get lunch."

"If you were hungry, why didn't you say something?" I scolded him.

He got that sly grin on his face. "Well, you know what they say about a dragon's hunger."

"Just make the call." I suppressed a smile and realized how glad I was to have him with me. Boya could always make me laugh, even in the worst of times.

We decided to meet the others at a local pizza parlor. We ordered six large pizzas with the works, a sixty-piece hot wing, and individual pitchers of tea, water, and juice.

Iscca picked up a wing, blowing a little fire on it to cook it even more. "The snake's name is Raul. He runs with the twins Ron and Don. Has a place over on Fifth, but everyone says he's been at the bottoms lately."

Ron and Don were cobras if I remembered correctly. I picked up a slice of pizza and bit a piece of the cheesy saucy goodness into my mouth.

It was so good that I closed my eyes for a second, just enjoying the taste before I began to speak. "The phoenix's name is Shai, and she hangs out at the bottoms as well."

Lin picked up a pitcher of tea and drank some down. "Pattern. This is good."

Ninia wiped her mouth with a napkin, after sitting down the pitcher of juice she'd just drunk from. I picked up my own pitcher of water and took a sip while I waited. "The wolves wouldn't talk," she finally said, "but we sniffed around enough to find out that the wolf in question's name is Eric, and he's unbonded, still looking for his mate."

"Which means he hasn't reached his full height of power," I said, catching on to what they were saying. Mated wolves were always more powerful than unmated wolves. Once mated the two wolves became one and drew on each other's strength and that of all their ancestors. An unmated one was just a lone wolf, easily defeated.

Steva's claws shined from the bright light in the restaurant, the tiny panther-shaped ring in his nose doing the same. "What do you want to bet he hangs out at the bottoms too?"

We talked like this for a while longer, until Iscca and Boya got in a fight over the last wing. It was okay until one of them mistakenly, or maybe not so mistakenly, burned the thing to ash. I shook my head, because I'd expected nothing less of the two of them.

The owner, a man of turtle descent, didn't find it so funny. He walked by and cast a sharp glance our way. "Dragons," he said as if he put up with this type of thing every day. "It's always dragons." He looked from Boya to Steva. "No burning my place down, yeah. Take the fire play outside. You're both too old for this shit." With that, he turned on his heels and walked away.

Both men looked properly reprimanded, and I laughed, glad to take humor wherever I could get it.

Lin took out his wallet and laid two crisp hundred-dollar bills on the table. The look he gave Boya was somewhere between amused and reproachful. "No more playing with your food. We'll talk later." He stood up from the table. "Ready to go?"

Boya blushed beet red, and then smiled, fumbling with his hands in his lap. He looked like a schoolboy with his first crush. "Yes, sir," he said getting up as well.

3

The bottoms held every type of creature and income bracket. Also, any and everything went down there, and neither law enforcement, like myself, nor the First Families tried to stop it.

It was deep in Spray Town and very far removed from any humans. Most people figured that's why the First Families didn't bother. Either that, or they figured magical creatures letting off steam in a controlled environment was a good thing. I wasn't so sure I agreed with them on that, but who was I to question the First Families?

While the rest of the city was knee-deep in the throes of winter, the bottoms was sweltering hot, with the sun shining bright and the birds singing.

Large elm trees surrounded the place and while the grass was dead everywhere else, it was green and lush at the bottoms.

An Elementer hung out here, more than one if I remembered correctly. Elementers had the ability to control the weather, from snow in summer, to random hurricanes, to heavy downpours on a bright clear day.

The bottoms had a few houses, but most people came out here to be outside. All around in different little huddles were couches, recliners, tables, and TVs. It was a large open space that looked like the inside of most living rooms, except everything was outside.

Some people had grills set up, with coolers of cold beer and other alcoholic beverages resting close by. Others cooked over pits of fire and rock. Some kept their drinks cool simply from water they'd frozen in the ground.

There were many different walks of life here, many different species. The rule of the day was always respect, though. You didn't horn in on someone else's huddle, and they left yours alone as well.

We'd parked at a distance hoping to get a read on the situation, knowing that going in blind wouldn't end well.

I closed my eyes and tried to identify temperature signals. I caught succubus, incubus, bear, wolf, banshee, siren, and so many others. I'd expected no less, but it was still a lot of people to have to deal with at once.

I shuddered to think about what we'd run into down there. They wouldn't be happy to see us, of that I was sure.

Either way, we needed to get on with it. Ninia, Lin, and I could change into the snake, phoenix, and wolf, the only problem was, we had no way of knowing if they were already here. If they were, then our game would be up before it even started.

"How do you want to play this?" I asked, turning to the others.

Boya took off his coat and threw it to the ground. "Well, since it's summer now, I say the first thing we do is get rid of these." Ninia closed her eyes, and suddenly we were all dressed in shorts and tank tops.

Steva grinned, looking down at his new clothes, then he

leaned over and kissed Ninia on the cheek. "Just make sure to change us back, dear. It ain't summer nowhere but here."

She tapped a finger to her chin. "There's no law here, and trying to impose it, will surely bring the First Families down on our heads. How are we going to do this?"

Lin walked a few steps closer to the bottoms, eyes closed, trying to suss out what he could. "Be ourselves. Ask what we want to know. Don't bring up the agency. We're not arresting anyone today. If we see the ones we want, we catch their scent and follow later."

He walked a little farther. "Spread out. Meet back in an hour."

Huddles were set up everywhere, but only one had a single occupant. A woman with rat DNA had her brown hair wrapped up in a scarf. She appeared to be in her forties and sat on a large green couch smoking a pipe and looking at a TV.

By the looks of it, she was indifferent to her surroundings and glued to the television, but something in her gaze told me that nothing went on here without her knowledge.

"Mind if I sit?" I asked, standing just outside her hurdle.

She waved her hand toward an empty chair, but before I could do anything, my stomach twisted, and pain shot through me, dropping me to the ground.

I wanted to scream at the unfairness of it all. The last place this needed to happen was the bottoms. If I destroyed it, or hurt anyone here, there would be hell to pay.

I tried to control the power this time, to hold it in, but my body had a mind of its own. I opened my mouth, and the screech of the banshee came pouring out. Bodies dropped as people screamed out in pain.

I was shaking now, sweat dripping from my brow and face. I didn't want this, wished I knew some way to stop it. It was...dehumanizing.

After a couple of seconds, it stopped, and I fell over, my breath coming in hard gasps. I could hear murmurs throughout the crowd and could feel the people of the bottoms start to close in on me. For some reason, I felt like the Grinch who'd stolen Christmas, and if I could've dug a hole and disappeared forever, I would've.

That wasn't an option, so I slowly came to my knees, mindful of the people around me. Then, my nails turned into claws like a panther. My back grew wings like a phoenix, and my mouth shot fire like a dragon. I swallowed the humiliation down, not knowing what else to do.

I hadn't wanted them to see me like this, hadn't wanted anyone to see me like this again.

Stunned gasps echoed throughout the bottom, and the air thickened with menace. My claws scraped the ground, the sound loud and foreboding.

I meant these people no harm, not really. My body, though, had different ideas, and I knew if I didn't get out of there quickly, there would be a bloodbath.

I closed my eyes, trying to calm myself, trying to slay the beast inside. A peaceful, soothing feeling floated through the air, and I realized it was Succubi and Incubi using their powers to control the crowd.

It wasn't just Ninia and Lin either, though they were doing it too. No, the other Succubi and Incubi were involved as well.

While the bottoms' residents were caught up in the lure of my fellow Cubi, I came to my feet. All around me people stared off into the distance, goofy grins on their faces. I let out a relieved breath and knew now was the time to go, while they were still distracted.

My claws at my side, and my mouth firmly shut, so as not to accidentally cause a fire, I began a careful walk back to the car. I'd only made it about two feet when my wings began to flap, and I felt myself rising in the air.

I was stunned at first but then decided to just go with it. The feeling was like no other. I'd flown with Boya before, and a couple of times with Iscca, but neither time had felt like this.

All I knew was freedom, as the wind whipped and my face and my body twisted and turned. This was me, I was controlling it, and that's what made it all the more fun. *Are you done yet?* Ninia's voice sounded in my head, interrupting my peaceful glide.

"Yes," I said, slowly bringing myself back to reality. This wasn't a game, and my life was still very much in danger. If I didn't find the soulbar, the First Families would kill me. If they found out that I'd touched the soulbar, and had taken some of its power, they'd kill me.

I flew to the ground, knowing I needed to get back on task. Still, it had been amazing to forget for a moment, and I knew that if I made it out of this alive, the one thing I would miss, was having those wings on my back.

The others were all gathered around the car, watching me pull myself back together. "You look worried," I said to Lin, who had a slight frown on his face.

He answered immediately. "You get better each time. Think the power is becoming part of you. Scared of what will happen if it does."

I tried to give him a reassuring smile, but I didn't really feel it, and it came out more of a grimace. I took a moment to think about his observation.

The first time, the power of the soulbar had crippled me to the point I'd passed out. The second time, it had taken me over completely, but I'd stayed conscious. This time I'd not only stayed alert, I'd also embraced the power and let it guide me.

A sick feeling settled in the pit of my stomach, and I began to understand why he looked so nervous. "You think the more it happens, the more in danger it is of becoming permanent?"

Lin wasn't one to sugarcoat things, but I could tell how much this bothered him. "Could be. Need more information."

Boya came up behind me and tapped me on the shoulder. "We did find out a bit before you had your little freakout."

"What?" I asked, my mind running in a million different directions.

Steva glanced from his claws to mine, a suspicious look on his face. I held my hands up. "These are not yours. I didn't steal them from you."

His brows creased as if he didn't understand what I was talking about. "Just strange to see you with those, that's all."

I looked down at them. They were long, sharp, and curved at the end. "Yeah." My voice was barely above a whisper. Lin reached out, and pulled me close, placing a small kiss on my forehead.

Ninia opened the car door. "Let's talk about it back at the house. I don't feel safe here."

Iscca waved a hand at our summer clothes. "Want to do something else first, Nin. The whole house will think we're mad if we go home dressed like this."

She rolled her eyes, but it was in a playful sort of way. "They'll probably just assume we'd been to the bottoms, but it wouldn't be you without the dramatics."

He smiled at her. "I take that as a compliment, dear, now hop to."

Her eyes fluttered, and soon we were all wearing what we'd arrived in. "Let's get out of here," she said.

Back home we sat in the den, a warm glow lighting up the fireplace.

"This is stupid," Boya said watching the flames leap up and dance over the wood. "We have central heat. What do we need this thing for?"

Ninia sat in the recliner by the door. "Are you jealous?" She laughed.

Iscca sat beside Boya on the love seat. "Of course he's jealous. It's not his blaze that started the fire. I'm jealous too," he said matter-of-factly.

I could never tell if he was serious or joking. It could be disarming at times. "You don't seem all that jealous."

He gave me a deadpan look. "Well, I am."

Ninia shook her head. "Dragon solidarity then?"

"That's right," Boya said, as he and Iscca high fived.

"Speaking of which." Steva sat in the brown recliner. "Am I wrong, or did other Cubuses help us out back there?"

"They helped calm things down," Lin answered. "Was talking to a few when it happened."

"You find out anything?" I asked.

"They haven't seen them in days, but all three do hang out there."

Ninia nodded. "I talked to a siren who said she'd seen them down by the water, Miller's Creek."

Miller's Creek was still in Spray Town. As a kid, on hot summer days, Lin, Ninia, and I, along with a few others, would go skinny dipping there.

A sly grin crossed my face as I thought of some of the stuff we used to get up to at the creek.

Ninia snapped her fingers. "Focus." I straightened up and tried not to look too guilty, but from the amused look on her face, she'd been thinking about the same thing.

Lin leaned over and whispered in my ear. "How 'bout

when the weather warms up we go there? For old times' sake?"

I smiled brightly, then remembered that with everything going on, I might not have a later. "Yeah, if I live that long." I'd tried to keep the bitterness out of my voice, but it'd crept in anyway.

Lin wrapped an arm around me and pulled me to him. "We'll fix this. I promise."

I lay my head on his shoulder, conscious of the undying buzz vibrating through both our bodies letting us know it was too soon to be touching like this. Sometimes, especially times like this, I wished we were not Cubi and could be together anytime we wanted. "It's not like you to make promises you can't keep." Because he couldn't stop this, not really.

His eyes were fierce when he looked at me. "We will fix this." He spoke in absolutes that brooked no room for arguments. So, I didn't say anything else about it.

Instead, I relaxed and decided to take comfort where I could. Lin wasn't usually optimistic, and he didn't normally put cart the before the horse, so the fact that he was so adamant now, did leave me with just a tiny bit of hope.

Iscca breathed fire onto his hand, and Boya reached out and stole it, playfully making the flames go up and down his arm, which I was sure he was doing just to get at Iscca. "Well, I learned," he said, pausing for a second when Iscca stole his flame back. "That a certain skunk has been having an affair with a banshee." Audible groans sounded throughout the room as no one cared about the local gossip coming from the bottoms.

Boya held his hands up. "Kia, babe, come on. You know I'm not gonna let you down like that. You know I've got your back, too. Now, just listen. The skunk told his sister, whom I talked to at the bottoms, that said banshee had not only been working with Rome, but they meet every night, around three A.M., at…"

"Miller's Creek," I finished for him.

He smiled like he'd expected nothing less. "That's why you and I make the best team, babe. That right there." He pointed two fingers from my eyes to his. "That connection. Nothing can beat that connection."

I gave him an endearing look then turned back to the others. "Well, I have to deliver the soulbar to Riverwalk tomorrow evening, so let's hope he really is at Miller's Creek."

Steva didn't look convinced. "What are we going to do if he is there? We barely survived him last time. This time we have to have a plan."

"Agreed," Lin said. "By now he knows we're coming. People talk. Especially at the bottoms."

Iscca nodded. "So, we don't engage. We just watch from a distance and listen."

Steva seemed to be getting more on board now. "And if we see the soulbar, we take it."

"Then we just have to deal with getting to the wizard and getting these powers out of you," Ninia said.

Their willingness to help hit me right in the chest, making me feel safe and protected. "Thank you," I said, my voice no more than a whisper. "Thank you for sticking with me through this."

Iscca scoffed at my uncharacteristic showing of emotions. "Well, what the hell else were we going to do?"

I laughed and so did the others in the room and just like that the tension broke. Still, I couldn't help wondering how different it would be if I'd had my mom and grandmother backing me up. I let out a sigh and reached over, slightly touching my hand to Lin's, not caring about the conse-quences.

I wondered how it would feel if I could actually trust my family with this? To have them help me? To even have them understand that mistakes happened and no one was perfect. It was peculiar to even think about, and something I knew would never happen.

They'd never forgive me for the shame I'd brought down on the family if they ever found out the truth. I thought about the number of people that hung out at the bottoms and wondered how many had truly understood what they'd seen.

No doubt a few of them had. Or maybe none. I ran a hand down my face as despair overwhelmed me again. "We'll fix this," Lin said, only loud enough for me to hear. "Not going to let you down."

"So, what do we do now?" Iscca asked.

Lin looked at the clock on the wall. "It's six now. We should rest until ten, be fresh for Miller's Creek at three. Maybe shake a few trees before then."

Steva nodded. "We are still in agreement that the creek is a trap, right?"

Ninia came to a stand. "Oh, it's definitely a trap, but maybe we can lay one of our own."

Steva came up behind her and placed his hands on her hips. He whispered something in her ear that caused her to laugh and make him kiss her softly behind the ear, before exiting the room. Iscca walked out right behind them.

Lin's eyes went from me to Boya, and then he left without another word.

"I need you," I said, holding out my hand to Boya. He took it in his own, then kissed me hard on the lips.

"And I need you." He ripped off my shirt, then picked me up and flew me to his bedroom.

He had both of us out of our clothes in mere seconds. "I can't lose you," he said, kissing my breast, his tongue teasing my nipple.

I reveled in his touch, so warm, so caring. "I'm not going anywhere," I whispered.

He stopped kissing me and looked down. He'd been putting up a brave front all day, but right here is where I saw how much he too was affected by this. "I can't lose you," he said again, his voice breaking this time.

"Shhh." I put my fingers on his lips, and he kissed them. "I'm not going anywhere. I'm right here. Boya, look at me. I'm right here."

He let out a deep breath, and I pulled him closer, kissing him hard, our bodies rubbing together, him hard, and me moist. "Come inside," I said, opening my legs a little wider and giving him complete access.

He whimpered softly and then entered me in one hard swoop. My eyes flew to the back of my head as his length and thickness filled me. I wrapped my legs around him and worked my hips meeting him thrust for thrust, pound for pound.

I didn't want it to end, but the way we were going, I knew it couldn't last much longer. We were both too frantic, desperate, and afraid. Only a few seconds later he was calling my name and coming. I followed not long after.

He went to the bathroom and came back with two wet cloths. I wiped myself down and then watched him while he did the same. "Get in bed." I threw the covers back, and he slid in, curling his body around mine, his hold possessive in a way it never had been before. "I'm not going anywhere," I said again, not sure who I was trying to convince more, myself or him.

I awoke a couple of hours later to Boya's voice on the phone. I pushed the covers from me and sat up in the bed. The clock on the wall read nine-thirty. So, I knew we needed to get a move on. Well, I did anyway, because Boya stood completely dressed and ready to go.

I went to the bathroom to wash up a bit, the cool water on my face helping me become more alert. When I came back out, Boya was still on the phone. The voice on the other end sounded familiar, and it only took me a minute to realize who it was.

He was talking loud enough that I figured Boya had to have his phone on speaker. Gull, Boya was talking to Gull, one of his frog informants. At the moment, the other man seemed to be having a fit. "I'm not meeting at my house, Boya. Not putting my wife and kids in danger. No. Meet me at Blackwood Forest, and I'll tell you what I know." That said, the line went dead.

Boya hung up and looked at me. "You get all that?"

I nodded. "What's got him spooked now?" The last time we'd dealt with Gull, it'd been over Rome, and he'd been scared shitless. Not something we'd been used to seeing from the man.

Boya shrugged. "Still Rome and everything that's going on, I guess. You know the sooner we catch this guy, the better."

I couldn't agree more.

We met up with the others in the living room and then split up into groups of twos. Boya and I together. Ninia with Steva and Lin with Iscca.

"Hope everyone rested good." Lin addressed us all. "From this moment on, no sleep, no food, nothing until the soulbar is found, and Kia is safe."

I didn't know how I felt about that. I didn't want any of them risking too much for me. Still, I knew if they didn't want to be here, no one could force them to be.

If they agreed to help me, it was because they genuinely wanted to, not because they felt obligated. Also, I'm sure they knew that I would do the same for each and every one of them. I couldn't see myself doing otherwise.

"Thank you, guys." My voice was a little more choked up than I would have liked, but at the moment, that was okay. "If we fail." I stopped for a second to clear my throat and try to banish the reasonable doubt from my head. "What I'm saying is… Look, no matter what, I know you guys tried your best. If we can't… If everything doesn't work out, don't feel guilty or bad." I took a deep breath as wetness began to sting my eyes. "When the time comes, just… I need you to let me go."

A bunch of voices began to speak at once, and I cut them off by holding up a hand. This time when I talked, I tried to put as much steel in my voice as I could, to let them know I meant what I said. "It's not up for debate. I won't see any of you hurt because of me. I'm okay. I'll be okay." I didn't even sound convincing to my own ears. "Just don't risk yourselves too much. That's all I ask."

Lin stared at me a moment, his face unreadable even to me, then he turned to the others. "Respect her wishes. Do as she asks. Please."

I looked at him, and a smile lit my face. He knew what it took for me to say those words, and what it would do to me if one of them got hurt trying to protect me. That. That right there was why I loved him so much.

4

Boya and I walked into the entrance of Blackwood Forest hoping Gull wasn't giving us the runaround. He'd been shaky lately, so who knew what this was really about. As always, we were on our guard.

The temperature had dropped a great deal, and not many people were out. The moon was waxing its way to full so the night sky was lit up.

Which wasn't really a good thing. Boya and I could see in the dark, but not all mystical creatures could. This moon phase gave people like Rome a leg up and made our job all the harder.

The park was filled with little creeks and ponds flowing over colored rocks and pebbles. Picnic tables and benches were conveniently placed every couple of feet, and some had grills set up beside them. A runner trail ran the length of the park, and on pretty days, people would walk their pets or cycle.

We took a seat on a brown bench close to the entrance, not wanting to wander too far inside. We'd been there maybe five minutes when Boya's phone rang.

"Gull," he said looking at the screen. An uneasy feeling settled over me as Boya answered the call. Why was Gull calling, instead of coming here as we'd agreed upon?

"Meet me in Ringgold at the flea market," Gull said as soon as Boya answered.

Boya blinked at his phone, which told me he was just as caught off guard as I was. "Why?" he asked the other man.

"Because I don't trust meeting anywhere in Spray. I thought about it, and it's just no good. Come to Ringgold, to the flea market, I'll be where the electronic sellers usually set up."

"That's over twenty miles from where we're at now, Gull. What kind of game are you playing? You said to meet you here." Boya sounded irritated, and I didn't blame him.

"I don't trust it!" Gull said, his voice a hushed whisper, then the line went dead.

Boya stared at his phone as if hoping it would give him some insight. "I don't know what he's playing at, but I don't like this."

I came to my feet, figuring, either way, we had to go. "You think he's leading us into a trap?"

He scrunched up his face as if that thought really didn't sit well with him. "Would he really do that? Gull?"

"Boya." I didn't feel like I needed to say more. He knew better than that. Anyone could turn, at any time, especially an informant, particularly one that could possibly be influenced by Rome.

He ran a hand over the back of his neck. "I know, I know. It's just... I don't know. We have to go regardless. Leave no stone overturned, right?"

"We driving?" I asked, not disputing his point.

He shook his head. "Nah, I'll let you ride. Come here, girl."

I smiled at his foolishness. "I'll be sure to hold on tight." I climbed on his back and got a good grip. His wings spread out and we began to rise in the air.

That feeling of lightness that I'd had earlier with my own wings came back, and for a while it was enough to make me forget everything and allow myself to get lost in the moment.

Boya's wings were beautiful. A deep rich red, they spanned about six feet, and were as powerful as the man himself. Sometimes, after I hadn't seen them in a while, I forgot just how extraordinary they were.

We touched down at the flea market, after about five minutes of flying. It was dark and deserted, which was about what we'd expected.

The wind was colder here, and I noticed that the ground was hard and stiff under our feet. Somewhere an owl hooted and I stiffened, wondering if it was man or bird.

Those with owl DNA could be pretty sneaky when they wanted to. Still, I had no clue what one would be doing out here in the middle of the night. Certainly not with Gull, as owls and frogs didn't usually work together.

The flea market was a large place and probably covered over ten miles. One could get anything from a magical blade to a bootleg DVD. Only open on Saturdays and Sundays, most vendors were here by seven a.m. and done by two p.m.

I shopped here from time to time as I'd found some of my best trinkets at the flea market. Gull had said meet by the electronics. That was where vendors sold laptops, phones, computers, and numerous magical items, like swords that you could program fighting moves into, to cameras that truly captured your aura.

"Gull," Boya called as we walked under the large tent. Nothing. No Gull, no yucky frog spit, the place was empty, dark, and creepy.

"Let's get out of here," I said. "I think Gull has jerked us around enough for one night."

Another owl hooted, and my whole body went cold. Certain owl calls, like this one, spoke of death and despair, much like the cry of the banshee, or the song of the siren.

Owls were camouflage beings, meaning they could move without sound and blend into any environment.

I didn't normally go inside Boya's head. It was an invasion of privacy, and I respected him too much to do it. Only in times like this, when our lives were at stake, did I speak to him this way.

He could be right in front of us.

He nodded slightly to tell me that he understood.

Let's back away slowly, I don't want him to know that we're on to him.

Before he could answer, another hoot sounded, and suddenly we were surrounded by owls, with yellow and white eyes.

Don't move, I warned Boya.

They had us in a circle, nowhere for us to run really. "Do you want it back?" a rich baritone asked us. The crowd parted and a tall owl with short black hair, who looked to be about thirty, stepped through, dragging Gull's seventeen-year-old daughter with him.

He had her in a chokehold, his sharp talons pressing dangerously into her neck. Her right eye was swollen shut, and she had a bruise on her face and blood seeping from her nose and ear. Her eyes widened when she saw us, and a fleeting look of relief fluttered across her face, as if everything would be okay, now that Boya and I were here.

Rage blinded me for a moment, and I had to fight to keep my emotions in check. The thought of this young girl being hurt to further Rome's agenda sickened me.

Boya had been dealing with Gull for years, which meant we'd practically watched his children grow up from toddlers to teens. Though never chatty, not after they'd gotten older anyway, they'd never been rude or disrespectful toward us.

Beside me, I could sense Boya tense. We hadn't prepared for this, and I wasn't sure how to handle it.

I closed my eyes and tried to use my allure, but because I'd been using so much of it lately, it was too weak to make any difference.

"Let her go," I said, teeth gritted, trying hard to restrain myself. I wanted to tear his head off, rip her away from him and get her to safety, but for now, I'd be smart and maybe this would end with no more harm coming to the girl.

The man ignored me. "Bring the rest forward," he said, voice raised. The crowd parted again, and Gull, his wife, and their youngest daughter who was fifteen, were thrown to the ground in front of us. The ladies seemed untouched, but Gull's right eye was swollen shut. His face was black and blue, and he had blood coming from an open wound on his cheek and right side.

I inhaled, shocked. He looked terrible and I wondered how long he'd be able to hold on before getting medical attention.

The younger girl had tears running down her face, but Chupli, Gull's wife's face was hard with the promise of vengeance and retribution.

Chupli was a mix of bear and cheetah. Her mother having bear DNA and her father was of cheetah descent. That meant her kids, were mixed with frog, bear, and cheetah. I wondered...

"What do you want?" Boya asked, his voice harsh, cutting through my thoughts.

The owl tightened his grip on Gull's oldest daughter. His voice when he spoke, was high-pitched and nasal, giving me the impression of a snotty schoolmaster looking down his nose at those he thought himself better than. "Give up this foolish quest to find the soulbar, and I'll let her go."

"Why?" I spat, still shaking with rage. "So, you can have it?"

He gave me a curious look. "Do you not know the power it holds? Do you not understand that in the right hands...? The First Families would be no more, and we'd all be free to live our lives as we see fit."

"The First Families have four soulbars, and they've been harnessing that power since the beginning of time. You think your one is any match for them?" I shook my head. "You're delusional."

"And you're stupid," he shot back. "Four soulbars spread over many, versus the most powerful soulbar there is, in one being. I'd be unstoppable."

"Or, at least I would," A female voice said, and a woman stepped through the crowd and into the circle. She was tall, had olive skin, and her hair was done up in a large plait that wrapped around her head turning into a bun up top.

She wore black jeans, with a black jacket and boots to match. She had on long silver skull earrings and a diamond nose ring. She looked powerful, regal even, and her eyes held intelligence and cunning.

The owl holding Gull's daughter bowed his head. "Kriste." His voice was filled with awe and reverence, and I knew why. Succubus, she was a succubus, but that wasn't all.

It took me a moment, but when I finally realized what she was, I gasped and took a step back, feeling as if I'd been slapped. "It can't be," I mumbled, though I was sure most of them heard me.

Her smile was both wicked and delightful. "I see you've met my brother, Rome. Yes, that is what this is all about, isn't it?"

My fists clenched. What the hell was it with this family?

First Rome and now his sister. Just like him, she was an absorber, and that alone told me this wasn't going to end well.

"I will deal with my brother, not you," she said as if we were one of her flock, only there to follow her commands. "He thinks he can handle the power of the soulbar, but he has always toiled under my feet."

"So, you can hold that power then?" I didn't try to keep the skepticism out of my voice.

"None of your business." Her tongue was sharp, and I almost felt as if I'd been spanked with a whip. "All I know is that the First Families can't get that power." She cocked her head to the side. "Why can't you see that?" The question seemed genuine.

She squinted and then tried to invade my mind. I exhaled and slammed her back immediately, pissed that I hadn't been prepared for something like that.

"Don't do that again," I warned, my teeth pulled back in a snarl.

She seemed unfazed. "Back off this quest you have to find the soulbar, and I'll let you leave here unharmed," she offered.

I knew it was a waste trying to take her mind, so I turned to her number one follower, the owl who held Gull's daughter. I eased in without preamble and found his thoughts thick and foggy. She had control of him, and it was hard getting through the murk. When I finally could make some headway, it was what I'd already known. They had no intentions of letting us leave here alive.

What they really wanted was the location of Lin, Steva, Ninia, and Iscca, so that they could dispose of them as well. I had no way of stopping her from getting into Boya's head and finding out, the only thing was, we didn't know where Lin and the others were.

They had their own leads to run down. But we did know where they'd be later, at the creek. We had to stop her before she found that last piece out.

I looked to Chupli and saw that she still held that same fire in her eyes I'd seen earlier. I kind of knocked on the door of her mind, asking permission to enter. A slight nod told me it was okay to go forward. *Can you fight? Can your daughters?*

Yes.

May I talk to them?

Yes.

Be ready.

I will.

I asked each daughter in turn before entering their minds. After talking to them, I turned back to their mother to let her know they'd be ready.

Kriste watched us with interest. An unbothered smile on her face. "Staging a little coup, are we? Let's see how far you get with that." She didn't sound worried in the least.

I started to respond, but then panic entered my mind, and I realized that Ninia was making contact with me.

Went to check out a couple of wolves. They have us on the chase, be careful if you come by Froad Street.

Dealing with a mess at the flea market in Ringgold. Stay safe.

My conversation ended with her and started with Lin, as he too was under attack. *Gonna shake them and still meet you at the creek.*

Well, he may be able to shake the snakes after him, I just wasn't so sure that Boya and I could do the same. *See you there.* I wasn't feeling very confident at the moment, and he must have felt it, but he didn't say anything, which was good.

What I got from him was his belief that Boya and I could handle this. I chuckled, if only to myself, because right now he had a lot more faith in us than I did.

The number one owl's phone rang, and he answered it

talking for only a few minutes. I used my powers to listen in, hoping to get some type of clue that would help us. It was the wolves and the snakes letting him know that they'd found Lin and the others, so they no longer needed to keep us alive.

I turned to Chupli and her girls, panic on my face, as I silently screamed, *NOW*.

Did I mention that cheetahs are super-fast? The oldest turned on the owl holding her, and using teeth as strong as steel, ripped his jugular out.

Her mom and sister did the same to the owls holding them, with lightning fast efficiency. They didn't stop with just one though. All around us, owls began to drop to the ground bleeding, as if caught up in a real-life game of dominos.

It was shocking, and I wondered why they hadn't freed themselves before now. They hadn't had backup before Boya and I arrived, and Gull was too hurt to help, was the only reason I could come up with.

As if on cue, Boya breathed out two balls of fire and tossed them to me, turning in the process to scorch the two owls, closest to him.

The men didn't even have time to scream before they were turned to ash.

Take your family and go. I sent to Chupli. Frogs could hop up to three miles doing one leap, plus she and her girls had cheetah blood, so I wasn't really worried about them getting away. The owls here had seen what they could do. They'd have to have a death wish to go after them now.

Chupli didn't waste any time, picking up her husband, who hadn't moved an inch since this thing started, she tucked him securely under her arm, and in one hop, her whole family disappeared from sight.

Only three owls were left standing, but they looked to be

the most vicious. One stood tall, neck thick and his hair cut in a black mohawk.

He had yellow eyes that looked even more sinister when he threw his head back and hooted. It was a dark, horrific sound that told of his anguish at seeing so many of his friends put down.

I swallowed knowing that this wasn't good. There was only Boya and I now, but it would have to be enough.

Tear them apart! Kriste mentally commanded them. The only reason I heard her, was because she'd connected with me when she'd said it, which meant she wanted me to hear. Mind games, just like her brother. Apparently the two got off on that sort of thing.

Well, just like before, I wasn't going down without a fight. I dropped to my knees, in order to confuse the one with the mohawk, then leapt onto his back and used my TK, to rip his heart out. I jumped down in time to see his eyes widen as he hit the ground.

From the corner of my eye, I could see that Boya had burnt the other two to a crisp. I dropped the owl's heart to the ground, and Boya and I stood side by side.

Ninia slammed back into my head, telling me that she and Steva were okay and would meet us at the Creek as planned. I immediately checked in with Lin, who told me that he and Iscca were on their way to Boya and me.

I stopped him, telling him we had everything under control and would meet him there.

Kriste stood alone now, but she didn't look scared. She put her hand in her mouth and whistled. An owl popped down from one of the tree branches and landed in front of her.

He had red hair and wore blue jeans and combat boots. He was medium height and very muscular. His eyes were yellow, and when he looked at us, I saw all my worst night-mares come to life.

See, this was why I didn't like messing around with owls. They were sneaky and scary, and unless you knew to focus your senses, you never saw them coming. Which made them one of the most dangerous beings to deal with.

He wrapped an arm around Kriste, and heaved her to him, as if ready to take flight. "I know when to cut my losses," she said as they rose in the air, "but this is not over. Not by a long shot."

I turned to Boya and sagged against him. "Let's get out of here."

5

B oya and I touched down in the middle of chaos. Ninia and Steva, having been closer, had already made it to Lin and Iscca. Boya flew above the scene, his long wings gliding through the sky.

Lin was whispering into the ear of a snake. The man grabbed his face, screamed in horror, and dropped to the ground, as Lin no doubt, read his worst fears, and then made the man believe he was living them.

Those with snake DNA could contort their bodies. A woman in a black coat, who looked to be about thirty, with a long ponytail and black-rimmed glasses, had wrapped her entire body around Steva.

His eyes popped and gagged, and my heart squeezed in my chest, as none of the others seemed to be paying attention. Frantically, I hit at Boya's back, trying to get him to get closer so that we could do something.

Before we got even halfway, Steva bared his claws, put both hands on either side of her, and ripped her to shreds. He then turned to the wolf slowly creeping up beside him and bit the man's throat out in one clean swoop.

Ninia had three on her, but they quickly became dust, as she used her allure to placate them, only to turn around and use her TK to rip their hearts out.

Iscca simply burned the face off everyone he came into contact with, and looked quite pleased to be doing so.

Boya swung lower, his powerful muscles, bunching under me, making me feel safe and secure. By the time we got close enough to do anything, there were only three attackers left standing, two wolves and a snake.

Boya opened his mouth, and fire hit all three, turning them to dust in an instant.

"What the hell happened?" I asked once Boya and I finally made it to the ground.

Lin's jacket was gone, and his shirt was half off him. He lifted the bottom of it and wiped sweat, and grime from his face. "Got cornered leaving Delmont place. Had been asking questions, but they seemed coordinated, like they knew we were coming."

I looked down at the now unmoving corpses. "I think they did. I think they were looking for all of us tonight. We just made it convenient for them by pairing off."

Ninia removed wolf guts from her hair. I looked at her strangely, wondering how in the world they'd gotten there, then decided it was probably best if I didn't know. "What do you mean?" she asked, still picking bits and pieces out.

"Oh, you're going to love this," I said, then I told them about Gull's family and Rome's sister.

"So, there's two of them," Steva asked, licking his claws clean, an incredulous look on his face.

"Might have more siblings," Lin said.

Iscca had smoke coming out of his nose and mouth. "I say we still go tonight. At least we know what to look out for now."

The thought of them all walking into danger to protect

me hit me so hard that I actually lost my breath for a moment. "I'm sorry, guys," I said, my voice thick. "If I hadn't touched it, if they hadn't stolen it, we'd be able to call for backup and not have to walk into this thing alone."

Iscca rolled his eyes. "Not this shit again. Look, what's done is done. We all fuck up sometimes, so whatever. Let's just get this over with, 'cause I'm hungry and Boya's cooking me pancakes and soup when we get home."

I smiled at Iscca because he'd loosened the thick knot that had been in my shoulders and made it easier for me to breathe. "That's disgusting." It really was an awful combination.

"And it's also not happening," Boya piped up, but he had a smile on his face as he looked at Iscca.

Ninia brought us back to the present. "What time is it?"

Steva pulled out his phone. "Twelve thirty. We should get a move on if we want to make it to the creek by one."

We arrived at the creek with ten minutes to spare. Rome and the others weren't due until three, so that gave us plenty of time to check the place over. Boya and Iscca took to the sky, to secure the perimeter and make sure we weren't hit with any unexpected surprises.

They flew back after a couple minutes and deemed the place clear of any immediate threats.

We stood in a small clearing. A large river flowed before us almost as silent as the night. Three picnic tables sat on the bank, along with large rocks big enough for at least two people to comfortably have a seat.

It was cooler here, where the water was.

Ninia took a look around. "He's going to go to the

Weeping Wet, to try and take in the power of the soulbar," she said.

The Weeping Wet was a river that held enormous power. It was forbidden by the First Families unless you were really hurt and it was the only way to save your life. The Weeping Wet amplified your abilities making you three times as strong as you normally were.

The effect only lasted a couple of hours, but with the soulbar, the power would likely be sealed inside of the person holding it.

I thought of what would happen to me if Rome was allowed to grow that strong. Then a shiver ran down my spine as I thought of what would happen to everyone if he took in that much power. "We have to stop him," I said, my voice filled with newfound panic. "We can't let him do this."

"That is why we're all here, K." Boya looked at me and winked, not in a cocky way, but more in a sense to calm me down and keep me grounded.

Lin stood in a defensive stance, his arms on either side of him as if bracing for attack. His feet were firmly planted on the ground and slightly parted.

He looked like he could tear you apart with his bare hands, and I felt better knowing he was on my side. "If they talked to the people at the bottoms," he started. "Then they already know--"

He didn't get to finish that thought, as the hooting of owls echoed through the park.

I braced myself, not sure what to expect or who to expect it from.

I heard the sound of flapping and looked up to see brown and gold wings circling around us. Owls. At least ten of them, both men and women. "Distraction," Lin said, eyes following the owl's every movement. "Rome's probably already at Weeping Wet. Let's go. Boya. Iscca."

The two dragons stayed behind, knowing exactly what he wanted them to do. The rest of us ran toward Weeping Wet, but I was still able to hear when Boya and Iscca took off to the sky. The smell of burnt owl flesh quickly followed.

We were probably about three minutes away when we heard the rustling of leaves and the sound of hard breathing.

Before we could react, they were on us, wolves, snakes, and phoenixes. "Distraction!" Lin shouted, then took my hand, while I took Ninia's, and she took Steva's.

They had us in a circle, but with the combined powers of Lin, Ninia, and me they were no match. We put a hush over them, alluring them until they were putty in our hands. Their bodies swayed from side to side, as they looked at us with happy, dopey grins on their faces. "Sleep," Ninia said, her voice sounding like that of three.

Immediately they dropped to the ground, curled up and smiling. "Dammit," I said as we stepped over them and walked on. Alluring drained us of a massive amount of power, and that's why we only used it as a last resort.

Now here we were going to fight Rome with only a fraction of our power. We were already at a disadvantage, this just made it a hundred times worse. Which had no doubt been a part of the absorbers' plan.

Up ahead we heard the flap of wings, and soon Boya and Iscca stood beside us. "They're finished," Boya let us know.

About five feet away from Weeping Wet, a bright light shone through the sky. It wasn't solid, but speckled with red, blue, green, yellow, and just about every other color of the rainbow. "We're too late he's already dipped it in," I cried.

"We still fight." Lin took off in the direction of the light, the rest of us right behind him.

Rome stood at the edge of the lake, the soulbar wrapped inside a purple silk cloth, as he twisted and turned it in the water, careful not to let any of it touch him, but diligent in his task all the same.

Around him stood owls, snakes, wolves, a few phoenixes, and his sister, smiling brightly as she watched on.

"We should have known they were working together as soon as we saw the owls," Boya said with a growl and I agreed.

Kriste was the first to notice us. Her head jerked back, and she tapped her brother on the shoulder. "It seems that we have company."

Rome didn't stop what he was doing. "We've come too far now. The power of the soulbar is right in our hands!"

She nodded. "No, we won't stop. Attack!" she yelled to the numerous beings surrounding us.

Phoenix, wolf, snake, and owl ran our way, all seemingly enraged and under the spell of Rome and Kriste.

Boya and Iscca unleashed fire on the leaders of the pack, and screams filled the air, as the smell of burnt flesh replaced that of forest and pine.

Steva had his claws out and was plying through wolf and snake alike, ripping out throats, and tearing through guts.

Lin's powerful hand went into the chest of one snake and dropped the man to the ground. He then grabbed a wolf to him and whispered something so hellish that the man began to claw at his own face as if trying to rip the image away.

Ninia, leapt through the air, landed on top of a phoenix, then used her telekinesis to snatch the woman's tongue out of her mouth, only to stuff it right back in, causing the woman to choke and gag until she stopped moving completely.

A wolf of medium height, long black hair flowing down her back, came at me from the right, while a tall snake with glowing yellow eyes, and short spiked silver hair, came at me from the left.

I closed my eyes and invaded their minds, weeding out their worst nightmares and sending them rapid-fire images of it. The wolf threw her head back and howled.

The sound like a knife blade down the spine of the night. She fell to her knees and then curled into a fetal position, her screams turning to whimpers, and then a low moan.

The snake stood shocked and still. Her eyes, wide with horror, her stance frozen, as she looked off into the distance at something only she could see.

The metallic smell of blood made its way to my nostrils, and I knew that some of my crew were hurt as well.

I trusted them to handle themselves, as my only mission was to get to Rome and Kriste so I could stop them from using the soulbar.

I walked with purpose, fighting my way through the horde, moving as quickly as I could.

I saw Lin with three guys on him, their powerful hands raining down blows on his back and head. He stumbled a bit, then wrapped his hand around one of their throats, and squeezed until the man's eyes popped out of his head.

As I said, my team could handle itself.

Rome and his sister stood opposite each other, a bit removed from the fight. The silk still covered the soulbar, but they each had their hand on the cloth as they held it between them.

"Not so fast." I was out of breath from the fight, and my hands clenched at my sides, wondering if I had enough power left to take on both siblings by myself.

Rome looked at me, a smile on his face. "Kia, I didn't think I'd see you again. I thought for sure the owls would have gotten you earlier."

Kriste smirked at her brother, and I shook my head, knowing I'd been played. She'd never wanted to hurt him.

Her little act had been just that, an act. If we thought they were working independent of each other, they figured we'd let our guard down, and it would be easier to take us over.

What they didn't know is that we never let our guards down, no matter the situation, and we were always ready for a fight. "I know you think that--" Fire shot out of my mouth, and flew past Rome's head. Red flames singed his hair a little but missed him on a whole.

This was not good, as I wasn't sure I could control it as well as I needed to. Not having a firm grasp yet, I went to my knees as the wings of a dragon sprouted from my back.

One of Rome's wolves charged me, probably hoping to get me while I was down, and I opened my mouth in his direction and shot fire at him. He stopped mid-stride, the flames taking him over until there was nothing left but dust.

My teeth grew to that of a panther, and large talons decorated my hands. My mouth opened again, and this time the cry of the banshee shrieked out, piercing the night with the screams of the dead.

Around me, I could hear the bodies dropping as the anguish of the banshee held them all in her grip.

In front of me, unable to fight it, Kriste and Rome both hit the ground, covering their ears, trying desperately to block out the sound.

They'd dropped the soulbar when they'd fallen, and I looked at it gleaming before me, well within my reach. I just had to get to it.

My scream continued, but just like with the wings I began to take control. Slowly I came to my feet. Everyone lay on the ground, my crew along with Rome's and Kriste's.

Gradually I closed my mouth, the sound dying away as I did so. I used my telekinesis, to call the soulbar. It came to my outstretched hand, still wrapped in the silk and frog spit. Letting out a sigh of relief, I held it firmly in my grip, glad that it was finally over.

Now that the cry of the banshee had quieted, those who were left breathing began to come to their feet. Lin, Boya, Ninia, Steva, and Iscca all stood, as well as one phoenix, three wolves, and two snakes.

I opened my mouth again, and the sweet song of a siren filled the night air. It lulled the wolves, phoenix, and snakes enough that they didn't even notice when Iscca and Boya set their whole bodies afire. They burned, still smiling, and dopey-eyed.

Rome and Kriste came to a stand, as they watched the last bit of their help turned to ash and blow away. Though they tried to play it cool, I could sense the rage leaking just below the surface.

They hadn't expected this. Hadn't prepared for me to have as much control over the powers of the soulbar as I did. It served them right, but the smug grin on both their faces made my stomach roll and let me know that this wasn't over yet.

Rome's smile was twisted and triumphant. "Always have a backup plan," he said like this was the part he'd been waiting all night for.

Kriste raised a brow as she looked at her brother. "I told you, Rome. Never waste a wolf, or snake, when a simple Samg will do."

He nodded his agreement, and she turned in a circle, her voice loud as she called: "Come out, come out where ever you are."

I heard a growl and then looked up to the trees to see two sets of reddish yellow eyes looking down at us. The trees were on opposite sides of the walkway, but both figures leapt at the same time, landing in front of me, twin snarls on their faces. Their hands were clawed, and they bared their teeth, looking as feral as I'd ever seen.

Tears fell down my face as I stared at them. I hadn't

wanted this for them. I wouldn't want this for anyone, but especially not these two who actually meant something to me.

"Why?" I asked, my voice heavy with emotion as I looked at Rome and his sister. "Why couldn't you just let them go?"

"Don't be so naïve," Kriste snapped, her eyes hot when she stared at me. "What did you think we were going to do? Let you take the soulbar and give even more power to the First Families? That's not how this works."

I turned to Lin, but his eyes were solely on Mitch and Misha. His mouth was pressed tight, and his eyes held heartbreak. He walked a few steps their way, and they turned to growl at him.

My anger intensified as I looked at Rome and Kriste. I wanted to hurt them, bad.

Rome looked prouder than a papa on prom day. "Didn't I tell you there would be casualties, Kia? Did you think I'd made a joke? I don't joke, but I guess you know that now."

Mitch and Misha stood rocking back and forth, some grunts coming out every now and then, but other than that, nothing. All signs of intelligence and knowledge were gone from their eyes. They were mere puppets now.

Puppets that Rome had made and molded into his own image. Pressure built behind my eyes, but I closed them until I regained control, not willing to do that here.

We'd left Mitch and Misha to his mercy, and he'd destroyed them. I didn't even know if what he'd done could be erased at this point. "I'm going to kill you," I said, barely able to suppress my rage. "I'm going to kill you both."

They smirked as if I'd just confirmed all their suspicions of me. "She's cute." Kriste smiled at me. "Does she have any other uses?"

Rome looked me over, an inquisitive look on his face.

"Hmmm, maybe, but I worry that she's more trouble than she's worth, you understand?"

Kriste nodded and sighed as if he'd just taken away her favorite toy. "You're right. We'd always be looking over our shoulder with this one." Then her eyes lit up as if she'd just had the most fantastic idea in the world. "Unless we broke her."

With my feelings back under control, I didn't wait for them to continue this ridiculous conversation. I shot fire out of my mouth knowing that it couldn't hurt them, but betting on it stunning them enough so that I could get the upper hand. Rome dove into the water, while Kriste jumped in the air, neither were hit by the flame.

"Rip them apart!" she said, still levitated about six feet off the ground. Rome came out of the water dripping wet with a look of disdain on his face as he went to stand by his sister.

You had to be in the Weeping Wet at least thirty minutes to strengthen your abilities, so at least we were good on that point.

His sister looked him over, probably making sure he was alright, and then turned back to the twins. "Rip them apart and bring me their skulls."

They advanced on us, and I stepped back, trying to think of how to end this without them getting hurt.

"We have the soulbar, let's just go!" Lin said, but he wasn't retreating. Instead, he advanced, coming to stand by me, not willing to let me face this on my own. "Get out of here! All of you! I'll handle Mitch and Mi--"

They were on him before he could finish the sentence. Misha dove and knocked him to the ground, her fingers clawing and scratching at his face. I heard Boya scream out a frantic, "Lin," but I didn't have a moment to spare him.

Lin put his arms up to protect himself, but Mitch knocked them down and began biting at his face. Lin, using as little power as he could, knocked them off him, and sent them sprawling.

They hit the dirt, then jumped back up grunting, and came for him again.

"Enough!" A voice shouted, and we all whipped our heads in the direction it'd come from.

I don't think I would have been more shocked if it had been the trees or swing sets, talking to us. Kevin shook his head at his children, his eyes lit with sorrow and regret. "Mitch, Misha, you must stop this," he pleaded.

While they were distracted, Boya and I helped Lin to his feet. His face had a few chunks missing, and he was dripping blood.

I put a hand to my mouth, horrified. We had to get him help, and soon, before he bled out.

None of this appeared to bother him though, as he seemed more concerned with the scene taking place in front of him, than his own personal health. "Kevin," he said, his voice a lot less powerful than it usually was. "What are you doing here?"

The tall man looked in his direction, and his eyes widened at the sight of the other man. They'd been lovers once, and the fact that it'd ended so badly had always left a sour taste in Lin's mouth. He loved those kids, and he'd loved their father too I believed.

Mitch and Misha grunted, their bodies rocking back and forth as they looked between their father and Kriste, not sure who to obey.

Kevin shot a stray glance at Lin, his attention still mostly on his kids. "I hadn't been able to get in touch with them in some time. Figured it had something to do with this mess you'd told me about earlier. When they finally did resurface, I began to follow them."

Kriste clapped her hands. "A family reunion, how nice." She turned to Mitch and Misha. "Now kill them all."

Lin pulled himself free of me and Boya. "Run. Get the soulbar to the First Families."

I didn't want to leave him but knew that I had to. Ninia and the others were still here, and I knew they wouldn't abandon him.

I needed to get the soulbar to Riverwalk. If I didn't, I was dead anyway. Still, somehow, I couldn't make my feet back away.

"Her, kill her," Kriste said before I'd made it two feet.

"Kill her and bring us the soulbar," Rome piped in.

The twins came at me swiftly, but I used my newly acquired wings to rise in the air above their reach. Only, they rose as well, phoenix wings on their backs just like my own.

I'd forgotten for a minute that besides being succubus and incubus, Kriste and Rome were also absorbers and could transfer any power they wanted, into any being they chose.

I tried to fly away, but a strong elbow to my face sent me plummeting. I still had the soulbar in my grip, so I wasn't ready to do any hand-to-hand combat. Instead, I used my succubus powers to stop my fall, then held out my hand and used my telekinesis to knock them back.

They tumbled for a second and then righted themselves, flying straight toward me. I would have to deal with them before I could get the soulbar to the First Families, there was no way around it. I wouldn't hurt them if I could help it, but I wouldn't let them kill me either.

A smash to my face knocked me clueless for a moment, and my eyesight began to blur. "What the--" It was them, they were super fast, somehow, I'd forgotten that part.

Before I could catch my breath, a hand wrapped around my throat and began to squeeze. Misha. I struggled, my breath coming hard, as my lungs fought for air. I felt a presence behind me and then Mitch was on my back, his arms wrapped around my chest, legs around my waist, holding me in place while his sister continued to choke me.

My body began to go limp, and my eyes rolled back in my head. I became lightheaded, so much so that I couldn't even panic. The soulbar slipped from my fingers, and I saw what was left of my life go with it. All Rome or Kriste had to do was grab it now, and this would be over.

Down below I could hear struggling and was able to get a clear enough picture to know that Rome and Kriste had the others under some type of spell. Both siblings had their hands outstretched, and a white glowing light engulfed Lin and the others.

I tried to tell myself to hold on because, in order to save them, I had to first save myself. I was weary though, my thoughts all jumbled and fogged up. Maybe it would be best to just let go, maybe that would solve everything. Maybe.

I stopped my happy acceptance of death, as power like I hadn't felt in years shook me to my soul.

"You fucking dare!" a voice said so loud and angry that even the trees begin to shake. The wind picked up, and Mitch and Misha were snatched from me and thrown to the ground.

I began to fall as well, but now that Kriste and Rome's spell was broken, Boya flew up and gathered me gently in his arms, guiding me safely to the ground.

My throat felt like someone had poured liquid fire down it, and at this point, it hurt to even breathe.

Rome and Kriste were levitated in the air being held there by my mother. My mother, she stood six feet tall, skin the color of ebony, hair black, curly, and flowing down her back.

She had a look of rage on her face like I'd never seen, and I shuddered just catching a glimpse of it. She had on a jean jacket, black heeled boots, and black jeans to match. "You dare touch a member of the Wyaque clan!" she screamed so furiously that the wind shook.

I blinked, not sure if what I saw in front of me was real. My mother had never once in her life stood up for me, never once gave any indication that she cared about me in the least, her, or my grandmother for that matter.

Maybe it was a lack of oxygen to my brain causing this hallucination, I decided as my eyes fluttered, and I figured that Misha still had me in the air choking me.

Rome and Kriste were frozen in my mother's grip, their faces wide with horror. "Did you think it would be so easy to kill *my* child!" she taunted them.

Yeah, you tell 'em, Mom. I settled in Boya's arms, and he kissed me on the forehead. "We're going to get you to Drem. He'll take care of you."

I nodded, and we began to back away. Kevin stood, his eyes shooting between my mom and his children as if he dared not make a move, for fear of upsetting either of them.

Lin stood between Ninia and Steva, putting his weight on them, his face was still bleeding, and he was starting to look pale.

Iscca stood right behind them, his eyes searching as if waiting for someone else to jump out of the bushes.

We heard the flap of wings and a large hooting sound from up above. There were six of them, three phoenixes and three owls.

They flew toward my mother, distracting her enough that she lost her grip on Rome and Kriste.

Two phoenixes quickly scooped the siblings up and disappeared before we could stop them.

My mom closed her eyes, and said a few words under her breath, when she opened them again they were blue and glowing. She pointed to the remaining phoenix and owls, and with a simple hand twist, popped their necks.

They dropped where they stood, and she looked down at them, a satisfied air about her.

She then turned to me, eyes hard and unforgiving. "Fix yourself and get the soulbar to the First Families. I won't have it being said that my child was the reason for the soulbar being lost." With that, she turned and walked away, without a backward glance.

As I watched her go my heart shuddered in my chest, and I wondered if I'd ever see her again. I wanted to call out, to tell her that I was sorry. To beg her forgiveness and try to make this right.

I walked about two feet before my legs gave out, and I fell to the ground, darkness clouding my vision and taking me under.

6

I awoke on a bright orange couch, with Drem, the wizard, looking down at me. "There. I'd say we're just about done." Drem was a man of medium height and build, and though he looked to be about thirty, the truth was he'd lived for thousands of years.

His skin was olive and his hair jet black and to his butt. Orange was his favorite color, so he wore orange pants, with an orange button up dress shirt.

His slender hands hovered over me, and I could see lights, every color of the rainbow, leaving me and flowing into the soulbar.

Sweat had broken out on his head, and he looked a little strained from the effort. "There," he said again, once all the light was gone and there was no more to transfer. "I've healed your sore throat too." My sore throat, right. Leave it to a wizard to describe being nearly choked to death as something as simple as a sore throat.

He backed up from me, and placed the soulbar, now wrapped in orange silk in my lap. "You don't have long to get it there. It's almost six."

"In the evening?" I sat up with a stir. Where in the world had the time gone?

He raised an eyebrow. "You've been out for a while, and this right here," he pointed from me to the soulbar, "is not easy work."

Now that I was up, I took a good look around the room. Everything was orange. Everything, from the couch, that Ninia and Iscca sat on, to the loveseat where Steva was perched. Other than that, the room was empty.

I tried not to panic, but not seeing the two I wanted most to be here left something sour in my gut. "Where are they?" I asked, pretty sure everyone in the room knew who I was talking about.

Ninia was the first to answer. "Boya is healing Lin. He was hurt pretty bad, remember?"

I blinked at her. "All this time?" I looked toward the door as if expecting to see them walk through at any moment.

She gave me a frank look then turned away.

Hmm. I'd just been to hell and back, and I at least wanted to see one of the two people that made me feel the safest. I reached out to Lin and he immediately answered back. *On my way, already. Felt it when you woke up.*

Boya?

Coming as well.

I sat back relieved but knew that feeling wouldn't last long. I still had to face the power of the First Families, and that was enough to almost make me wish I was still in the park fighting for my life.

At least Drem had managed to get the power out of me, but I wondered... "Will there be any lasting effects?" I asked him. I felt okay for the moment, better than okay actually, but I wasn't sure how long it would last.

Drem flicked his wrist. "I don't know. This is new territory for me as well." He shrugged. "I mean, I got it all, but some may have already mingled with your blood and central nervous system. Who knows?"

"Could you sound a bit more concerned?" I asked, my teeth grating at his flippant manner. This was my life we were talking about here.

"No, I cannot." His voice didn't sound harsh or mean, just accepting. "You messed up, not me."

"Yeah, yeah, yeah, we all know the story," Boya said walking into the room, Lin right beside him.

Lin's face was healed, and he looked like at least some of the weight had been lifted from his shoulders. "What happened to the twins? And Kevin, what the hell was that about?"

Lin leaned over and gave me a quick kiss on the cheek before sitting on the couch. "Drem healed them. Got them out of Kriste and Rome's allure."

"He also made it impossible for them to be allured again, by Rome or anyone else."

Boya took up the narrative. "And… He let them keep a few powers so that they could defend themselves if need be."

I looked to Drem, who sat watching myself, Boya, and Lin with interest. "Is that wise, and were they okay with that?"

He gave me a put-upon look, letting me know he didn't like being questioned, but he still answered. "First off, they're Samg, so their bodies are made of stronger stuff anyway, but yes, I adjusted things a bit so it wouldn't be a problem. Second, they're the ones who asked for it, and their father agreed, so… any more questions or will you finally leave now? It's been a grueling couple of days locked away in Riverwalk with the First Families, and I'd like to unwind."

"Why were you there?" I asked, coming to my feet. I had twenty minutes to make it to Riverwalk and time was steadily ticking.

"None of your business," he answered in a voice, that said I should know better to even ask.

I held my arms out to him. "Thank you."

He gave me a "you've got to be kidding," look. "I'm not hugging you, now off with the lot of you. Go."

With nothing more to say, we gave him one last thank you and left.

7

I walked into Riverwalk alone and expected. Head down, I allowed the guards to lead the way. It was quiet here, and out of the corner of my eye, I could see the large silver buildings and perfectly manicured lawns.

All the First Families were extremely wealthy, and spared no expense on their living and work environments.

They led me into a ten-story white building and placed me inside a large room. The quick glimpse I'd gotten, before being shoved through the door, told me that the hallways were silver, and black crystal made up the floor.

A few people had walked by, but none had paid me any attention, and I wondered if they'd even known I was there.

The room I was in held a massive black table, big enough to take up half the floor. I counted over fifty black chairs around it.

The floor was gray carpet and the walls the same black as the table. I sat in the first chair I saw, my heart beating out of my chest, hoping I could pull this off.

This place felt unfamiliar and unwelcoming, and I wondered what took place in here.

After about ten minutes a door opened, and my grand-mother, along with a siren, and a pantue entered. Pantues are descended from pigs. They are highly intelligent, and their counsel is very much sought after.

I swallowed hard and took a good look at them. The siren had skin the color of ivory and red hair flowing down her back. She wore a simple white gown, with white slippers.

The pantue was more of a tan color and wore a navy-blue shirt and tie, both looked down at me like I'd just set fire to the world. My grandmother joined them in this.

"You have the soulbar?" she asked, her voice sounding not that much older than mine, but then again, she didn't look that much older than me, so…

She had black hair like my mother, yet her skin was the same brown as my own.

"I have it," I said, trying to keep my composure. I took it out of my bag and handed it over, hoping this would put an end to everything and I could go home.

"No problems?" she asked, and from the look on her face, I could tell she already knew the answer.

The pantue and siren didn't say a word because I was Wyaque Clan and it was up to my grandmother alone to mete out my punishment.

That should have been comforting, but knowing my grandmother as I did, it wasn't. Panic rose in my throat as I imagined all the ghastly things she could do to me. If I could just explain to her, try to make her understand. "Mema, look, it was a mistake. I didn't mean to touch the soulbar, I didn't even know what it was when I first saw it." I cursed under my breath, mad at myself for always reverting to a five-year-old child whenever her or my mom were around.

She put one finger to her mouth, the pantue and siren standing stonily at her side. "Hush, Kia. I forgive you for touching it. Accidents happen, but what I don't forgive you for is making your mother clean up your mess, and not alerting us to the fact that you had in fact touched and lost it."

Righteous indignation boiled in me like a volcano, and for a moment I wondered if Rome and Kriste didn't have a point. "Well, maybe if you guys, didn't take everything so--" my throat closed up stopping me from finishing. What the hell was with everybody and going for my throat lately?

"Shhh," My grandmother said, once again putting a finger to her mouth. "You don't get to judge. All you have to do is listen and follow. Here is how it's going to be. You will only have sex the fourth week out of every month, for the next three months."

I let out a gasp, and my hands began to tremble as her hold on my throat loosened. "That's a death sentence, and you know it." My voice was low and filled with shock and anger, as I tried to process what she'd just said.

She didn't even blink, just kept looking down at me with that indifferent expression on her face. "It will be difficult, yes, but there've been Wyaque, before you that have faced worse.

"Pay this simple debt, and all is forgiven. I and the other members of the First Families will stay mentally linked with you the whole time." To make sure I didn't slip into a strip club and get my rocks off, no doubt, I thought bitterly.

"What if I can't?" I asked, scared of her answer.

"Then you'll die. If you have sex before the fourth week of the month, the First Families will kill you. If you're not succubus enough to withstand this punishment, then you will die anyway." With that, she, the pantue, and the siren left the room.

I sat in stunned silence, wondering how the hell I was going to tell Boya and Lin this news. My breath shuddered as

I thought about it. I wasn't strong enough. I couldn't do this, there was no way I could do this.

The First Families had just sentenced me to death, and not one of them gave a damn.

I was still pondering my fate a couple of minutes later when the guard walked me out. I kept my head down the whole time, not wanting any of them to see the shame and despair upon my face. The guard, a beefy man of lion descent, took me as far as the gates. "Leave," he sneered, before closing them shut in my face.

I walked to my car, which was parked two streets over, with a heavy heart, and wondered how the hell I would survive for the next three months.

ACKNOWLEDGMENTS

A special thanks to my beta readers, and editors for making this book what it is. Thank You!

ABOUT THE AUTHOR

N.R. Hairston resides in Southern Virginia with her family. She enjoys writing, reading, cooking, and spending time with her family.

Please be on the lookout for upcoming books by N. R. Hairston.

If you enjoyed this book, please consider leaving a review.

Subscribe to N. R. Hairston's newsletter to get exclusive short stories, and be the first to hear about deals and promotions. Click here!

I hope you enjoyed reading this book. If you'd like to discuss it you can find me in these places:

Website
Blog
Twitter
Tumblr